THE RECRUIT
(BOOK THREE)

By Elizabeth Kelly

Chapter 1

"He's avoiding me, Douglas."

The old Lycan sighed and sipped at his cup of tea. "He's ashamed at what he's done, Hannah. He needs some time to figure it out."

Hannah stared into her own cup of tea. "He shouldn't be ashamed. He saved my life. If he would talk to me for just one damn minute, I'd tell him that myself. I'd tell him how grateful I am for what he did and how much I love him. But he won't even step foot in the facility."

Douglas reached out and squeezed her hand. "Generally speaking, it's frowned upon by other Lycans when one of our kind turns a human. Will is reacting to that. He knows you love him."

She gave him a curious look. "Why is it frowned upon?"

He looked decidedly uncomfortable and she pressed him further. "Douglas? Why is it frowned on?"

He stood and poured them both more tea. "They, and trust me when I say that not all Lycans feel this way but a great majority of them do, believe that humans are weak. And humans who have become Lycans through a bite are thought to be, well, unpredictable and dangerous."

Hannah didn't reply and Douglas sat down next to her. "Centuries ago, it was common practice for Lycans to turn humans. They did it for a variety of reasons – sometimes it was just for sport, sometimes they had no choice, and at one very dark time in our past, they did it to keep the bloodlines going."

"What do you mean?"

"There was a – a type of Black Plague that swept through the Lycan race many, many years ago. It took out sixty percent of our population and in desperation, Lycans began turning humans."

"So why is there such a problem with it now?" Hannah asked.

Douglas gave her a hesitant look. "There is some truth to the belief that humans who have been turned are unpredictable and dangerous. There have been many documented cases of them turning on other Lycans and humans. They can have a difficult time controlling their Lycan side, especially during the full moon, and many of us who were born Lycan began to worry that their inability to control their wolf would expose us to the humans. There were more than a few who were afraid of these – these hybrid Lycans for lack of a better word."

Hannah stared thoughtfully at him. "Are you afraid of me, Douglas?"

He shook his head. "No. You're strong and have a good heart. You won't hurt me or anyone else."

She gave him a small smile. "Truthfully, I don't feel that much different."

He nodded. "That's because it's only been a few days, Hannah. Over the next week or so you're going to start noticing changes. Your sense of smell will heighten, your eyesight will improve and you'll be faster and stronger."

She gave him a look of doubt and he patted her hand gently. "It's true. I know it's hard to believe, but it will happen. Some humans just take longer than others. I knew of one human, years ago, who took nearly six months before he shifted for the first time."

He took a sip of tea. "When you do shift for the first time, it can be painful and disorienting. You shouldn't expect to have full control of your Lycan side immediately. Constance and I, and Will, will teach you how to control it. You'll be fine. I promise."

"Will won't be able to help me do anything if he won't even talk to me." She said moodily.

He cleared his throat nervously. "There's something else you should know, Hannah. There are quite a few people in the facility who believe that Will turned you because of his issue with humans and Lycans mating. They – they think he did it on purpose so that you could be together without any of the stigma attached."

She gaped at him. "Are you kidding me?"

He shook his head. "I wish I were. There's been enough talk about it that the Board of Directors has become involved. They're considering firing Will as an instructor and asking him to leave the facility. The rumour is that when the new head of the facility arrives, he'll be evaluating Will's performance closely and making a decision on whether to keep him or not."

"They can't do that!" Hannah stood up abruptly. Her hands clenched into fists and knocked her cup of tea off the island counter. It shattered on the floor but she paid no attention to it as she glared at Douglas. Her eyes were fading from brown to green and Douglas held his hands up in a soothing manner as her body began to swell and hair sprouted on her cheeks.

"Calm down, Hannah."

"Calm down?" She arched her eyebrow at him and then growled. "You want me to calm down, old man? The man I love — the man who saved my life and countless other lives — is going to be thrown from the very facility that he's spent half his life defending and you want me to calm down?"

"Yes." Douglas said firmly.

She was panting harshly and the seams of her t-shirt were beginning to rip. She glanced down at herself and then gave Douglas a look of fear and confusion. "Douglas? I feel so strange."

"Take some deep breaths, Hannah. I know you're upset about the situation with Will but your anger and your fear is bringing on your first shift. This is neither the time nor place for it. If you relax, it will stop."

She shook her head, her eyes wide with a combination of fear and anger. "I can't."

"You can." He replied.

She made a soft moaning noise that turned into a low growl. "I won't let them hurt Will. He turned me to save my life, not because he had some hidden agenda. If they even try to accuse him of that or kick him out of the facility, I'll make them pay. All of them."

"Enough, Hannah! Pull yourself together and focus!" Douglas said sharply.

She snarled at him as her teeth turned to fangs and her nails lengthened to sharp points. "Don't tell me what to do, old man.

Douglas stood up and backed away as Hannah's body continued to swell. She growled again as she fell to her hands and knees. She glanced up at him and gave him a look of agonizing fear. "Help me, Douglas."

"Control it, Hannah. Take deep breaths and clear your mind." Douglas slid around the counter.

She ignored him, her entire body rippling and shaking, as she lifted her head and howled. She shifted completely into her wolf form, her clothes ripping apart, and snapped her teeth before leaping to the top of the island. She stared at Douglas, growling deep in her chest, and he swallowed thickly as he stared into her eyes.

"Don't do this, Hannah." He said softly. "Remember who you are."

She grinned at him, her large teeth flashing in the lights above her head, and fear rippled through him. The

Hannah he knew had been swallowed completely by the wolf within her.

Douglas took a step backwards. His ass hit the fridge and he swallowed thickly as his own body began to swell. He didn't want to shift. If he did, this night would end in either Hannah's death or his own. But as Hannah crouched down and growled softly, he could feel the shift happening.

"Hannah," he growled, "stop. Do not make me – "

There was a loud knocking on his apartment door and Hannah whipped her head around as the door opened and Selena stepped into the room.

"Professor? Is Hannah in here? Chen is – "

She stopped and stared wide-eyed at the dark brown wolf crouching on the counter. Its green eyes glowed at her and it barked loudly before leaping off the counter. It stalked toward her and Selena pulled her gun and aimed it at the wolf.

"Professor?" She strained to see around the advancing wolf.

"Selena, get out of here!" Douglas shouted. "It's Hannah! She's not – "

With a loud snarl, Hannah leaped at Selena. There was the sharp bang of gunfire and Hannah yelped in pain and surprise as her body was knocked backwards. She hit the floor of the apartment with a muffled thud and Douglas, his ears ringing, staggered toward her.

She was shifting back to her human form and he grabbed a blanket from the couch and threw it over her naked body as Selena dropped to her knees beside her.

"Hannah? Honey, I'm sorry." She peeled back the blanket and examined the bloody wound in Hannah's shoulder. She breathed a soft sigh of relief when the bullet pushed out of Hannah's flesh with a wet plop and landed on the floor.

"You shot me." Hannah whispered hoarsely.

"I did. I'm sorry." Selena gave her a faint smile and stroked her hair back from her face as Hannah struggled to sit up.

"Lie still, Hannah." Douglas said sternly. He pushed her back to the floor and used the edge of the blanket to wipe the blood from her shoulder. "Give your body time to heal itself."

They could hear the muffled shouts of the others in the facility and Selena glanced at Douglas. "You should let the others know that everything's fine."

Douglas nodded. "Right. Of course. I'll just, uh, tell them it went off accidentally."

His hands trembling slightly, he left the room as Hannah stared up at Selena. "I shifted."

"Yeah, I saw that." Selena replied. She frowned when Hannah began to cry and stroked her arm soothingly.

"It's okay, honey. Don't cry."

"I almost killed Douglas and I tried to kill you." She whispered brokenly.

"You didn't."

"But I tried. I – I couldn't control it. I knew what I was doing was wrong and there was a part of me that tried to stop but there was a bigger, stronger, part of me that liked it. I wanted to bite you, I wanted to – "

She stopped and squeezed her eyes shut as Selena stroked her arm again. "It'll be alright, Hannah."

"Will it?" She whispered without opening her eyes. "What if I never learn to control it? Douglas said that humans who are bitten can't always control their Lycan sides. What if I'm not strong enough to stop from hurting people? To stop the shift?"

"You will be." Selena said firmly. "You just need time. For God's sake, Hannah, you were just bitten three days ago. You can't expect to have full control right away."

"Will that be a good enough excuse when I hurt someone?" Hannah asked softly.

"You're not going to. Will and Douglas will teach you how to control it. They – "

"Will won't even speak to me. He hasn't been back to the facility since that night." Hannah said miserably.

Selena snorted. "Yeah. I know he saved our lives and I know you love him but God, that guy can be a real idiot sometimes."

A faint smile crossed Hannah's face and Selena squeezed her arm before examining her shoulder. She gave a low whistle of appreciation. "It's already starting to heal. How does it feel?"

Hannah moved her shoulder gingerly. "Fine." She cracked one eye open and stared at Selena. "You knew that shooting me wouldn't kill me, right?"

Selena hesitated before grinning at her cheerfully. "Mostly. I mean, I figured it wouldn't but…"

"Cold, Selena. Really cold." Hannah replied.

Selena laughed. "Let's not forget you were about to try and rip off my face."

Hannah winced and Selena shook her head. "Sorry. Listen, it's going to be okay, I promise. Here, sit up."

She helped Hannah into a sitting position before glancing over at the torn and ripped clothing that littered the floor of the kitchen. "You're gonna need a bigger wardrobe. Or just walk around naked."

"Don't joke, Selena." Hannah frowned. "I – I'm dangerous and the state of my clothing is the least of my worries right now."

Selena sobered and sighed heavily. "I know, Hannah. It's just – so many of us are dead, we lost at least half of the recruits in the attack and the other half are scared shitless and want to bail. Richard is dead, we've got a new guy coming in, Chen's hand was cut off, and you're a fucking

Lycan. If we don't try and find something to laugh about, we're going to go insane."

Tears were starting to form in Hannah's eyes again and Selena gave her a brief hug. "That reminds me. I was looking for you to give you some good news."

"Oh yeah? What's that?"

"Chen's awake."

Hannah stiffened before scrambling to her feet and wrapping the blanket around her body. "I need to see him. I need to see him right now, Selena."

"I know, but maybe you should stop at our room and put some clothes on first. What do you say?"

Hannah smiled faintly. "Yeah, okay."

Chapter 2

"Chen?" Hannah sat down gingerly on the side of the hospital bed and stared at Chen's pale face.

"He may have fallen asleep again." Barb said quietly. "He's very weak."

She squeezed Hannah's arm. "How do you feel?"

"Fine." Hannah smiled up at her. "I'm glad you're okay, Barb."

Barb sighed. "I count myself lucky that I was at the farmhouse and that the damn leeches didn't swarm it, as well. I just wish that Richard had been there with me."

Tears began to form in her eyes and Hannah stood and hugged her tightly. "I'm sorry, Barb."

Barb wiped briskly at her face. "Your mom and dad and the twins are at the farmhouse. I haven't been back there yet but your mom's been texting me. She's worried about you."

"I know." Hannah said guiltily. Her mom had been texting and calling her cell phone repeatedly and other than sending a single text telling her mom she was fine and not to worry, she hadn't spoken to either of her parents. Mannie had taken the twins to the farmhouse and instructed them to stay put, and she knew that she needed to go there and see them and her parents.

"You should go and see her." Barb said sternly.

"I will." Hannah promised. "I just – I don't know how to tell them that I'm, you know…"

Barb shook her head. "They're your parents, Hannah. They'll love you no matter what you are. Besides, you're still you."

Although Hannah wasn't entirely sure that was true, she just smiled at Barb and sat back down on Chen's bed. "Thanks, Barb."

"You're welcome, honey. I've got some other patients to check on. I'll be back in a bit." She drew the curtain around the bed and Hannah reached out and took Chen's hand. She stared at his left arm, at the bandage that covered the stump and felt a wave of nausea and guilt go through her. It was her fault that Chen –

Chen shifted in the bed and opened his eyes, staring blearily at Hannah.

"Hello, master." She said softly.

"Hello, Hannah." His voice was hoarse and laced with weariness and she squeezed his hand tightly.

"How do you feel?"

"Tired. My arm hurts."

"I'll get Barb. She'll give you some more meds for the pain." She started to stand and Chen tightened his grip on her hand.

"No. Do not leave me."

"I won't, master." She smiled at him before kissing his cheek.

"How did you kill him?" He suddenly asked.

"I stabbed him through the heart with my shiny sword." Hannah gave him a half-hearted smile.

"I knew you were faster than him." Chen replied.

"I wasn't." She said softly.

"What do you mean?"

"He stabbed me in the chest."

He stared unblinkingly at her and she gave him another tentative smile. "Will, he was there and he, well he…"

She trailed off and he sighed softly. "He bit you."

"Yes."

He didn't say anything and she gnawed at her bottom lip. "I'm sorry."

"Sorry for what?"

"I don't know." She said miserably. "I'm sorry that I couldn't stop him from taking your hand. I'm sorry that I wasn't the person you trained me to be."

He shook his head immediately. "You have nothing to be sorry about, Hannah."

She shrugged and stared at their clasped hands for a moment. "You should try and get some more rest, Chen. I'll sit with you until you fall asleep, alright?"

He nodded and closed his eyes. She studied his pale, drawn face before her gaze dropped to his left arm, and blinked back the sudden tears.

* * *

"Come in!" Mannie snapped.

Reid opened the door to Richard's office and poked his head in. "Hey."

"Hey."

He hesitated and then sat down in the chair across from Richard's desk. Mannie was typing something on the computer and he waited patiently for him to finish.

When he was done, Mannie sat back and rubbed at his forehead wearily. "What's up?"

"Just checking in to see what the plan is."

Mannie laughed bitterly. "The plan? I have no fucking idea, Reid."

Reid frowned. "You're temporarily in charge, Mannie. We need someone to take control of the place. The recruits we have left are freaked out. They're talking about – "

"I know!" Mannie shouted. "Jesus, you think I don't know what a fucking gong show it's been the last three days? Half our recruits are dead, Richard is dead, Chen is missing his goddamn hand, Will's gone AWOL, and Hannah's a fucking werewolf! You think I don't know how fucked we are?"

"Okay, okay, calm down." Reid held his hands up in a soothing manner. "I just thought maybe the Board of Directors had spoken to you."

Mannie, breathing hard, closed his eyes for a moment. "Jesus, I'm sorry, Reid. It's just, Alison is dead and I..."

He trailed off and Reid nodded solemnly. "I know, man. I'm sorry."

Mannie took a deep breath and blew it out harshly before staring at the blood-stained carpet behind the desk. "The new guy should be here by the end of the week. They're sending a clean-up crew today, and they're bringing in recruits from some of the other facilities to help us patrol until they can install better security equipment."

Reid shook his head. "The security equipment should have been in place months ago. They were idiots to think that we didn't need it. We're a training facility for God's sake! You'd think they would have put extra effort into protecting their new recruits."

"Yeah, well, lesson learned." Mannie said quietly.

"Do you think the vampires will attack again?"

"Honestly, I have no idea. I don't know if there are other leeches out there who know where this place is, or if that fucking Samuel brought his entire army with him. We have to assume that others do know. I talked briefly with Hannah after the shit was all over and done with, and she said that although Samuel didn't come right out and say it, he implied that he was part of a bigger group. That vampires across the country were working together and that they would take out the facilities one by one."

"There's no way that's happening." Reid protested. "Vampires can barely stand each other. Do you honestly think they could form large groups country-wide without killing each other?"

"That asshole Samuel managed to do it." Mannie replied.

"Yeah." Reid sighed.

"The Board of Directors wants us to try and get things back to normal as quickly as possible. They've informed me that we're to return to training classes by tomorrow."

"Tomorrow?" Reid shook his head. "They do realize that one of our instructors is lying in the hospital missing his damn hand and another is running around the woods, right?"

"They know about Chen. I haven't said anything about Will." Mannie replied.

"Why not?"

"Because the Board of Directors is already freaking out that Will turned Hannah. I have no fucking idea how they found out, but they know and they're not happy about it."

"He saved her life." Reid said quietly.

"Yeah, but there's been talk that he did it for other reasons too."

Reid stared thoughtfully at him for a moment. "We were both there when he turned her. Do you think he did it for a reason other than to save her life?"

Mannie shook his head. "No. And honestly, if I had been in his place, I would have done the same thing. You'll do whatever it takes to save the woman that you lo −"

His voice broke and he stared at Richard's desk as Reid waited patiently. After a few moments he cleared his throat roughly and shuffled some papers on the desk. "The Board wants us to get back to normal as quickly as possible, thinks it will be better for the remaining recruits, and I can't fight them on this. Besides, the new guy will be here soon and he'll do what the Board wants, so we might as well try and get the recruits back into a normal routine before he arrives."

"I'm not sure − "

There was a knock on the door and at Mannie's shout to come in, Selena entered the office. She nodded to Reid before sitting down in the chair next to him.

"You wanted to see me?"

"Yeah. How's Hannah doing?"

"Fine." Selena said cautiously. "She's visiting Chen right now."

"Good, good." Mannie nodded distractedly as he opened a file folder on Richard's desk and combed through the papers. "Listen, this is a hell of a time to say congratulations but we're trying to get things back to normal as quickly as possible."

"What are you talking about?" Selena frowned at him.

"You've passed the program. You're no longer a recruit." Mannie gave her a small smile. "Richard meant to tell you before..."

He trailed off and Selena grimaced. "Thanks, but I'm quitting the program."

"You're what?" Mannie gaped at her.

"I'm quitting. I'll pack up my things and be gone by the end of the week." Selena said calmly.

She walked toward the door as Mannie stood up. "Selena, wait! You can't quit. We need you now more than ever."

"I'm sorry. I've made my decision." She slipped out of the room as Mannie stared at Reid.

"What the fuck just happened?"

"I'll go and talk to her." Reid left the office as Mannie collapsed back into his chair and dropped his head into his hands.

* * *

"Selena! Hey! Wait up!" Reid jogged down the hallway as Selena quickened her pace.

He tugged her to a stop. "Just hold on a minute, okay?"

"What, Reid?" She asked impatiently.

"Listen, I know what happened was awful, and I know we lost a lot of good people but quitting isn't going to make you feel better."

"I'm not quitting because of what happened here." She replied.

"Then why are you?" He asked.

"Why did you kiss me?" She asked abruptly.

"What?"

"Why did you kiss me?" She repeated.

"Hell, I don't know. I was pretty sure we were going to die and it seemed like a good idea at the time."

"Right." She pulled her arm free. "Goodbye, Reid."

"Selena, wait!" He took her arm again and pulled her into Chen's training room. He shut the door and leaned against it. "Tell me why you're quitting."

"It doesn't matter, alright?   I just – I can't do this anymore." She shoved at his large body. "Get out of my way."

"No, not until you tell me why you're quitting."

She glared at him. "Get out of my way, Reid. I won't ask you again."

He shook his head. "You can't just – "

She scowled at him and when she tried to punch him in the stomach, he blocked her arm and swung her around until her back was pressed against the door. She kicked and punched wildly at him and he grabbed her wrists and pulled them above her head, pinning her against the door with his hands and body.

"Tell me, Selena."

"Fine!" She shouted. "I'm quitting because I'm useless at this, alright?"

He blinked in surprise. "Are you kidding me? You're one of our best, Selena."

"Bullshit!" She spat at him. "I go into every single fight terrified that I'm going to die. I'm – I'm so scared that I can hardly think straight."

"We're all frightened." He said softly.

She snorted angrily. "That isn't true and you know it, Reid. Hannah isn't afraid, and neither is Will or Chen or Mannie."

"Just because they don't show it, doesn't mean that they
– "

"Did you know I was in the military?' She interrupted.

He nodded as she sighed heavily. "I was really good at my job. You know that? I was one of only two women in my unit, and one of the greatest days of my life was when one of the guys in my unit told me he trusted me to have his back more than anyone else. I was tough and I wasn't afraid. I knew what I had to do, what I needed to do, and I did it."

She sighed again. "With this though, I just – I can't do it. Hannah's a civilian with no prior training and she's better at killing vampires than I am. She was a college student for God's sake! I'm a liability, Reid. Every time I go hunting, I put the lives of the people who are with me at risk because I'm afraid and I don't know how to stop being afraid."

She started to cry and he hesitated before releasing her arms and pulling her into his embrace. She stiffened against him and then put her arms around his waist and clung tightly to him as he rubbed her back.

"Don't compare yourself to Hannah or anyone else, alright? Besides, you saved my life, and when it counted you did what needed to be done. You were right there beside Mannie and me in that common room killing vampires, remember?"

She continued to cry and he held her a little tighter. "Don't quit, Selena. Give it a few weeks, alright? I know you think it has nothing to do with what just happened but I think you're wrong. Take some time to really decide what it is you want. You're a damn good vampire killer, you just need to realize that."

"I hate this." Her voice was muffled against his shirt and he stroked her curly dark hair.

"We all do. But you've been bitten. If you leave, the leeches will find you sooner or later. It's better for you to be here where you're protected and have friends to help keep you safe. Right?"

"I guess." She sighed.

She leaned back and stared up at him. Her cheeks were wet and he wiped at them gently with his thumbs. She inhaled sharply and her gaze dropped to his mouth.

He cleared his throat nervously. "Selena, I think – "

She stood on her tiptoes and pressed her mouth against his. He jerked in surprise and her arms tightened around his waist before she pushed at his lips with her tongue. With a soft groan, he parted them and she slid her tongue into his mouth and touched his delicately.

He cupped her face with one large hand, his fingers tangling in the softness of her hair and kissed her back. She moaned into his mouth and the soft sound had his cock hardening in his jeans. He kissed her deeply before licking her bottom lip with his tongue. She moaned again and he sucked lightly at her top lip as she pressed herself against his erection. He cupped her small, firm breast through her t-shirt and she arched her back and shivered against him. He trailed a path of soft kisses down her throat before licking her warm skin.

"Selena." He whispered.

She pushed away from him, her face red and her mouth swollen from his kisses, and gave him a look of shame mixed with desire. "I'm sorry. I shouldn't have done that."

Before he could reply, she yanked open the door and ran from the room.

Chapter 3

Hannah slammed the door of the truck shut and stared apprehensively at the farmhouse. Her pulse thudding heavily, she started up the steps of the porch. The door flung open and her mom charged out on to the porch and threw her arms around her.

"Oh, Hannah." She kissed her repeatedly on the cheek as she squeezed her tightly and Hannah's eyes started to water when her mom burst into tears.

"We were so worried. Come in, right now."

She followed her mom in and was immediately surrounded by her father and the twins. Reuben, barking shrilly, was dancing at her feet and her mother scooped him up and scolded him lightly as her dad hugged her tightly.

"Hi, baby girl."

"Hi, dad." She smiled at him and he kissed her forehead before stepping back and letting Luther and Tyrone at her. She hugged them tightly, kissing first Tyrone's cheek and then Luther's before smiling at them.

"You two look great."

Luther rolled his eyes. "You saw us four days ago."

"I know. It feels longer." She kissed them again and they both groaned and pushed away from her.

"She's got a point." Tyrone said. "The last time she saw us we were covered in ash and blood from the vampire ass we kicked."

He held up his hand and Luther fist bumped it before turning back to Hannah. "Hey, has that cold stone fox been asking about me?"

He wiggled his eyebrows at her as Tyrone punched him in the back. "She's a wolf, you idiot."

"I know!" Luther scowled at him before punching him in the arm. "You think I don't know what my future wife is?"

"Please! One little kiss don't mean she's gonna lie on her back and spread her – "

"Tyrone!" Jim said sharply.

Tyrone shut his mouth with a snap and gave Natalie a guilty look. "Sorry, ma'am."

"That's alright, dear." Natalie patted his arm. "But let's remember that a gentleman never speaks poorly of a woman. Right?"

"Right, ma'am." Tyrone replied.

Natalie curled her arm around Hannah's shoulders and led her into the kitchen. "Come sit down, honey. We'll have a cup of tea. Your father is determined to give you a lecture for staying away so long and you know that normally I'd remind him that you're a grown woman and free to live your own life, but not this time I'm afraid. You really do owe us an apology."

"I'm sorry." Hannah said sincerely. "I shouldn't have been avoiding you, it's just that – "

She took a deep breath and smiled at her dad. "Go ahead, lecture. I'm ready."

Her dad shook his head and squeezed her hand as he sat down next to her. "I'm just glad you're okay, Hannah Banana."

"Softie." Natalie muttered under her breath before smiling cheerfully at the four of them. "Who wants pie with the tea?"

Luther and Tyrone jumped up and hurried into the pantry to grab the pie as Natalie put the kettle on and took down five plates.

"Is Heather okay?" Hannah asked suddenly.

"She's fine. She was actually out here earlier this morning for a visit. We've been staying at the farmhouse with the boys and I asked her to stay too but she wanted to go back home." Natalie replied.

"Are you okay, Hannah?" Her father gave her a sympathetic look and squeezed her hand again. "Barb told us about Richard and about Chen losing his hand. How is he?"

"I'm not really sure. He woke up yesterday and I visited with him for a bit but he was still a little groggy. We didn't really talk about his hand."

Her throat burning and tears threatening again, she accepted the steaming mug of tea her mother held out to her. She sipped cautiously at it as Luther and Tyrone dug into their pieces of apple pie.

"Poor Chen." Natalie sighed. "I wanted to go and visit him but Mannie won't let us into the facility right now."

"They're still doing clean up." Hannah replied. "Trust me, you don't want to see the place."

"So many lives lost." Natalie sighed again. "How is Will? I'm surprised he didn't come with you."

Hannah winced. "Listen, mom, dad, there's something I need to tell you. It's um, it's kind of complicated but when I was fighting Samuel, he stabbed me. Will was there and he – "

She paused, feeling her cheeks heating up and her hands trembling. How exactly did one tell their parents that their daughter was a Lycan now?

"He - and I want you to know that he did this to save my life – he, well…."

"He bit you. We already know, dear." Natalie popped a forkful of pie into her mouth and chewed delicately before staring at Luther.

"Luther, dearest, you have apple on your face."

He swiped at his face and she grinned and wiped away the chunk of apple with her thumb.

"Thank you, Natalie." Luther said politely.

"You're welcome, dear. Why don't you and Tyrone have another piece each but that's it. Supper will be ready in a few hours. You're staying for supper, I assume?" She arched her eyebrow at Hannah.

Hannah, her mouth open and her eyes wide, stared at her mother and then at her father. He was washing down the last bite of his pie with a swallow of tea and he winked at his wife. "The pie was delicious, Nat. Thank you."

"You're welcome, honey."

"Mom..." Hannah reached out and touched her mother's hand.

"Yes?"

"I – you understand what this means, right?"

"Of course we do." She frowned at Hannah.

"It means you're gonna wolf out and howl at the moon." Tyrone snickered as Luther grinned at her.

"You should shift right now – let's see what you look like."

"No!" Hannah took a deep breath. "I – I don't have a lot of control over it right now. I've only shifted once and I – well, let's just say it didn't go well."

"That's alright, honey. You'll get the hang of it." Her father patted her hand before carrying his plate to the sink. He rinsed it and placed it in the dishwasher before lifting the kettle. "More tea, Nat?"

"Yes, please." She said cheerfully. She smiled at Tyrone when he took her empty plate and carried it to the counter. "Thank you, Tyrone. You're such a sweet boy."

"Not that you aren't either, Luther." She went on hastily. "You know I love both my boys."

"We love you too." Tyrone said shyly. His face red, he dropped a quick kiss on her cheek before sitting back down beside Luther. He ignored his brother when Luther elbowed him in the ribs and muttered, "pussy" under his breath.

Hannah stared at the four of them before leaning forward. "Mom, you know I'm not the same anymore, right? I'm a Lycan now and I – "

"You're still our Hannah. And honestly, we're just grateful you're alive. We don't care what you are. Well, obviously we're thankful you're not one of those horrid leeches." Her mother replied with a frown.

"You're not afraid of me?"

"Why would we be?" Her father gave her a blank look.

"I don't know, I just…" Hannah trailed off.

"Is that why you've been avoiding us? Because you thought we'd be scared of you?" Her mother shook her head. "Oh Hannah. You know us better than that."

"Although," she frowned in sudden thought, "I do hope this doesn't mean you'll stop eating vegetables. I know Lycans like meat but it's important to maintain a healthy balance. You have to promise me you'll keep eating your vegetables, dear."

When Hannah didn't reply, she raised her eyebrows at her. "Promise me."

"I promise."

"Good." Natalie smiled in satisfaction and took another drink of tea.

Hannah, feeling a strange mixture of fierce gratitude and shock, stared at her uneaten piece of pie. "How did you know I was a Lycan?"

There was no reply and she glanced up to see her parents giving her an odd look.

"Mom? Dad? How did you know?" She persisted.

Jim frowned at her. "Will told us. Didn't he tell you?"

"What?" She stared at him in shock and pushed her plate away." You've seen him? When? How?"

"He came by the farmhouse the morning after the attack at the facility. We had just gotten here ourselves and Mannie had just dropped the boys off to us." Natalie said gently. "He was in his wolf form and terribly upset. It took us forever to convince him to shift to his human form and talk to us."

"He's terribly upset?" Hannah snapped. "He just took off after saving my life. He's been roaming around the woods for the last four days avoiding everyone except my parents, apparently, and I had no idea if he was even okay. He just leaves me to deal with this alone, and he's terribly upset?"

Her voice was rising and Jim gave Natalie an uneasy look before holding Hannah's hand. "Honey, I know you don't want to hear this right now but Will feels awful for what he did."

"Well, he shouldn't." Hannah snapped again. "He saved my life and if he wasn't being such a stubborn jackass, I'd tell him that myself."

She made herself take a deep breath. "Why did he come to the farmhouse?"

"He wanted to tell us himself what he had done." Jim replied. "He didn't want there to be any misunderstanding about why he bit you."

"The poor boy. You know, I actually think he expected Jim to just haul off and hit him." Natalie shook her head. "We, of course, were just grateful that he had saved your life."

"Has he been back?" Hannah asked.

"No. We haven't seen him since. Honestly, I assumed that he was going back to the facility to check on you."

"Well, he didn't." Hannah retorted.

"I think he just needs some time." Natalie said softly. "He's changed your life forever and I know it was done to save you, but it's a still a difficult thing to process."

"He's still a jackass."

"Oh, undoubtedly." Natalie grinned at her. "Did I ever tell you about the time that your father decided he would cut my hair?"

Her father groaned and stood up. "That's my cue to leave. Boys? Shall we retire to the living room and watch football?"

The three of them left the room as Natalie settled back in her chair. "It was just after we were married, long before you came along, and your father had just started his own accounting practice. It wasn't doing great and we were tight on money so we started looking for ways to cut expenses. Your father had the brilliant idea that he would cut my hair. I was, as you can imagine, skeptical but I did need a trim so I took a chance."

"And?"

"Oh my gosh, it was awful! Your father couldn't cut a straight line to save his life." Natalie said dramatically. "He just kept cutting and cutting – just to even up the edges - and finally I just ripped the damn scissors out of his hand. I went to the bathroom mirror, took one look at myself, and burst into tears. I looked like a lead singer from a terrible nineties rock band. Do you remember how bad their hair was?"

Hannah couldn't stop the grin. "Yeah, I remember."

"I was so mad at your father, I wouldn't talk to him for a week straight. He felt terrible, of course. Kept begging for my forgiveness and asking what he could do to make it better. He even booked me an appointment at my regular salon to get it fixed, but I refused to go at first. I was just being petty and miserable, but eventually I got over myself and went to the appointment. After all, I had said he could cut my hair."

Hannah smiled again. "I can't believe you never told me that story before."

"Well, I didn't act very kind in it, did I? I wasn't keen on telling either you or your sister that I could, from time to time, be a spoiled brat." Natalie laughed.

"The point is, Will feels just as terrible for what he's done as your father did for giving me that haircut. It's going to — "

She stopped. "Oh dear, that wasn't a very good analogy at all was it? I thought it was but I hardly suppose that being turned into a Lycan and getting a bad haircut is in any way remotely similar."

She sighed. "I'm sorry, Hannah."

"It's fine, mom. It was a good story." Hannah squeezed her hand.

"Will loves you. He won't be able to stay away for long, even with the guilt he feels. And when he returns to you, you can give him the tongue-lashing he deserves for running away and then tell him that you love him and he has nothing to feel bad about." Natalie said firmly.

Hannah didn't reply and Natalie frowned at her. "Does he need to feel bad about it?"

"No. It's just – I'm afraid, mom. I got angry and upset yesterday and I shifted for the first time and nearly killed Douglas. If Selena hadn't shot me, I think I might have."

Natalie twitched a little. "Selena shot you?"

"Yes. Don't worry. It won't kill me if it isn't a silver bullet."

"Fascinating!" Natalie said brightly.

"But I can't control it. I don't want to hurt people but when I shift, I just... Douglas says that some humans who are bitten become dangerous. They never learn to control it."

"You will." Natalie said firmly. "You've never given up on something you wanted before, and this will be no different. Now, let's go sit with your father and the boys for a bit and then you can help me start dinner. Alright?"

"Okay. I love you, mom."

"I love you too, dear."

Chapter 4

Hannah joined Selena at the cafeteria table, ignoring the stares of the recruits scattered among the other tables.

Selena eyes widened at the giant slab of steak on Hannah's plate and Hannah gave her a guilty look. "I'm craving meat like you wouldn't believe."

"Yeah, I'm not surprised." Selena grinned at her. "At least you're still eating vegetables." She stared at the small amount of steamed broccoli on the plate.

"Only because my mother made me promise to continue eating my veggies." Hannah laughed as she cut into the steak.

"How are you feeling?" Selena asked curiously as she ate her chicken.

Hannah shrugged. "Honestly? Really weird. I have this crazy amount of energy. I did a 10 km run this morning without breaking a sweat. Douglas said my eyesight and hearing would improve and it has. I can hear everything and it's nearly impossible to sleep. I don't know how to drown it out – people are so fucking loud, Selena."

She glanced around at the other people in the cafeteria. "I swear I can hear all of them chewing." She grimaced. "And last night I could hear Leanne having sex with someone, and her room is three doors down from ours."

"Glad to see some things don't change." Selena rolled her eyes.

"It's good to have a routine again." Hannah replied. "The recruits started training yesterday and I think everyone is feeling a little better because of it."

"Yeah, maybe." Selena toyed with the salad on her plate. "Have you met any of the recruits they sent down to help us patrol?"

"A couple of them. I just finished patrol and there were a few on patrol with me. I think the other recruits have been sharing information because they were decidedly nervous around me."

She chewed happily at a piece of steak before swallowing and smiling at Selena. "By the way, I hear congratulations are in order. Mannie said that you had graduated."

"Yeah."

"He also said that you told him you were quitting."

Selena sighed and pushed her plate away. "Reid convinced me to stay."

"Good. We need you."

Selena shook her head. "I'm not sure that's true. I'm – I'm not like you, Hannah. I freeze up and I'm afraid and I – "

"I'm afraid too. I told you that before." Hannah said firmly. "Besides, you don't freeze up. You saved Reid's life, and Mannie and Mallorie and Ryan. Not to mention a bunch of the babies. You're good at this, Selena. As good, if not better, than the rest of us."

"Maybe." Selena said moodily.

"What are you doing tonight? We could go to the farmhouse and visit with my parents and the twins for a while. I know they'd like that."

Selena shook her head. "Thanks but I've got the late shift in patrolling tonight. I want to sneak in a quick nap before – "

She stopped, her face flushing, when Reid sat down next to Hannah. "Hey."

"Hi, Reid." Hannah smiled at him. "Where have you been? I feel like you're avoiding me."

"No. Just busy." His gaze flickered to Selena and Hannah watched curiously as his cheeks reddened. "Hello, Selena."

"Hey, Reid." Selena mumbled. She had suddenly become fascinated by the table surface as Reid cleared his throat.

"Have you heard from Will?"

"No."

"He'd better get his ass back here before the new guy shows up tomorrow." Reid replied. "It won't exactly make a good impression for him to be missing in action, and Jordan's a hard ass."

"You know him?" Hannah asked.

Reid nodded. "He was second in command at my old facility in LA. Honestly, I'm surprised he agreed to come here. The small town scene didn't really seem to be his thing. But, he was anxious to move up so maybe he figures this is his only chance."

"What's he like?"

"I didn't know him that well, to be honest. He seems like an okay guy, just a real stickler for the rules and," he hesitated, "I know he doesn't like the idea of allowing supernaturals to be involved with the facility. He's not an outright racist, but he doesn't believe that we can trust any supernatural."

"Great." Hannah sighed. "Just great."

"I'm sure it will be fine." Reid said soothingly. "Just don't piss him off and when Will decides to show his hairy face here again, maybe tell him to keep his wolf under control."

"Right." Hannah replied grimly.

He squeezed her shoulder reassuringly before glancing at Selena again. She was still studying the table and he cracked his knuckles nervously before standing.

"I should go. See you later, ladies."

"Bye, Reid." Hannah smiled at him as Selena gave him a brief wave without looking up.

It wasn't until he had left the cafeteria that she raised her gaze, and she blushed hotly at the look Hannah was giving her.

"What?"

"What do you mean - what?" Hannah replied. "What's going on with you two?"

"Nothing!" She said quickly. "There's nothing going on with us. Why would you think there's something going on with us? There isn't. I hardly know the guy."

Hannah took another bite of steak and stared thoughtfully at Selena. "Are you going to tell me or do I have to ask Reid?"

Selena glared at her and took a large drink of water. "Alright, fine. We kissed, okay?"

A grin crossed Hannah's face. "That's great."

"No, it isn't."

"Why not?"

"Because." Selena scowled at her again.

"Because why?"

"Oh for the love of – because I learned the hard way that getting involved with anyone in this program means heartbreak, because Reid's an instructor, because he has a thing for you!" Selena snapped.

"He doesn't have a thing for me." Hannah replied.

"Please, don't even try and tell me that – "

"He might have had a thing for me at one time," Hannah interrupted, "but trust me – he doesn't now. He knows I love Will and besides, he's not real fond of Lycans. He tries to be accepting but..."

She trailed off and took a quick glance around before leaning closer to Selena. "C'mon, girl. Spill your guts."

Selena sighed before resting her chin on her hand. "The night that Samuel attacked the facility, Reid, Douglas and I went to the common room. Mannie and the others were in there and they were being decimated. There were leeches everywhere and all three of us knew that we were going to die when we stepped into that room. You know?"

"I do." Hannah said gravely.

"Anyway, Reid looked at me and basically just said, fuck it, that no one lived forever and then he kissed me and we ran in."

Hannah grinned. "He has a way with words."

Selena snorted softly. "Anyway, after I told Mannie that I quit, Reid came after me to convince me to stay. I asked him why he kissed me that night and he said he didn't know, that it seemed like a good idea at the time."

Hannah rolled her eyes before motioning at Selena with her fork. "Go on."

"He took me into Chen's training room and kept questioning me and finally I told him the truth. Then, like a complete idiot, I started crying. Reid hugged me and God, it felt good to be hugged by him. The guy's body is hard as a rock but he was so warm..."

She trailed off and stared absentmindedly at her dinner plate as Hannah waited patiently.

"He wiped the tears from my face and I was staring at his mouth and, I don't know, I just lost my damn mind and kissed him." Selena dropped her face into her hands. "I'm such an idiot."

"What did he do?" Hannah asked curiously.

"He kissed me back. The next thing I know we've got our tongues in each other's mouths and he's got an erection, and I'm ready to just rip his clothes off and take him right there." Selena's voice was muffled.

Hannah laughed. "Nice. He likes the saucy girls. What happened then?"

"I came to my senses, told him I was sorry and I shouldn't have done that, and ran away." Selena said miserably.

"Oh." Hannah patted her arm gingerly. "That explains the awkwardness."

"Yeah." Selena sighed.

"Why did you stop? Is it because of Tyler?" Hannah asked gently.

Selena shook her head. "No, I don't think so. I mean I miss him terribly and I still love him, but it's more because of what I said before. Falling in love with someone at this place means heartbreak and loss sooner or later."

She gave Hannah a quick look. "Not that I'm falling in love with Reid, because I'm not."

"I know." Hannah smiled at her. "Reid's a pretty good guy but he doesn't seem like the settling down type to me so it's probably better if you don't fall for him."

"Yes, I know, that's why I – "

"Of course, that doesn't mean you can't boink the hell out of him. I bet he's super fun in the sack." Hannah said cheerfully.

Selena blinked at her. "Reid's an instructor."

"So? You're not a recruit anymore."

"It's not a good idea, Hannah. Besides, it's still against the rules."

Hannah shrugged. "Fuck the rules. The rule-makers are idiots if they think they can keep people from having sex in this place. People need to blow off a little steam and sooner or later, the higher-ups will figure that out."

She looked earnestly at Selena. "You're a grown woman so I'm not going to tell you what to do, but I do think that a little no-commitment nookie might just be what the doctor ordered. And it sounds like Reid would be a-okay with it."

A small smile crossed Selena's face. "I know you think that I need – "

She paused, watching curiously as Hannah stiffened and dropped her fork to her plate with a loud clatter. She raised her head and inhaled deeply.

"Hannah? What's wrong?"

"He's back." She said softly.

"Who? Will?" Selena turned and looked around the cafeteria. There was no sign of the large Lycan and she turned back to Hannah. "How do you know that?"

"I can smell him." Hannah inhaled again before standing. "I have to go, Selena."

Selena caught her hand. "Are you alright?"

She dropped Hannah's hand when the woman smiled at her. Her eye teeth had become sharp fangs and her eyes had lightened to a brilliant jade.

"I'm fine." She said dreamily as her eyes began to glow. "I'm just fine."

"Hannah – "

Hannah made a low, soft, growl and Selena watched as she turned and ran nimbly from the cafeteria.

* * *

Hannah stood outside the door of Will's apartment and took another deep breath. Despite the barrier between them she could easily both smell and hear Will. She closed her eyes, listening to the rasp of his jeans as he pulled them over his hips and the louder purr of the zipper.

He won't need those.

Lust had exploded in her belly from the moment she had smelled him. Despite being in the hallway where anyone could see her, she slid her hand into her pants and underwear and cupped her warm center. Her fingers were soaked instantly and she grinned again, baring her fangs, as she reached for the door handle.

It was unlocked and she entered the room, shutting the door firmly behind her as Will looked up from the middle of the living room. He didn't look surprised to see her and smiled nervously.

Mine.

Her nostrils flaring, her desire beating within her like a steady, unrelenting drum, she stalked toward him. She could feel her need to shift bearing down on her, and she touched her fangs with the tip of her tongue. Her anger with him had been buried beneath her overwhelming need to claim him and his eyes widened as he caught the scent of her need.

"Hannah – "

"Mine!" She growled at him and grabbed him by the front of his shirt. She mashed her mouth down onto his, her fangs cutting into his lips, as she thrust her tongue deep into his warm mouth. She ripped his t-shirt in half, the fabric tearing with a low purr, and yanked it from his body before pulling her mouth away from his and tracing his hard chest. Her fingernails had lengthened into sharp claws and he let his breath out in a low hiss when she ran them along the waistband of his jeans.

"Hannah, I – "

She flicked the button open on his jeans and thrust her hand under the material. She wrapped her fingers around his length, he was already hard and pulsing, and squeezed firmly.

"This is mine." She growled.

"Yes." He said immediately. "But we need to talk first. We need to – "

"No!"

He grunted with surprise when she gave him a hard shove and knocked him to the floor.

She stripped off her clothes, slicing her bra in half with her fingernails when she couldn't undo the clasps fast enough, and straddled him. She reached between them and yanked the zipper down on his pants before pulling his cock free.

She growled again and he moaned harshly when she rubbed the head of his cock against her swollen clit.

"Jesus, Hannah." He groaned. "Just wait, honey, we need to – "

He cried out when she impaled herself on his thick cock. She growled happily and snapped her teeth at him as her eyes glowed in the dim room. She bounced on his cock, using her legs to thrust herself back and forth as his hands circled her waist and he arched his back under her.

She braced her hands on his chest and rode him madly as their bodies slammed together. Will, his own eyes glowing, suddenly growled and flipped her on to her back. He plunged in and out of her, the veins in his throat standing out in stark relief as he fucked her hard.

She moaned and gasped and growled as her fingernails raked long, deep scratches into the flesh of his back. He had never been so rough with her and as he bent his head and nipped at her breast with short, stinging bites, she dug her nails into his back until he hissed in pain and lifted his head.

"You're mine." She snarled at him.

"Yes, yours." He tangled his hand into her hair, pulling her head back roughly and sucked hard on her throat.

His fingers found her clit and he rubbed the swollen nub firmly as she arched her back and wrapped her long limbs around his waist. She squeezed his cock tightly and he gave a harsh bark of need before tugging on her clit.

The pleasure exploded within her as the colours of the room began to sharpen and Will's harsh panting grew to an almost unbearable level. She was starting to shift, she could feel it, and she fought desperately against it.

"Will!" She shouted his name as her orgasm flooded her body and unable to stop herself, she lifted her head and sank her fangs into the meat of his shoulder. His blood filled her mouth, warm and surprisingly sweet, and his entire body shuddered before he climaxed with a loud, hoarse howl.

Chapter 5

Hannah, her heart finally beginning to slow, stared up at the ceiling. Will was still lying on her, his hard body fitting every soft curve of hers perfectly, and she smiled happily before running her hands over his back. Wetness coated her fingers and she lifted her hands, her soft smile turning to a look of horror at the red that covered them.

"Oh my God!" She pushed at Will and he rolled off of her. "Oh my God, oh my God!" She nearly shouted. Blood was dripping from his shoulder where she had bitten him and, nausea and fear rolling in her stomach, she jumped to her feet and ran naked to the bathroom.

She returned with a towel and pressed it firmly against his shoulder as he sat up. "Shit! Will, I'm so sorry!"

She could feel the tears threatening and she blinked them back fiercely as she leaned over him and examined his back. What she saw horrified her. There were deep, bloody scratches all over his back and she moaned softly. What had she done?

"Will, get up!" Still holding the towel against his shoulder she climbed to her feet and urged him to his.

She nearly yanked him to the bathroom, her worry and fear making her rough, and he made a soft sound of reassurance. "Hannah, it's fine. Honey – "

"It's not *fine*!" She snapped at him. Despite her efforts, the tears were starting to slide down her face. "I scratched the shit out of your back, Will! I – I *bit* you!"

"Hold this!" She made him press his hand against the towel on his shoulder.

She wet a washcloth before turning him around and wiping softly at the scratches in his skin. As she wiped the blood away, she was dismayed to realize that she was close to shifting again. Her panic and her shame was heightening her need to shift and she made a soft moan of panic.

"Hannah?" Will immediately turned and pulled her into her arms, dropping the towel to the floor. "It's okay. Shh. Calm down."

"I can't." She moaned. She was vibrating in his arms and she moaned again when the light in the bathroom was suddenly too bright.

"Take a deep breath, honey." He pushed her head against his uninjured shoulder and she wrapped her arms around his hips and buried her face into his neck. His scent, warm and familiar and utterly intoxicating, filled her nostrils and she took breath after breath. After a few moments she realized with an odd mix of wonder and gratitude that the urge to shift had passed. Will's presence, his scent and his warm, hard body, had calmed her.

She pressed herself tighter against him and he stroked her naked back with his callused hands. Her wolf, she wondered if other Lycans thought of their wolves as separate beings inside of them, made a soft growl of lust and her eyes widened. She wanted him again, she wanted him inside of her while she bit him and scratched him and marked him as hers, and God help anyone who tried to stop her.

The scent of Will's arousal, strong and undeniable, filled the room and she made a low, soft growl before reaching between them and squeezing his cock. He groaned harshly and she stroked him firmly as he stiffened in her hand.

She would take him again and again. She would mark him fully with her scent until every bitch knew that he belonged to her. He was hers and –

She tore away from him with a soft gasp and backed away as far as she could in the small bathroom.

He reached out for her and she shook her head desperately.

"Don't touch me, Will." She moaned. "I – I'm not myself right now and I don't want to hurt you."

"You won't hurt me." He said soothingly.

"I already did." She whispered. Her eyes drifted to the bite on his shoulder and she drew in a shuddering breath of relief. It had stopped bleeding and was beginning to heal.

"It's fine. It will heal quickly." He smiled at her as her eyes dropped to his cock. It was hard and ready to go, and she bit at her bottom lip as the need to take him surged within her.

Take him. Take him now. Take him before another female tries to claim him.

The voice, one she didn't recognize, chanted steadily in her head and she squeezed her thighs together in a vain attempt to stop the aching between them. It only made things worse, as did the smell of Will's arousal, and she put one hand over her mouth and nose.

She growled when Will took a step closer. Her eyes flashed bright green at him and she lowered her hands and dug her claws into the wall behind her.

"Come any closer, Lycan, and I will take what is mine." She snarled softly.

Will's eyes turned a dark yellow and he grinned at her. Another bite of lust went through her at the sight of his sharp fangs. "Not if I take what is mine first."

With a hoarse growl she lunged at him. He caught her and slammed her up against the wall, hard enough to make a crack appear in the plaster, as she wrapped her legs around his waist. He kissed her hard on the mouth as he trapped her wrists above her head with one hand.

She fought against him but even her new-found strength was no match for his and she gave a low howl of pleasure when he thrust his cock into her. He plunged in and out, banging her body against the wall as he kissed her deeply.

She kissed him back eagerly, her tongue battling with his as he fucked her hard and fast. She squeezed her legs around his waist and made a harsh yip of excitement when he pushed his hand between them and stroked her clit.

Her orgasm roared through her, completely unexpected, and she bit him again as he thrust back and forth. He growled and nipped her painfully on the neck as a second wave of pleasure washed over her. Her pussy squeezed his cock until, with another hoarse growl, he stiffened and came deeply inside of her.

Panting hoarsely he rested his forehead against hers and stroked her side soothingly. "Better?"

"Yes." She whispered. "I think so."

"Good." He took a deep breath and eased out of her before lowering her to the ground. "Are you – "

"Fuck!" She suddenly shouted. "I fucking did it again!"

She was staring at his other shoulder, blood was dripping down his chest, and she grabbed a second towel and dabbed at the bite delicately. "Jesus, Will. I am so sorry."

"It's fine, Hannah, I swear." He stroked her hip as she chewed at her bottom lip. "It's natural for Lycans to bite during sex."

"You've never bitten me." She said softly.

"You weren't a Lycan before. I would never bite a human in that way."

"You still haven't bitten me." She pointed out. Her hand rose to her throat and she rubbed at the spot where he had nipped her. Although she could feel the indents of his fangs, he hadn't broken the skin.

"Old habits." He said briefly. "I'm used to controlling the urge to bite you when we mate."

"Right." She sighed. "Tell me how you control it and how you stop from shifting when we mate. Please. I – I think part of me keeps biting you because it stops me from shifting but I hate making you bleed."

"It takes practice." He replied. "But I swear to you, I don't mind the biting."

She didn't reply and he took her hand. "Hannah, we need to talk about – "

"I'm hungry." She interrupted him as her stomach growled loudly. "Let's eat first and then we'll talk."

* * *

Selena leaned against a tree and listened carefully. She had thought she heard something to her right and she studied the area carefully. The night vision glasses lit up the forest with a soft glow and she squinted as the bushes about ten feet away shivered delicately. She drew her gun, her pulse beginning to quicken, and aimed it at the bushes. A rabbit, its nose quivering delicately, emerged and stood on its hind feet. It sniffed the air as she released her breath in a soft rush.

"Stupid rabbit." She muttered. "Why the hell aren't you tucked away in your nice, warm burrow? It's the middle of the – "

A branch snapped behind her and she whirled, her finger first tightening on the trigger and then relaxing when she saw Reid.

"What the hell, Reid!" She snapped at him. "I could have killed you."

He shrugged carelessly and moved to stand next to her. "Sorry."

"What are you doing out here?" She scowled as she took a step away and tucked her night vision glasses on the top of her head. The moon had drifted out from behind the clouds and there was more than enough light to see him. She was too aware of the heat of his body, of the way his jeans hung on his hips and his shirt clung to his upper chest, and she snorted angrily to herself.

"I'm on patrol. Just like you are." He gave her a curious look. "What's your problem tonight?"

"I don't have a problem!" She snapped again. "Although you'd think you would be smart enough not to sneak up on a person with a gun."

"I wasn't sneaking up on you." He protested. "I was walking my rounds. You're in my section."

"No, I'm not." She frowned at him. "Mannie told me to cover the west side and I – "

"You've drifted a little south." He interrupted her.

"Fine. See you later."

She sighed loudly when he trailed after her. "What do you want, Reid?"

"I think we should talk about what happened earlier."

"There isn't anything to talk about. I made a mistake."

"A mistake? That's all I am to you?" He clapped his hand dramatically to his chest. "After we shared that beautiful moment in the training room, all you can say is that you made a mistake? You've cut me deep, Selena."

She tamped down her laughter and made herself frown at him. "Are you always this dramatic?"

"I was going for funny, but I'll take dramatic." He grinned easily at her as he fell into step beside her. "Seriously, though. We should talk."

"Why? Can't we just chalk it up to a momentary bout of insanity and leave it at that?" She asked grumpily.

"You don't look insane to me." He studied her carefully in the moonlight.

"That's why I said *momentary*." She rolled her eyes.

"Yeah, maybe. But do you want to know what I think?" He asked cheerfully.

"No."

"I think," he carried on as if he hadn't heard her, "you've got a thing for me. I think you want to be naked and underneath me."

She gaped at him as her cheeks went bright red. "Excuse me?"

He winked at her. "It's nothing to be embarrassed about. I'm used to lovely ladies like yourself wanting to jump me. It's my cross to bear, and you should know that I'm an excellent lover."

"It's been my experience that if you have to tell me you're an excellent lover – you're not."

"Ouch. You're a mean little thing, aren't you?"

When she didn't reply, he grinned at her. "Don't worry, I like it."

"Oh goodie." She replied sarcastically. "Listen, not to be rude, but we're supposed to be patrolling, not talking about fucking each other."

"Whoa! I never said anything about fucking." He gave her a shocked look.

"I – like hell you didn't!" She sputtered indignantly. "You just said I wanted to be naked and underneath you."

"Yeah, but I didn't say anything about fucking. Sounds like someone's projecting." He replied.

She stared at him with her mouth open for a moment before shutting it with a snap. "You're impossible."

"Did you know I play the guitar?" He said suddenly. "I do a mean Elvis impression."

She watched as he mimed playing a guitar before gyrating his hips at her.

"Hey, little lady." He did a surprisingly good imitation of Elvis' voice and a smile crossed her face when he curled his upper lip at her before pretending to slick his short hair back.

He grinned delightedly. "A closet Elvis fan, I see."

She forced herself to stop smiling at him. "I hate Elvis, and you're delusional if you think that guitar playing will make a woman drop her panties."

"It worked in college." He shrugged. "Well, when they were actually wearing panties. Curiously enough, women were rather anxious to go commando around me."

"Oh my God, you were totally one of those hipster douchebags, weren't you?"

He nodded. "Guilty as charged. I used to have long hair and the coolest fringed leather jacket. It was seriously the best jacket ever. I've been looking for its replacement for years but – "

"How on earth did you go from being a hipster douchebag to this?" She interrupted impatiently.

He shrugged again. "Same story as most people in the program, I bet. I was attacked by a vampire when I was walking home one night from my job as a barista."

She snorted. "Of course you were a barista."

He laughed. "Anyway, a vampire attacked me and was about to drain me dry when this woman came along and saved my life. She kicked the shit out of that leech before finally stabbing him through the heart with a stake."

He rubbed thoughtfully at his smooth jaw. "I thought I was going crazy, obviously, but Sharon convinced me that what I had seen was real. She was on assignment in LA and I stayed with her for a few weeks while I tried to sort out what I had seen. It can be a bit," he hesitated, "jarring to realize that there are vampires and werewolves, not to mention other paranormals, in the world."

"Yeah." She muttered.

"Sharon urged me to try and go back to my normal life but there was no fucking way I could do that. One night in bed, I – "

"In bed?" She raised her eyebrow at him.

"What can I say? The ladies love hipster douchebags."

"Not all of us."

"*Anyway*, I told her that I wanted to join the program. She took me to the facility and the rest is history. I was turned into the hard body, smokin' hot, killing machine you see today."

He gave a short bow and she snorted loudly. "What about college?"

"I dropped out, obviously. I was only taking general studies and was mostly using it as an excuse to get laid. Honestly, before the vampire attacked me, I had been just drifting through life. My parents were killed in a car accident just after my eighteenth birthday and I really had no idea what I wanted to do with my life. Joining the program gave me something to focus my energy on, something to help dull the pain of losing them, you know?"

"I'm sorry for your loss." She said softly.

"Thanks. I spent a few years travelling the world on different assignments but I was a natural with guns and when I was offered the job to be the new weapons instructor, I took it. I enjoy teaching."

"Do you miss LA?"

He shrugged. "I was tired of the city. LA is full of fake people and the women – let's just say there was nothing real about them. And I mean nothing."

He suddenly grinned. "Thanks to spending most of my life in LA, I can count on one hand the amount of times I've seen and touched tits that were real. What is with women and fake breasts? It's like handling rubber."

His eyes dropped to her small breasts, and she blushed and crossed her arms over her chest. "Stop looking at my tits."

"I can't help it." He said cheerfully. "Yours felt great."

"Shut up!" She groaned. "We agreed to forget that happened, remember?"

"I never agreed to that." He replied immediately. "C'mon, Selena. I'm attracted to you and you're attracted to me."

"Sorry, I'm not."

"Bullshit!" He grinned at her as she flushed again.

"Listen, I'm not into guys who are in love with someone else, alright?"

"Who am I in love with?"

"Hannah."

He burst out laughing. "I am not in love with Hannah."

"Why? Because she's a Lycan now?" She glared at him.

He gave her a puzzled look. "No, because she's in love with Will. Being a Lycan has nothing to do with it. Did I give it a shot with her? Hell, yes. She turned me down flat."

"I'm turning you down flat."

"Ahh, your lips say no but your eyes say yes." He wiggled his eyebrows at her and she had to stop herself from grinning again. "What's wrong with having some fun?"

"I'm not looking for just a fun time. If you want to have fun with someone, try Leanne. She's always willing."

He shuddered a little. "Yeah, tell me about it. She's already hit on me a few times. She's a nice girl but definitely not my type."

"I thought women in general were your type."

He shook his head. "There's so much about me that you don't know, Selena. I've got layers."

"Like an onion?"

He gave her a delighted look. "No, layers like a parfait. A delicious, creamy parfait."

She rolled her eyes as they skirted around a fallen log. "Listen, Reid, this is – "

She gave a squeak of surprise when he suddenly pushed her to the ground, dropping down on top of her.

"Hey!" She shoved at his hard chest, ignoring the tremble of desire that went through her. "Get off me! What are you – "

"Shh!" All trace of humour had vanished from his eyes and he lifted his head and stared over the top of the fallen log with the gaze of a predator. "Something's out there."

She raised her own head and scanned the dark forest. After a moment, she whispered, "I don't see anything."

He frowned. "I heard something as we were – "

He paused and a small smile crossed his face. "Cool."

"What's cool?" She strained to see in the dark and was just reaching for her night vision glasses when he caught her hand and put his mouth to her ear.

"Look to the left, slowly." His warm breath made her shiver and she carefully turned her head.

Dots of light could be seen flickering through the trees and as they grew closer, she breathed, "What are they?"

"Fireflies." He murmured.

She frowned and whispered, "They're much too big to be fireflies, Reid."

He chuckled softly. "Paranormal fireflies, Selena. Have you never heard of them?"

She shook her head as the bouncing bits of light flew toward them. She jerked in surprise when they grew close enough for her to see them clearly.

"Wow." She whispered.

"Like I said, cool." He shifted against her and groaned softly when she absentmindedly parted her thighs so he could settle between her legs. She didn't notice. She was captivated by the fireflies, and he studied her face in the glow of the firefly light before turning back to the fireflies.

The fireflies were, in fact, tiny naked people no bigger than his thumb. They glowed with a soft yellow light and Selena watched delightedly as they flickered from plant to plant. Their wings fluttered rapidly and they made a low humming sound as they flew.

"What are they doing?" She whispered as about a dozen of them hovered over a low bush dotted with purple flowers.

"Drinking the nectar." He couldn't resist stroking her firm thigh through her leather pants. "They're addicted to the stuff."

He frowned slightly. "In fact, I'm pretty sure they must be drunk on it because they rarely show themselves to humans."

"Maybe they don't know we're here." She replied.

"They know." He cupped her thigh in his hand and pulled experimentally as she studied the fireflies.

Her thighs widened further and he lifted her leg and pressed it against his hip as his cock hardened in his jeans.

"There's so many of them." She whispered.

He pressed his erection against her core and was rewarded by her hips arching. He uttered another soft groan and kneaded her thigh as, without realizing it, she began to gently press her pelvis against him.

"They're so tiny, so delicate." She whispered. "I wish I could – "

She held her breath as two of the fireflies glanced up at them and then slowly flew toward them. They weren't flying in a straight line, they were weaving and bobbing about unsteadily, and Reid lowered his mouth to her ear again. "See, they're drunk."

She smiled as the two fireflies hovered in front of her face. They were both female and their long dark hair went down to their ankles. They studied her as carefully as she studied them before the smaller of the two whispered into the other's ear. They both laughed, a tiny sound like tinkling bells on the wind, and she smiled at them as they laughed again.

"They like you." Reid whispered into her ear. She pressed her hips against him again, barely registering his resulting moan, and stared delightedly at the fireflies.

"I like them too." She raised her hand slowly toward the fireflies. They gave each other startled looks and immediately zipped away to join the others still gathered around the flowers.

"Damn it." She muttered.

"They're very shy." Reid reminded her in a throaty whisper as his hand moved to her ribcage and rubbed slow circles.

She sighed and stared up at the night sky as her pelvis pushed and retreated in a gentle motion against Reid's erection. "I know, I just – "

Her eyes widened as she finally realized what her body was doing. "Shit!" She whispered and pushed again at his chest.

He captured her hands and raised them above her head, pinning them lightly to the hard ground before smiling down at her. "What's wrong?"

"What's wrong? What's wrong?" She scowled at him, the fireflies forgotten momentarily. "I was dry humping the weapons instructor in the middle of the damn forest, that's what's wrong!"

"Was?" He bent his head and licked her mouth. "I hate to tell you this, sweetheart, but you're still dry humping me."

She realized with horror that he was right and forced her traitorous hips to stop moving. "Get off me, Reid."

"Are you sure?" He nuzzled her neck and she shivered against him.

"I – I'm sure." She was a little ashamed at the obvious need in her voice and bit back her groan of disappointment when he sighed and sat up. The fireflies froze in the moonlight and then scattered into the trees, their light gradually growing dimmer, as Selena scooted backward on her butt before standing up.

She wiped at the ass of her pants as Reid rose gracefully to his feet. "Selena, I – "

"No." She shook her head and backed away from him. "I need to get back to my patrol section. Please, Reid."

He sighed again before nodding. "Be careful, alright?"

"I will."

He disappeared into the dark.

Chapter 6

"You're not eating the strawberries."

"I'm sorry?" Hannah ate the last of her steak and licked her fingers before staring at Will. He had gone to the cafeteria kitchen and brought back two steaks and a carton of strawberries.

"The strawberries." He pointed to the untouched bowl of strawberries in front of her. There was an odd tinge of sadness in his voice that she didn't understand, and she studied him carefully before reaching for a strawberry and popping it into her mouth.

She chewed the sweet fruit and swallowed before reaching for another. "You owe me a really big apology, Will."

"I know. I'm so sorry, Hannah. Please believe that I bit you because I was desperate to save your life, not to – "

"I know that." She interrupted irritably. "I know why you bit me and I'm more grateful for you saving my life than I'll ever be able to say. You owe me an apology for just running out on me afterward."

He winced. "I'm sorry. I was upset and I needed to think, to clear my head, and – "

"I know." She softened and reached out to squeeze his hand. "I can only imagine how terrible it was and what a difficult decision it was to make. I love you, Will."

"I love you too." He replied hoarsely.

"Still, you shouldn't have just left like that. I needed you." She sighed. "But considering that I faked my own death and left you, I'd say that what I did was still a hell of a lot worse."

He laced their fingers together as she picked up another strawberry. "How are you feeling? Have you – have you shifted fully yet?"

"Yes." She bit into the strawberry, licking the sweet juice from her lips, and then stiffened before inhaling. "Stop that, Will."

She could smell his arousal and her body had reacted instantly.

Take him!

"Sorry." He replied.

"Listen, I have a whole new respect for you and your ability to resist temptation when we weren't a couple."

He smiled a little and she returned his smile. "I mean it. I swear to God, I'm dying to fuck you again already and smelling your arousal really isn't helping."

"It can take some getting use to." He replied. "But you will get better at resisting it."

"I hope not." She said candidly. "I like fucking you."

He laughed. "I like fucking you too."

Her eyes drifted across his naked chest and he growled softly as his hand tightened around hers. She took a deep breath and did her best to ignore the voice screaming inside her head to jump on Will.

"Rein it in, big fella. We need to talk, remember?"

"Right, talk." He rolled his shoulders and stretched his neck like he was a boxer preparing for a fight and she laughed softly before sobering.

"I almost killed Douglas."

"What?" He blinked at her in surprise and she nodded.

"We were talking about you and how the Board of Directors thinks that you turned me because of the stigma of humans and Lycans mating. Douglas said that the new guy is going to be keeping a close eye on you and that they're rethinking the whole "Lycan" in the program thing. They're threatening to kick you out, Will."

She could feel her anger rising and she closed her eyes and took a few deep breaths before continuing.

"When Douglas told me, I – I got angry and it brought on my first shift. Only," she stared at the counter and when she tried to tug her hand free he held it more tightly, "I couldn't control it. I couldn't think past the anger and the hurt and I – I wasn't even really thinking, you know? I mean, there was a small part of me - the human part - way down deep inside my head but no matter how hard I tried, I couldn't get past the wolf. And the wolf wanted to tear Douglas apart."

She gave him a small smile. "Am I crazy, Will?"

He shook his head immediately. "No, honey. It takes time and practice to learn to control your Lycan side. And I told you before, it's harder for humans who are bitten."

"Yeah." She sighed. "Anyway, I was about to attack Douglas but luckily Selena showed up and shot me."

"She what?" He shouted in astonishment.

"She shot me."

His nostrils flared and his eyes glowed as hair grew on his cheeks. Her wolf snarled in response, wanting to shift with its mate, and she swallowed thickly. "Will, don't! If you shift, I will too."

He closed his eyes and after a moment, the hair disappeared from his cheeks and he gave her a small smile. "I'm sorry. But Selena shouldn't have shot you."

"Yes, she should have. I was out of control. I was about to attack her too and I didn't give her a choice, Will. Besides, she knew it wouldn't kill me."

"It could have." He tried to keep his voice even. "If she had shot you in the chest, there was a strong possibility that you would have died. Not all humans who are turned are as strong as those of us born Lycan. You need to remember that, Hannah."

"I will." She said absently. "Besides, she shot me in the shoulder. It was fully healed by the next day."

He didn't reply and she gave him a look of heartbreaking fear. "I can't control it, Will. I can't. What if I get angry again and I hurt someone?"

He moved around the counter and pulled her up against his broad chest. "It's only been a few days, honey. You can't expect to have any type of control after that short amount of time. I'll help you learn to control the shifting. I promise you. Okay?"

"Okay." She sniffed and rested her head on his chest, her fingers stroking through the dark hair. "How do you get used to how loud people are? And how awful some of them smell?"

He laughed. "I'll teach you some techniques to block the constant noise but as for the smell – I'm afraid you just have to get used to it."

"Right." She continued to rub his chest. "I know you went to see my mom and dad."

"I needed to tell them what I had done. I wanted to ask for their forgiveness and explain why I had done it, but they – they were just happy you were still alive."

She rubbed her cheek against his skin. "Did you really think they would be upset with you?"

"I didn't know." He admitted.

"The new head of the facility will be here tomorrow." She said suddenly. "You need to watch yourself around him, Will. Reid says he's not fond of Lycans or other supernaturals, and I think he's just looking for an excuse to kick you out."

"I'm not going anywhere, honey. I promise you." He stroked her dark hair as she leaned against him.

After a few minutes, he kissed the top of her head. "It's late. We should get some sleep."

She shook her head. "I want to fuck you again. Why did becoming a Lycan turn me into a sex addict?"

"It hasn't. It's just that our Lycan side is led by the most basic of needs – food, shelter, mating. That's all that matters to a Lycan."

She frowned at him. "But Douglas, he loves art and music and knowledge. And I don't see Constance running around stuffing her face and fucking like a bunny."

He laughed loudly. "Again, it's all about learning to control it. We've been learning to control our Lycan side since we were children. You can't compare yourself to Constance or Douglas or any other Lycan you meet. And Lycans are capable of enjoying plenty of other things – like Douglas with his art and his music – we just prefer food and mating more."

He kissed her forehead. "As you learn to control your Lycan side, more of your other loves and interests will surface again."

"Do you promise?" She whispered.

"I promise."

"Good." She took a deep breath. "Now, let's get back to that mating thing. What do you say?"

She ran her finger down his spine and he growled softly before nodding. "Yes, definitely yes."

She suddenly paused. "Wait, I – are you sure? I keep biting and scratching you and I don't think that's something I can stop."

"I already told you," his hand cupped her breast and squeezed roughly, "I don't mind the biting or the scratching, but the only way to get better at not biting during sex is by practicing."

She grinned up at him as he lowered his mouth to hers and nipped softly at her bottom lip. "Lots and lots of practicing."

* * *

Will walked into the infirmary and hesitated. Curtains were drawn around a few of the beds and he had no idea which one Chen was in. He searched the room for Barb as Constance stuck her head out from behind one of the curtains.

"Will!" She smiled in delight and quickly ran over to him. She hugged him tightly. "I'm so glad you're back."

"Hi, Constance. How are you?"

She shrugged. "I'm okay. How are you?"

"Better."

"Good." She sniffed him. "Hannah found you, huh?"

He nodded. "Yeah."

"Everything okay with you two?"

"Yes, I think so. What are you doing in here?"

"Visiting Ryan."

"How is he?"

"He'll live." She sighed softly. "He was hurt pretty badly but he's strong, you know?"

Will studied her closely. "You really like him, huh?"

She smiled briefly. "I do, actually. He's not bad, for a human."

He laughed as Barb entered the room from the far door. She walked toward them as Constance smiled at him. "I'd better get back to Ryan."

"Welcome back, Will." Barb squeezed his arm and he kissed her briefly on the cheek.

"Thanks, Barb. How are you?"

"Getting better. Are you here to see Chen?"

"Yes."

"Good. He's in that bed there." She pointed to the last bed on the left and touched his arm as he started to walk toward it. "I'm worried about him, Will." She said in a low voice. "He's so quiet and he's barely eating."

"He's always quiet." Will pointed out.

"I know but this is different. You'll see." She said solemnly. "Both Hannah and Mannie were here this morning to visit but even that didn't seem to cheer him up. Maybe you can get him to open up to you."

"I'll try." Will gave her a reassuring smile before walking to Chen's bed. He stuck his head in the opening of the curtain.

"Hello, Chen."

The sword instructor opened his eyes and gave him a brief smile. "Hello, Will."

Will sat down in the chair next to the bed as he stared at Chen's arm. It was covered in a bandage and he sighed heavily. "I'm sorry about your hand."

"Thank you."

Chen stared up at the ceiling and Will sat in silence for a few moments before clearing his throat. "How are you feeling?"

"Fine."

"Just fine?"

"Yes."

"Do you want to talk about what happened?" Will asked quietly.

"I do not."

"It might help."

Chen shook his head and changed the subject. "Hannah was here this morning. She seems more content now that you have returned to her."

"I shouldn't have left her like that."

"It was a cowardly thing to do." Chen said softly.

Will winced before nodding. "Yeah, I'm an idiot."

When Chen didn't reply, he cleared his throat again. "So, when do you get to leave the infirmary?"

"I don't know. Barb tells me there is a physiotherapist arriving tomorrow from the New York facility. Apparently he is to teach me how to navigate life with only one hand."

There was a note of bitterness in Chen's voice and Will touched his leg lightly. "Chen, I really think we should talk about what happened. I know how hard it is and I – "

"Do you, Lycan?" Chen suddenly asked. "I find that hard to believe considering you still have all four of your limbs."

"You're right. I'm sorry, that was a stupid thing to say but I – "

"I'm very tired, Will. Would you mind leaving? I'd like to take a nap." Chen interrupted.

Will nodded. "Yes. I'll come back tomorrow, okay?"

"Sure." Chen had already closed his eyes and Will gave him an anxious look before standing. He squeezed the Asian man's shoulder gently.

"I'll see you tomorrow, Chen."

Chen nodded and, with a troubled look on his face, Will left.

* * *

"Will!"

Will shut the infirmary door as Mannie jogged down the hall toward him.

The two men embraced and Mannie pounded him on the back. "Good to see you, man."

"You too, Mannie."

He studied the smaller man carefully. He looked tired and there were dark circles under his eyes. "I'm sorry about Alison."

"Thanks." Mannie replied briefly. "The new guy, Jordan, arrived this morning. He wants to meet with all the instructors in Richard's office in about half an hour."

"Alright. I'll be there."

"Listen, watch your step with him, okay? He seems nice enough but – "

"I know. He's not fond of Lycans."

Mannie hesitated. "People around here think you turned Hannah for reasons other than to save her life. It's gotten back to the Board of Directors, and this Jordan guy is going to be evaluating you and questioning you about your motives."

"I've heard." Will sighed. "You know I turned her only to save her life, right?"

"Yeah, man. I know." Mannie clapped him on the back. "Listen, I've got to go. After our meeting with Jordan, you and I need to talk about the progress of the babies. After what happened, the ones that are left are nervous and timid. I'm not sure they're going to ever graduate."

Will nodded. "We'll work with them. There's not that many of them and we can give them some individual instruction if needed."

Mannie shook his head. "We've got a new crop of recruits coming in the day after tomorrow."

"What? Isn't that a little soon?" Will frowned.

"The Board of Directors and Jordan believe it's best to get back to normal as quickly as possible."

Will snorted. "They weren't here when the shit went down. A lot of good people died, Mannie, and the ones who are left need time to grieve."

"Yeah, we do." Mannie said solemnly. "But that's not going to happen. I'll see you at the meeting."

* * *

"Good afternoon. My name is Jordan Hart and I'm the new head of the facility."

Jordan was tall and thin with gray hair and dark brown eyes. He smiled at the group of instructors. "First, let me start off by saying I understand how difficult the last couple of weeks have been, and both myself and the Board of Directors appreciate your willingness to get things back to normal as quickly as possible."

He leaned back in his chair and folded his hands across his trim abdomen. "I'll be speaking with each of you individually over the next week or so but for now, I thought it would be best if we had a group meeting and I went over the new plans for the facility."

"New plans?" Mannie raised his eyebrow at him.

"Nothing too extreme, I can assure you." Jordan said cheerfully. "You probably noticed the crew that arrived yesterday to start installing the new security measures around the facility and surrounding areas. We're confident that with this new technology we can stop any future vampire attacks from decimating the facility."

"It would have been nice to have this new equipment in the first place." Reid muttered sullenly.

"Yes, well, lesson learned." Jordan replied.

He leaned forward and shuffled through a few papers on his desk. "Your previous head, Richard, did a remarkable job of keeping the facility running smoothly and I fully intend to follow in his footsteps. There will be a few changes in how we train the recruits, nothing major I assure you, and I'll be implementing those changes over the next few weeks. For now, we're going to do what we can to bring things back to normal. As of this moment, this place is the only training facility we have and based on recent information, we're anxious to expand and bring in more recruits."

"What information is that?" Douglas asked softly.

Jordan studied him carefully. "Douglas, is it? You teach the history of the supernaturals to the recruits?"

"Yes."

"On the same night that this facility was attacked by Samuel and his followers, the Atlanta facility was attacked as well."

"What the fuck?" Mannie asked in surprise. "Alison uploaded the virus to our system so how the fuck did they know where the Atlanta facility was, and why the fuck are we just hearing about it now?"

Jordan raised his eyebrows at him. "We're uncertain as to how exactly they found out the location of the facility but we have people working on that. The actual attack was not nearly as devastating as the one here. All things considered, our people in Atlanta controlled and eliminated the vampires with relative ease."

He studied each of them. "Because of the simultaneous attacks, we're running under the assumption that what this Samuel said was true. There are pods of vampires banding together across the country in an attempt to destroy each individual facility. Each facility has been put on high alert with, again, the assumption that their locations have been compromised."

"Have other facilities been attacked?" Constance asked.

"No. Whether that's because the vampires do not know the location or because they're waiting for us to lower our defenses, we don't know."

He cleared this throat briskly. "Regardless, the issue we face now is getting this facility back into shape and training our future recruits. The Board of Directors has asked that we increase the amount of recruits we train and I personally believe that's an excellent idea. They've been making great effort to recruit new people which, as the vampires have become bolder in their attacks in the last few years, has become much easier than in the past. There will be two new groups of recruits arriving early next week. And, as I mentioned earlier, there will be some changes to how we train. We're hoping to cut the training time in half, enabling us to get the recruits out and hunting in record time."

"Are you fucking kidding me?" Mannie snapped. "We can barely keep up with the current load of recruits, not to mention that half of them are traumatized by what happened. If we want them to graduate, we're going to have to spend more time with them and that's not going to happen if you're dumping new people on us."

"I understand your concerns, Mannie, but you do need to look at the bigger picture. Vampire attacks have increased substantially in the last year. If we're to control their population, we need more people."

"Sending out half-trained recruits to be slaughtered by vampires isn't going to increase our chances of winning the war." Will said grimly.

Jordan gave him a cool look. "The Board of Directors has faith in yours and the other instructors' abilities to adapt to the new training schedule, and ensure the recruits are properly prepared for hunting."

"And you? Do you believe we are?" Will asked.

Jordan smiled thinly. "I believe some of you, more than others, are capable of it. Time will tell if I'm correct."

"Why not just hire more instructors?" Constance asked.

"We'd like to keep costs as low as possible. Although – "

Will rolled his eyes. "Yes, because allowing innocent recruits to die is cost effective."

Jordan ignored him. "Although, we will be looking at hiring another weapons instructor as we feel that you would be much better suited to training the babies full time, rather than splitting your time between that and weapons training."

"Why is that?" Constance asked softly.

"The Board of Directors didn't share that information with me."

"The Board of Directors doesn't believe that a Lycan can properly train a human on stake or gun use." Douglas said. "Isn't that right, Mr. Hart?"

Jordan gave him a considering look as Douglas snorted loudly. "We're nothing but mindless beasts who use our claws and our teeth. We couldn't possibly teach the humans how to protect themselves against the leeches with guns and knives."

Jordan shook his head before smiling at Constance. "As I was saying, the Board of Directors has not shared with me their reasons. But I can assure you that we have the utmost faith in your abilities to train."

Douglas snorted again and Will elbowed him gently in the side as Jordan gave him a frosty look. "If you have issues with how Lycans are being treated within the program, I would suggest we talk about it in private at a later date."

He glanced at his watch. "I think that's enough for now. I'll be calling a meeting tomorrow in the gym to introduce myself to the recruits and I expect all of you to be there. We'll continue with our patrols until the new security system is up and running, and I'll be speaking with Will, Mannie and Constance in the next few days about the new batch of recruits arriving. In the meantime, if you have any questions or concerns, don't hesitate to come see me. I maintain an open door policy and I welcome your thoughts and suggestions. Alright?"

The others nodded and Jordan glanced at Will. "Would you mind staying for a moment, Will?"

Will returned to his seat and waited patiently as the others filed out. When the door had shut behind them, Jordan rested his hands on his desk and stared gravely at him.

"I wanted to speak with you about the incident involving our recruit, Hannah Torrington. The fact that she is now a Lycan is – "

"I turned her to save her life." Will interrupted harshly. "Not because I was worried what others would think about a Lycan and a human being in love, despite what you may think."

Jordan laughed. "Someone's been telling stories about me."

"Stories or the truth?" Will raised his eyebrow at him. "Everything I've heard about you indicates you have trust issues with Lycans. In fact, it's my understanding that my job here is on the chopping block and you're the one holding the axe."

"It is my job to ensure that the facility runs smoothly and I will be keeping a close eye on each of the instructors, Will. Richard was the head of this facility for a very long time and we are well aware of how close you two were. He considered you a very good friend and while that is admirable, I'm not here to make friends. I'm here to run the facility. If that means making difficult decisions regarding the employment of some of the long-term instructors, then so be it."

"Let me guess – the first instructors to be accused of not doing their job will just happen to be Lycan."

"I don't have the hatred for Lycans that you believe me to have, Will." Jordan said quietly.

"Do you not?" Will asked skeptically. "Then perhaps you need to do a better job at controlling the rumours about your dislike for my kind."

Jordan sighed loudly. "About ten years after Richard created the program, he and the Board of Directors decided to bring other Lycans into the program. He'd had nothing but good things to say about you and while the Board was initially hesitant, they knew how effective you were at killing the leeches."

Will stared at him in disbelief. "Richard never said anything to me about this."

"No. He wouldn't have. The decision was made to keep it quiet, in case it didn't work out as well as it had been working with you. Lycans are volatile by nature and while there is a certain amount of peace between us and them, at that time they were still mostly regarded to be as dangerous, if not more, as the leeches themselves."

He cleared his throat. "Richard's success with you, however, and his unwavering belief that Lycans could be taught to destroy the leeches for us, prompted the Board to – "

"Taught?" Will interrupted. "We are not dogs for you to train. If this is how you approached them, I can only imagine the response."

Jordan sighed irritably. "You're deliberately twisting my words, Will. Just listen, would you?"

Will grunted softly as Jordan continued. "They approached a pack of Lycans living in California and although initially they were resistant to the idea of working with humans, after a few weeks two of the younger Lycans agreed to it. They were brought to the LA training facility. I was a recent graduate and I worked quite closely with them, Lafen and Marco were their names, in training the newest batch of babies. It went well for the first few months. Both Lafen and Marco proved to be excellent leech killers and although their training methods were crude, they were effective."

Richard and the Board began to discuss the possibility of bringing in more Lycans to the other facilities. They even arranged a meeting with another pack of Lycans. Two nights before the meeting, Marco and Lafen shifted and systematically hunted down and murdered the entire batch of babies they had been training."

"Jesus." Will muttered. "Was it a full moon?"

Jordan shook his head. "No. Marco had fallen in love with one of the recruits. Our understanding was that she returned his affection for a while before deciding to move on. In retaliation, the Lycans murdered her, her new lover, and seven other innocent people."

"You can't base all Lycans on their behaviour." Will said. "Just because they lacked the control doesn't mean that others do not."

"Perhaps. Richard did speak highly of your ability to control your wolf side. However, even he could not deny that only a few months ago you put your entire team in danger on a regular basis by refusing to exercise proper protocol during the hunts."

"I thought the woman I loved was dead. I was grieving for her. It's hardly the same as being spurned." Will said angrily.

"Yes, that's true. The Board did take that into consideration and that, along with Richard's absolute refusal to fire you, is the reason you still have a job."

Guilt flooded through Will. He had treated Richard horribly near the end, and to hear that even then Richard had defended him filled him with regret and sorrow.

"Which leads me to my next point. I've done my research on Lycans, Will. I know very well the dangers that a human who has been turned can present. We are anxious to keep Hannah in the program, she has proved repeatedly that she's an effective hunter, but the Board will not allow another incident like the one with Lafen and Marco to happen again. Obviously with the hiring of Douglas and Constance, we're giving it another try. But I'll be honest – I have my doubts about them as well. Alan was found mutilated beyond recognition. Douglas has admitted that he killed the man."

"Alan was responsible for the deaths of dozens of recruits!" Will snapped. "He deserved what was coming to him."

"I'm not saying he didn't." Jordan said patiently. "But the manner in which Douglas killed him was disturbing to say the least. Plus, we cannot forget that Lycans are also working with the leeches."

Will sighed heavily. "What do you want me to say? You obviously will never trust my kind."

"That isn't true." Jordan said carefully. "Despite what I have witnessed in the past, I am more than willing to give the Lycans here a chance. But, that being said, I am concerned about Ms. Torrington. Her ability to keep her control is obviously not going to be on par with yours and the others."

"She can learn." Will said immediately. "She's tough and she's strong, and it won't take long for us to teach her how to control the shift."

Jordan stared silently at him for a long moment. "I hope you're right, Will. I really do."

There was a soft knock at the door and Jordan checked his watch before calling for the person to come in. Hannah entered the room and she and Will stared at each other in surprise as Jordan smiled.

"Ms. Torrington. Thanks for coming by and seeing me. Will – we're done for now. Thanks."

"I'd like to stay." Will said immediately.

"Oh, that won't be necessary." Jordan replied. "I just need to have a brief meeting with Hannah."

"I don't care. I'm – "

"It's fine, Will." Hannah was still standing by the door and she gave him a quick smile. "I'll talk to you later, alright?"

He headed toward the door and paused before kissing her lightly on the mouth. "I'll see you soon."

"You bet." She gave him another confident smile but he could see the anxiety in her eyes and he squeezed her hand reassuringly before leaving the room.

Jordan stood up and she crossed the room to shake his hand. "Welcome, Hannah. I'm Jordan Hart and it's great to finally meet you. Why don't you have a seat and we'll get started."

Chapter 7

Douglas opened his door and smiled at Hannah. "Hello, Hannah."

"Hello, Douglas." She gave him a nervous smile. "I – I came to apologize for what happened earlier. I'm sorry it's taken me so long."

"That's alright." He said immediately.

"It isn't. I nearly killed you and I can't tell you how sorry I am. I feel terrible for what I did."

He shook his head. "I understand, Hannah. Besides, it turned out fine."

"Only because of Selena. If she hadn't come in when she did, I – "

"Do not worry about it." Douglas interrupted. "Now, why don't you come in and have a nice cup of tea."

"Are you sure you want me to come in?" Hannah asked hesitantly. "I'll understand if you prefer I didn't."

"Don't be silly." He stepped back and motioned for her to enter his apartment. "Besides, Will and Mannie are here and I know Will wants to talk to you."

She crossed the room to Will. He hugged her tightly and kissed her briefly on the mouth. "How did it go?"

"Fine." She sat down next to him and smiled at Mannie. "Hey."

"Hey, Hannah. How are you feeling?"

"Okay. How about you?"

He shrugged. "As good as I can."

She squeezed his hand gently, inwardly relieved when he squeezed back, and accepted the cup of tea that Douglas handed to her.

"What did Jordan want?" Will asked anxiously.

She sipped at her tea. "He wanted to talk to me about the, as he put it, recent changes happening in my body."

Mannie snorted laughter. "Fuck, he makes it sound like you're going through puberty."

Hannah grinned. "Yeah, he sort of did, actually."

"What did he say?" Will asked a bit impatiently.

"He mostly just wanted to know how I felt about it, if I was angry with you, did I think I had sufficient control over my Lycan side."

Will rolled his eyes. "I told him it would take time. The man's an idiot if he thinks you can just control it easily after such a short period."

"I think he's just worried that I'm going to freak out and kill a bunch of people. Honestly, the man's got a point. I don't have control over it." Hannah said softly.

"You will, honey. I promise you." Will replied immediately. "We'll go out tonight and start practicing."

Hannah nodded before taking another sip of tea. "He also asked me to take over the kenjutsu training until Chen is back on his feet."

Will blinked at her in surprise and she smiled a little. "You've got the same look on your face that I did."

"It's not a bad idea." Mannie mused. "After Chen, you're the best we've got with a sword and it would be good to keep the others training while he recovers. I know Chen thought Henry from the current batch of babies has potential with the sword."

"I told him no." Hannah replied.

"What? Why?" Mannie asked.

"Because I'm not good enough to train, Mannie. Chen's dedicated his entire life to the sword. I've been doing this for less than a year. There's no way in hell I'm anywhere near his level and I never will be. Having me train a new person will just got them killed. Besides, Alex and Paul have been training with Chen longer than I have. There's no way they'll just accept that the person who started after them is going to continue their training."

"You're better than them." Will pointed out.

"That isn't the point." Hannah persisted. "I wouldn't be happy about having someone with as little experience as I have acting as a teacher and neither will Alex or Paul."

"What did Jordan say when you refused?" Douglas asked.

"He just told me to take some time to think about it and to talk to Chen about it. He said he would meet with Alex and Paul and ask them how they feel about working with me."

"You don't have to train them," Will said, "you could just be their sparring partner."

"Maybe." Hannah said moodily. "I'm just not comfortable with it and I don't want Chen to think I'm stepping on his toes."

"Hannah, have you considered the possibility that Chen may not go back to teaching?" Mannie asked hesitantly.

Hannah glared at him. "No, I haven't. And I won't allow Chen to think that way either. He doesn't need two hands to either teach the sword or kill vampires. Do you think he's less of a person now, Mannie? Is that what you're saying?"

Her anger, so quick to rise to the surface now, was getting harder to control. She bared her fangs at Mannie who sat back and gave Will a nervous look.

"He's faster and better at the sword than I'll ever be, even with only one hand, and I won't let you or anyone else try and tell me differently. If we're to get Chen back to the way he was, we can't treat him like an invalid. And if I see any of you acting like he is, I swear I will – "

"Enough, Hannah!" Will said sharply. His hand squeezed her upper arm and she turned to him and snarled as her eyes glowed.

"Stop it." He growled at her. "Do not let your anger get the best of you."

She snarled again before closing her eyes and bowing her head. He kept a firm grip on her arm, nodding reassuringly to Mannie and Douglas as Hannah breathed deeply for nearly five minutes. Finally, her body relaxed and she raised her head.

She gave Mannie a shameful look. "I'm sorry, Mannie."

"Yeah, no problem." He said nervously. "Listen, I'd better go. I want to talk to Constance before we start our training session this afternoon. Will, you're meeting us in the gym, yeah?"

"Yes." Will was still holding Hannah's arm and Mannie gave her another nervous smile before nodding to Douglas and leaving the apartment.

Will released her arm and Hannah buried her face in her hands. "Fuck! Now Mannie's afraid of me."

"It's okay." Will said soothingly.

"Is it?" She asked softly.

"Yes, you'll see." He kissed her forehead and stroked her back.

* * *

"Chen?" A man, slender and dark-haired, poked his head around the curtain surrounding Chen's bed.

Chen nodded and stared silently at the man as he sat down in the chair next to the bed. He had bright green eyes and a short, neatly-trimmed goatee and he smiled cheerfully at Chen.

"Hi. I'm Andrew Resener, your physiotherapist."

"I thought you were arriving tomorrow."

"I got in a day early and thought I'd drop by and say hello. It's nice to meet you." Andrew replied.

Chen nodded and closed his eyes. Andrew waited patiently and when Chen didn't open his eyes, he stood and began to remove the bandage from Chen's arm.

"What are you doing?" Chen frowned at him.

"I'd like to take a look at your arm." Andrew smiled.

"I would prefer if you did not."

Andrew laughed. "I understand but it's kind of my job." He continued to unravel the bandage, ignoring Chen's look of anger. "Okay, let's see what we're dealing with."

He studied Chen's stump as Chen turned his face away and stared at the curtain.

"Well, there's some swelling, but that's to be expected." He said cheerfully. "Barb did a great job with the suturing, considering the circumstances and that she's more of a general practitioner and not a surgeon."

"How does it feel? Are there any pressure points in the dressing?"

Chen shook his head no as Andrew continued to study his arm. "Good. What about the pain? On a scale of one to ten, what would be the level?"

"Eleven." Chen said bitterly.

"I'll talk with Barb about your current pain medication. It's possible that we can increase the dosage a little. Are you feeling any phantom limb sensations?"

Chen sighed. "Can you leave? I'm tired."

"I'm sure you are but I'm going to need a few more minutes. Answer the question, please." Andrew said firmly.

Chen glared at him and Andrew gave him another one of those annoying cheerful grins. "Glaring at me and giving me the silent treatment isn't going to make me go away, Chen. I'm here to help you adjust and I get paid whether you're a willing or unwilling participant in your rehab. Although, just between you and me, things will go a lot smoother and faster if you participate."

"It's been a week." Chen suddenly snapped. "Do you really expect me to just accept what has happened and move on with my life?"

Andrew shook his head. "No, of course not. But I do expect you to actively participate in your rehab. It's the first step to acceptance."

Chen snorted loudly as Andrew raised his eyebrows. "Phantom limb sensations – are you feeling them?"

"Yes." Chen said shortly.

"I'm not surprised. Phantom limb sensation is more common in adults, especially if it's been a traumatic amputation. Is it pain or do you mostly feel like your hand is still there?"

"Like my hand's still there." Chen grunted.

Andrew nodded. "Well, the good news is — that will lessen with time. Your brain needs some time to, essentially, rewire itself to adjust to the change. If it doesn't, there are a few things we can try — antidepressants, muscle relaxers — but for now, we'll adopt a wait and see approach."

He bent and studied the end of the stump. "I think removal of the sutures could probably be by the end of next week, the skin has really healed quite nicely, and then we'll use a compressive sock to help reduce the swelling. It'll also help mold your limb so the prosthesis fits more comfortably."

"I'm not using a prosthetic hand." Chen said immediately.

"Eh, we'll see what happens." Andrew replied. He sat down on the bed, his hip pressing against Chen's side and smiled at him.

"Now, this is going to hurt a little but it's important that I start stretching your limb. Ready?"

Chen didn't reply and Andrew carefully gripped his arm. Chen twitched and Andrew made a soft soothing noise under his breath as he began to massage and rub his arm.

"Please stop doing that." Chen said grimly.

"Nope." Andrew grinned again at him. "This is very important, Chen." His hands kneaded and squeezed and rubbed. "How's the pain? Really bad?"

"No." Chen said shortly.

"Good." He shifted closer when Chen tried to move away. "Hold still, please."

Chen closed his eyes. There was some pain but Andrew's hands were warm and surprisingly strong, and he told himself the weird tingling in his stomach was from nothing more than having his arm touched. With the exception of Barb, who really had only changed the bandage on a daily basis, no one had touched his arm at all.

He couldn't look at his arm without the bandage on it and, as Andrew's hands continued to stroke and stretch his arm, he studied his face instead. There was another of those weird tingles in his stomach when Andrew met his gaze and smiled at him. He had perfect white teeth and Chen studied his lips for a moment.

"So, I hear you're pretty good with a sword."

Chen was oddly fascinated by the movement of his lips, and he groaned out loud when Andrew wet the bottom one with his tongue.

"Did that hurt?"

"What?" Chen dragged his gaze from his mouth. "No, it didn't hurt."

"Good. Just a few more minutes and then I'll stop." Andrew said reassuringly. "I was saying that I've heard you're good with a sword."

"I used to be." Chen muttered. A sharp pang of loss went through him and he choked back the bitter bile rising in his throat.

"It says in your chart that you're right-handed. Did you use only your left hand for sword fighting?" Andrew asked curiously.

Chen frowned at him. "No."

"Well, then it isn't 'used to be', after all, is it?" Andrew replied.

"I used two swords." Chen snapped.

"All the time?"

Chen hesitated before admitting grudgingly, "No, not all the time."

"Good. You'll be back on your feet and chopping up vampires again in no time." Andrew winked at him and Chen gave him a dirty look before closing his eyes.

He was too tired to argue and he had a feeling that the therapist wouldn't listen anyway. He felt an odd sense of disappointment when Andrew stopped massaging his arm. "I'm just going to put another bandage on your arm and then I'll let you rest. I'll be back later this evening to massage and stretch it again. It's important in these first few days that we do frequent massage and stretching exercises. As your strength improves, we'll look at getting you to take a more active role in the therapy. I'll be showing you some exercises to help increase circulation and strengthen your muscles. Sound good?"

"No." Chen grunted again and Andrew laughed.

"I know you think being uncooperative will make me leave, but it won't, Chen. In fact, I kind of like the grumpy ones. You're more challenging."

Chen snorted. "I'm not – "

"Master?" Hannah stuck her head between the curtains. "Can I talk to you – oh, I'm sorry. I didn't realize you had company."

Andrew held his hand out. "I'm Andrew Resener, Chen's physiotherapist."

"It's nice to meet you." Hannah shook his hand briefly. "I'm one of Chen's students, Hannah."

"You've graduated." Chen said bluntly. "You are no longer my student."

Hannah just shrugged and studied the end of Chen's arm. "It's healing nicely, master."

He didn't reply and Andrew patted his shoulder. "It really is. I'm just going to bandage it and then I'll leave you two alone."

"Oh, I can come back later." Hannah said hurriedly.

"No need. I was just finishing up." Andrew pointed to the chair beside the bed. "Have a seat, this won't take long."

He wrapped Chen's arm carefully. When Hannah took Chen's right hand and held it firmly, he hid his surprise that Chen didn't pull away from her. She rubbed his arm lightly with her other hand and gave him an encouraging smile. Although Chen didn't return her smile, Andrew could feel his body relaxing slightly.

"Alright, that should do it." Andrew stood and smiled at Hannah. "Nice to meet you, Hannah. Chen, I'll see you later this evening."

"Bye, Andrew." Hannah said softly. Although Chen didn't reply to Andrew, Hannah didn't miss his glance at the man's ass as he disappeared behind the curtain.

She waited until she heard the door to the infirmary close. "He's good looking, huh?" She said casually.

When Chen glared at her, she smiled innocently at him. "What? I'm just saying - the guy's cute."

"What did you want to talk to me about, Hannah?" He asked tiredly.

She hesitated before stroking his arm again. "I met the new head of the facility, Jordan Hart, today."

"And?" Despite his depression, he was curious about the man.

"I don't know. He was nice enough but I guess we'll see, right?"

"Yes."

"He, uh, he asked me to take over the sword training until you were ready to instruct again."

He looked at her in surprise and she shook her head. "I know, right? I told him absolutely not."

He studied her quietly for a moment. "I think you should."

"No." She frowned at him. "I won't do it. If I try and train Henry, he'll die. You know that."

"You're better than you think." He said softly. "Besides, they will need someone to take up the training when I leave."

"When you leave?" Hannah squeezed his arm. "You're not going anywhere, master."

"I can't stay here." He said angrily. "I will never again be effective with the sword, and it is ridiculous to think that a man with one hand can train others. As soon as I'm healed, I'm leaving."

"No, you're not." Hannah said firmly. "I'll tie you to a chair if I have to, Chen. You need to give it time. Do the physio, let your body heal, and see what happens then. You're better at the sword with your right hand only than I am using both of mine. Do not try and tell me otherwise just because you're feeling sorry for yourself."

"Enough, Hannah. I'm tired."

"I know you are. But you can't keep driving me away. I love you, Chen, and I won't let you push me out of your life."

He blinked in surprise before sighing wearily. "I love you too, Hannah."

"Good. Listen, you promise to actually try at physiotherapy and I'll promise to be a sparring partner with Alex and Paul so they're not too rusty when you return. Okay?"

"You will also start training Henry."

She shook her head. "No, master, I told you – I can't do that."

"Are you really refusing to do what I ask of you?" He frowned at her and she blushed a little.

"If I promise to start Henry's training, do you promise to finish it?"

He nodded and she frowned at him. "Say it, master."

He rolled his eyes. "Fine, I promise. Now leave me be, please. I'm tired."

She grinned happily at him and kissed his smooth cheek. "I'll see you tomorrow."

Chapter 8

"Are you ready, Hannah?"

Hannah eyed Will nervously. They had waited until dark before leaving the facility and traveling deep into the woods.

"Not really. I don't even know how to shift on purpose." She sighed.

He nodded. "It can take a great deal of concentration at the beginning." He stripped out of his clothes and after a moment, she followed his lead.

"Close your eyes and take some deep breaths. Try to think about your wolf and allowing it free. Don't fight it. Just allow it to happen."

"Right." She muttered. She closed her eyes and concentrated.

After nearly five minutes, she sighed loudly and opened her eyes. "I can't, Will. I just – I don't even know where to begin."

He didn't reply. He was staring at her naked body and his cock was full and erect. She could feel the answering call of desire in her own body and she smiled lazily at him. "I want you, Will."

"I want you too." He growled.

She gave a soft gasp of surprise when spun her around roughly. He dragged her back against his body, one hand cupping her breast and the other reaching between her legs. He thumbed her clit harder than he normally did and she growled softly at him even as wetness pooled between her legs.

He ignored her growl and bit her lightly on the back of the shoulder. She moaned, her nipples hardening in delight at the feel of his sharp fangs, and he slid two fingers deep into her pussy. She gasped again at the sudden invasion and tugged at his hand.

"No, this is mine." He breathed into her ear. He cupped her throat gently with one big hand and held her firmly as he moved his fingers in and out in a quick, hard rhythm.

She moaned and twisted in his arms and when he pushed her to her hands and knees on the ground, hard lust exploded in her belly. She spread her legs eagerly as he dropped to his knees between her legs, and gave a loud howl of delight when he pushed his cock into her slick entrance.

He held her firmly around the hips, his cock sliding in and out of her in a hard deep rhythm, as Hannah arched her back and pushed back against him. To her surprise, she was already close to coming and when he slid his hand between her legs, leaned over her and sank his fangs deep into the back of her neck, she howled hoarsely as she climaxed explosively. Dimly she was aware of his own hoarse howl and his warm seed spilling into her but the shift was happening and she was trying desperately to stop it.

Will was suddenly kneeling in front of her and he cupped her face with his warm hands. "Let it happen, honey."

"Will..." She moaned as her back arched and hair began to sprout on her face and body.

"It's okay." He whispered soothingly.

She closed her eyes, fear and excitement coursing through her body at the same time, and Will watched as with a loud growl, she shifted to her Lycan form. She crouched on the ground for a moment, staring unblinkingly at him and he gave her a reassuring smile.

"It's alright, my love." He whispered before shifting. He nuzzled her throat and she whined softly before licking his face.

She stood a bit shakily and stretched as she looked around the forest. Will barked quietly and she turned toward him. He grinned at her and then turned and bolted into the trees. With a sharp bark, she chased him through the trees.

The moon, half full and shining brightly through the trees, called to her and she skidded to a stop. She stared rapturously at it, whining again when it disappeared behind the clouds. Will bumped her head with his and she licked his face again before suddenly darting away. The urge to run was too strong to deny and she panted happily as she loped through the forest. Will ran beside her and she breathed deeply of the clean, night air as they moved easily across the ground.

A scent caught her attention and she stopped, lifting her head and inhaling deeply as Will returned to her side. It was the scent of a deer and she growled deep in her throat as an urge to hunt - an urge to kill - overtook her. Will nudged her with his head and she snarled at him. He growled back and bit her in the shoulder until she whimpered and collapsed to her belly. He held her there with his teeth until she whimpered again in submission. He licked the shallow wound in her shoulder, it was already beginning to heal, before inhaling and slowly moving away.

She followed him, every nerve in her body singing for the deer's blood, and she gave a soft yip of excitement when the deer's scent grew stronger. Will growled and nipped her again and she bowed her head before creeping after him.

They followed the deer's scent for nearly half an hour until Will stopped and crouched to his belly. She did the same and could barely hold in her excitement when the deer stepped around a tree. Beside her, Will's body was vibrating with excitement and she panted lightly as he gave her a quick look. Moving as one, they stalked silently toward the deer.

* * *

"Leanne? What are you doing?" Selena flopped down in one of the armchairs in the common room and stared at the redhead.

Leanne was sitting alone in the room and holding a large bottle of whiskey.

"What's it look like I'm doing?" Leanne took a large gulp of whiskey.

"Why are you drinking whiskey straight out of a bottle?" Selena asked patiently.

"I couldn't find a glass." Leanne snickered softly before sighing. "Dwight broke up with me."

"Dwight from the babies?"

Leanne nodded. "Yeah."

I'm sorry. I didn't realize you two were dating." Selena replied.

"Yeah, apparently Dwight didn't either. He'd heard the rumours about me and figured I was good for a roll in the hay. I mean I was, obviously, but we've been sleeping together for nearly a month. I kind of thought it was starting to mean something."

Selena gave her a look of sympathy and Leanne snorted loudly. "Don't look at me like that, Selena. I know what you and Hannah and the other women think of me."

"Leanne – "

Leanne drank another swallow of liquor. "I hate being alone, okay? Does it make me a bad person to want someone to keep me warm at night? To want someone to make me feel good, to maybe even love me a little?"

Selena shook her head. "No, it doesn't. I'm sorry, Leanne. I was being a judgemental shrew."

Leanne shook her head. "Fuck, who am I trying to kid? I deserve it. You're Hannah's best friend, and I tattled on her and Will like a little kid having a temper tantrum. Why wouldn't you hate me?"

"I don't hate you."

"No?" Leanne laughed bitterly and Selena reached out and swiped the bottle from her.

She took a long drink, crinkling her face at its taste, before handing the bottle back to Leanne. "No, I don't. And I think you've got the right idea tonight. Do you mind sharing?"

Leanne shook her head. "My dad always told me to never drink alone. Bottoms up, Selena." She tipped the bottle to her lips, drank deeply, and handed it over.

* * *

Selena staggered down the hallway, running her hand along the wall to steady herself. She stopped in front of a door and studied it before pressing her ear against it. The faint sound of guitar playing could be heard and she smiled with satisfaction before knocking.

The guitar stopped and she smiled again when she heard Reid's footsteps. He was going to be —

The door opened and, still leaning against it, she fell forward into Reid's hard body. He caught her instinctively and frowned at her. "Selena, what are you doing here?"

"What? I can't knock on your door? It's a free world, you know." She pushed away from him and weaved into his apartment, glancing around curiously. It was on the small side and she eyed his unmade bed with interest before studying the posters on the wall. Most of them were of musicians and she trailed her hand along the neck of the guitar propped up against the couch.

"It's two in the morning."

"What are you? The time police?" She rolled her eyes before nearly tripping over the small footstool next to the couch.

"Are you – are you drunk?" He asked in disbelief.

"No, just tipsy." She giggled. "Now Leanne on the other hand – wasted. The girl can't hold her liquor."

She toyed with the buttons on her shirt, a small smile crossing her face when his gaze dropped to her breasts.

"Where is Leanne?"

"I dropped her off in her room. She's sleeping it off." She shrugged.

"Why are you here?" He asked cautiously.

She pouted at him. "What? I can't drop by for a visit? I thought we were friends."

"We are." He acknowledged. "But you should probably go back to your room before you do something you regret."

"Like what?" She asked innocently.

He shook his head as a small grin crossed his face. "You know what. Here, I'll walk you back to your room."

He reached out to take her arm and she grabbed his hand and placed it on her breast.

"Whoa! Selena, this isn't a good idea."

She kept his hand on her breast with surprising strength for her size. "Hey, I'm just trying to be nice. Aren't you the one who said you've never felt a real breast before?"

"No." He said patiently as he struggled not to stroke his thumb over her hard nipple. "I said I hadn't felt that many."

"Well, here's your chance to feel another. Go on." She purred at him.

He closed his eyes and prayed for strength. "That's very sweet of you, Selena, but you're drunk and I'm not – "

He gritted his teeth when she threw herself against him and rubbed her small firm body against his. "I'm not drunk. I'm tipsy. There's a difference."

"No, there isn't." His hands were circling around her waist and she leaned into him before reaching behind him and squeezing his ass.

"Your ass is amazing." She said softly.

"Thanks. Now that we've groped one another, what do you think about heading back to your room? We'll go for a little walk, I'll tuck you in to your nice warm bed and – "

"Will you sing me a song?" She asked.

"Uh, sure, if that will get you to go to your room, I'll sing you a song." He replied. He was starting to feel a bit desperate. Selena's warm body, her hands kneading and stroking his ass, was giving him an erection despite his best intentions.

She suddenly gave a soft coo of delight before rubbing her flat belly against his cock. "Ooh, someone is happy to see me."

"Selena..."

Sweat was breaking out on his forehead as she slipped her hands under his shirt and traced her fingers over his back. Her fingers were unbelievably soft and why did she have to smell so fucking good?

She stood on her tiptoes and tugged his head down to her mouth. "You were right, Reid. I do want you. I want you so badly I can't sleep. Every night I crawl into my cold bed and I think about your mouth and your hands. Every night I slide my hand between my legs, and I rub my wet pussy and pretend it's your hand touching me until I come so hard I can barely breathe."

"Selena!" He hissed out. "Please..."

"It's not enough for me anymore, Reid." She sucked lightly on his earlobe. "I need you. I need you between my legs, and I need your cock in my pussy. Please, can you do that for me?"

"Yes." He said hoarsely. "I can do that for you."

"Good boy." She whispered.

"But not tonight." He said firmly. "Another night when you haven't been drinking."

She glared at him. "I told you I'm only tipsy."

"I know but that's still not – "

She yanked his head down and sucked roughly on his lower lip. "God, I love your mouth." She muttered. "Do you know that? You have the nicest lips."

He groaned and pulled her body up against his before slamming his mouth down over hers. He devoured her mouth hungrily, licking and kissing at her soft lips as she moaned sweetly. When she thrust her tongue into his mouth, he sucked firmly on it, and she arched her hips into him.

She tasted like whiskey and bad choices, and with a loud groan he forced his mouth away from hers. "Seriously, we need to stop."

She frowned at him. "No, we don't."

"Yes, we – "

She grabbed the front of his shirt and yanked hard. The buttons flew off and she gave a soft squeal of delight before pressing her mouth against his bare chest. He groaned again and then cursed loudly when she sucked firmly on one flat nipple. His back arched and he cupped her head, threading his fingers through the dark curls as she sucked and licked.

"I think you like that." She whispered. She licked her bottom lip as her hand squeezed between them and she cupped his cock.

"Hmm, something else wants a good sucking." She winked at him.

"You are fucking killing me, woman!" He moaned.

She giggled softly before suddenly stripping her shirt off. He stared hungrily at her breasts and, his hands shaking, cupped them gently. He ran his thumbs over her nipples, feeling them harden against the soft material of her bra and she moaned loudly.

Her hands had moved to his belt and they were unbuckling, unbuttoning and unzipping. She slipped her hand into his jeans and wrapped her fingers around him.

"My goodness. You're nice and thick, aren't you?" She made a soft sound of delight and he moaned as she stroked him firmly.

"Sit down, Reid." She surprised him by shoving him hard in the chest. He dropped with a loud grunt to the couch, and she quickly knelt between his legs before reaching into his jeans and tugging his cock free.

"Selena, wait!" He gasped out as she bent her head.

"I don't want to." She said primly before sliding her mouth over his cock.

At the feel of her wet, hot mouth, he cried out and forgot entirely about her making her stop. He forgot about her being drunk and being worried that he was taking advantage of her, and arched his hips up off the couch.

She made a muffled sound of surprise as his cock slid further into her mouth before she sucked enthusiastically. Her soft tongue traced the head of his cock as she slid her hand around the base of him and pumped firmly.

"Fuck!" He moaned as he threaded his fingers through her hair again and held tightly. She licked his entire cock before taking just the head into her mouth and sucking in a wet, hot rhythm that had his toes curling. He panted and moaned above her, his hips rising up and down helplessly as she brought him closer and closer to the edge.

"Selena!" He gasped. "I'm going to come!"

She stopped immediately and he made a soft groan of dismay as she climbed into his lap. She rubbed her pussy against him and grinned.

"We can't have that, now can we, Reid?"

"I think we can." He muttered.

She laughed and kissed him. He could taste himself on her mouth and it drove his need higher. He crushed her against his broad chest as he stroked her tongue and nipped lightly at her lips.

She reached between them and rubbed his cock. "I need you to fuck me, Reid. Right now. Will you? Will you make me feel good?"

"Yes." He whispered. "Hell, yes."

"Good." She stroked his face with her soft fingers. "Take me to your bed. Make me yours."

An odd little shiver went down his back at her words and he studied her carefully before tracing her bottom lip with his thumb. "Mine."

"Yes."

Without another word, he held her firmly and stood up. He carried her to the bed and set her down gently. He lay down next to her and placed his hand on her flat stomach as he kissed her upper chest lightly. She moaned in response and he moved to her throat, licking and sucking gently at her soft skin.

"Do you have a condom?" She muttered.

He sat up. "Yes, don't move. I'll be right back." He stood up from the bed and gave her an almost anxious look. "Don't go anywhere."

She grinned as she traced her hands lazily along the quilt on his bed. "I'm not going anywhere, handsome."

He turned and nearly ran to the bathroom. He popped open the medicine cabinet, groaning softly when the box of condoms wasn't there.

"Fuck! Where the hell is it?" He muttered as he pawed through the contents of the medicine cabinet.

"Son of a bitch!" He bent and ripped open the door of the cabinet under the sink. He tossed things out carelessly as he rifled frantically through the cabinet for nearly five minutes.

"Oh come ON!" He nearly shouted with frustration. If he didn't find the condoms he was about to be stuck with the worst case of blue balls in the goddamn history of blue balls. He muttered another curse and stuck his entire head into the cabinet. There was a muffled shout of triumph and he emerged clutching a box of condoms.

"Thank you, God." He tipped a salute to the ceiling before leaving the bathroom.

Selena was curled on her side and he dropped on to the bed beside her and placed a soft kiss on her bare back. "We are good to go, sweetheart."

There was no response and he placed his hand on her hip and shook her lightly. "Selena?"

She made a soft snoring noise and he leaned over her. She had passed out, and he groaned and collapsed on his back and stared up at the ceiling. His balls throbbed and his dick was hard as a rock, and he was still holding the now-useless box of condoms in his hand.

He sighed and dropped the box on to the floor beside the bed before tucking his hands under his head and taking a few deep breaths. Selena mumbled something in her sleep before turning and snuggling up to him. She put her arm around his waist and buried her face into his throat before slinging one thigh over his.

"Nighty night, handsome." She murmured.

He sighed again before putting his arm around her and stroking the soft skin of her back.   "Goodnight, sweetheart."

* * *

The dark brown wolf backed away from the fallen deer. They had eaten their fill of meat and Will barked sharply at her as she made a low whine. He watched as the wolf began to shiver and shake and its whine turned into a hoarse cry as Hannah shifted back to her human form.

Will quickly shifted, wiping the blood from his mouth as Hannah stared in horror at the dead deer. "What - what have I done?"

She touched the blood smeared across her face. "Oh my God, I – "

She turned and staggered a few feet away before bending over and vomiting. Will hurried over to her and rubbed her back soothingly as he held her hair back. She continued to vomit until there was nothing left and she was dry-heaving wretchedly.

She wiped her mouth with a shaking hand and gave him a miserable look. "Oh god, Will."

She stared at the mess of guts and blood she had vomited up and Will picked her up and carried her away. "Don't look at it, my love."

She started to cry, her naked body shaking in the cool air, as Will made soft noises of comfort. They were close to a small creek that ran through the forest and he sat her down next to it before dipping her hands into the water. He scrubbed them clean as she cried silently before using the clear, cold water to wash the blood from around her mouth.

"Honey, it's okay. Don't cry." He pulled her into his embrace. She wasn't cold, her Lycan half was keeping her warm, but she was shaking uncontrollably and the tears were still flowing down her cheeks.

"I'm sorry, I'm so sorry." She moaned. "I don't know why I did that. I just – I saw the deer with, well with my human half I guess, and there was so much blood and I ate the raw meat and – "

She dry heaved again, slapping her hand over her mouth as Will rocked her back and forth.

"You have nothing to be sorry about. This is my fault. I should not have allowed you to hunt so soon. I'm sorry, my love."

They sat quietly until Hannah's crying had slowed to the occasional sniffle. She wiped her hand across her nose before sighing quietly. "I suck at being a Lycan."

"You don't." He kissed her forehead. "Most humans who are turned take months to start hunting. I should not have taken you hunting with me. It was stupid of me."

"I don't – I don't think I ever want to hunt again." She said softly.

"That's fine. You don't have to." He replied soothingly. "Being a Lycan does not mean you have to hunt, Hannah. Alright?"

She nodded and curled closer into his warm, naked body before staring at the moon. "The moon is so pretty." She whispered.

"It is." He agreed.

"I'll hunt when the moon is full, won't I?" She said sadly. "Even if I don't want to – I won't be able to help it."

"Maybe, maybe not. You're strong, Hannah. If your human side is that opposed to hunting, it may be able to stop the Lycan in you from hunting."

"I don't think so." She whispered. "I'm not as strong as you think I am, Will."

"You are." He replied firmly. "In another month or so, when you have better control of your wolf, you'll understand."

He hugged her tightly and then stood up, dropping her gently to her feet. "We should grab our clothes and go back. Okay?"

"Okay." She gave him a wan smile and he kissed her again before leading her away from the creek.

Chapter 9

"Hey, Will. Is Hannah with you?"

It was early the next morning and Will eyed Selena before wrinkling his nose. "She is. Come on in, I was just leaving to meet with Mannie."

Selena gave him a weak smile and moved toward Hannah who was sitting at the island and drinking a cup of coffee.

"Hannah, I'll see you later, alright?" Will called.

She nodded and gave him a tired smile. "Bye, honey."

She clapped her hand over her mouth and nose before sliding off the bar stool and moving away from Selena.

"Oh God, Selena. Don't take this the wrong way but you smell terrible."

She lowered her hand and took a tentative sniff in Selena's direction. "Why do you smell like whiskey and," a small smile crept across her face, "Reid?"

"Aspirin." Selena whispered hoarsely. "Please, Hannah, for the love of God get me some aspirin."

Hannah disappeared into the bathroom and returned with a bottle of aspirin. She poured Selena a glass of water and handed it and the aspirin to her.

"My head hurts so badly." Selena moaned. She took some aspirin and drank the rest of the water in four large gulps. "Fuck me."

"It smells like Reid did." Hannah laughed.

Selena groaned and rested her head on her arms. "I'm an idiot."

"No, you're not. Tell me what happened."

Selena squinted at her. "Well, first I – ", she paused, "wait, what's wrong? You're not looking that hot yourself."

"I'm fine. Tell me what happened." Hannah replied.

Selena shook her head and then groaned before cupping her forehead. "You first. I need a minute for the aspirin to kick in."

Hannah sighed. "Will took me out last night in the forest to try and help me control the shift. Only I couldn't even shift. I had no idea how to make it happen. Finally, Will had to have sex with me and then I shifted."

"Weird."

"Yeah, I know. Sex makes me want to shift. Anyway, we had sex and then we shifted and we were just running through the forest. It was kind of nice, you know? The moon was out," a dreamy look came over Hannah's face, "and it was so pretty. I wanted to stare at it forever."

She stared silently into her coffee cup for a moment. "Then we caught the scent of a deer and we – we hunted it and murdered it and then we ate it."

She glanced at Selena. The dark-haired woman was giving her a solemn look and Hannah smiled faintly. "Then I shifted back to my human form and barfed everywhere."

"Oh, Hannah."

"It was awful, Selena. Even now, just thinking about how I ate its guts and it's..." She trailed off and rubbed at her forehead. "I'm not really getting the hang of this whole Lycan thing."

"You will." Selena said quietly. "It takes time."

"Yeah." Hannah replied irritably. "That's what everyone keeps telling me."

She sat down and took a sip of coffee. "Tell me about your night. Even looking the way you do, it had to be better than mine."

Selena rested her head in her hand. "Last night I found Leanne drinking alone in the common room. She was having a bad night, I guess you could say, and we talked a bit and then I started drinking with her. We both got pretty drunk and I helped her to her room and put her to bed. I was going to just go to bed myself but then I somehow ended up standing outside of Reid's apartment."

Hannah poured a second cup of coffee and pushed it across the island to her. "Go on."

"Reid let me in, we started talking, and then I made a total and utter fool of myself."

Selena sipped cautiously at the hot coffee. "He tried to take me back to my room but I refused to go. Instead, I started making out with him and grabbing his ass and at first he tried to resist but I was, uh, pretty persistent. I told him I wanted him to, uh, fuck me and he was all – no problem."

Hannah laughed. "Of course he was."

Selena blushed. "He actually said he would sleep with me but another night when I wasn't drunk."

"Good man, Reid." Hannah said cheerfully.

Selena gave Hannah a miserable look. "Then I might have, maybe, given him a blow job."

Hannah raised her eyebrows at her. "Either you did or you didn't, girl. There's no maybe in blow jobs."

Selena dropped her face into her hands again. "I did. I totally did." She whispered.

After a moment she lifted her head. Hannah was drinking her coffee and studying her fingernails.

"Well?" Selena asked.

"Well, what?"

"Aren't you going to tell me how terrible I am?"

"For giving a man a blowjob? Honey, you're not the first girl to drink too much and do something she regrets."

"I don't regret it."

"Then what's the problem?"

"I – I don't know! Reid's an instructor and a playboy, and I told him that I wasn't interested in just casual sex. And then the next thing I know, I'm in his apartment and he's pinned to the couch with my mouth on his – "

She groaned. "Fuck, I really am an idiot."

"No, you're not." Hannah said patiently. "And I'm sure that Reid had no problem with you changing your mind and having happy mouth time with his junk."

Selena groaned again. "Anyway, then I asked him again to fuck me and this time he was all for it. He carried me to the bed, we were making out, and he went into the bathroom to get a condom."

"So you did sleep with him?" Hannah asked.

Selena shook her head. "No. That's the last thing I remember. I passed out."

"Oops." Hannah grinned at her. "What did Reid say this morning?"

Selena gave her a look of panic. "I – he didn't say anything because I woke up before he did and I just grabbed my shirt and got the hell out of his apartment."

"Selena! You have to talk to him about this." Hannah scolded.

"I can't! I – I'm so embarrassed and I would never have gone to his apartment if I hadn't been drunk." Selena wailed.

"Really? You're telling me the only reason you would have sex with Reid is because you're drunk?" Hannah said skeptically.

"Yes?" Selena said hesitantly and Hannah snorted loudly.

"Bullshit, Selena. You need to talk to Reid."

"I know." She sighed. "I just, I need a few days to figure out what I'm going to say."

Hannah reached out and squeezed her hand. "It'll be okay, honey."

"Yeah, maybe." Selena said morosely.

"It will be. Listen, I don't mean to be rude but you seriously need to shower." Hannah grinned at her. "Even if I wasn't a Lycan, I'd be able to smell you."

Selena laughed. "Yeah, yeah, I know. Time for the walk of shame back to my room. Thanks for listening, Hannah."

"Anytime, honey." Hannah replied.

* * *

"You've been avoiding me all morning."

Selena gave a sharp gasp and jerked wildly before glancing behind her. "No, I haven't."

She had just finished target shooting and was putting the gun back in the small room that housed the guns used for training. Lost in her thoughts, she hadn't heard Reid enter the room or the door shutting behind him.

"Yes, you have." Reid said firmly. "We need to talk."

"Reid, I have a really bad headache and I'm tired and I'd just like to be left alone, okay?"

"Sorry, sweetheart, but you're not going anywhere until we talk about what happened in my apartment last night."

She placed the gun on the shelf and took a deep breath. "Yeah, about that. The thing is – I don't really remember what happened."

"You don't remember." He repeated.

"Not really. I mean, I remember coming to your apartment and talking to you but after that it's pretty much a blur. It must have been embarrassing though because I woke up in your bed without my shirt."

She gave him an embarrassed look over her shoulder. "I'm sorry for bothering you when I was drunk. I shouldn't have done that."

He stepped closer and when she tried to move away, he placed his hands on the shelving and blocked her in.

"I think you're lying, Selena." He said softly.

She continued to stare at the shelf in front of her, trying to ignore the feel of his hot breath on the back of her neck. "I'm not."

"Really? You don't remember tearing my shirt off?"

"No."

"You don't remember telling me that you masturbated every night while you thought about me?"

"N-no." She stuttered. "And that isn't true. I – I don't think about you when I, um, masturbate."

"More lies." He said sternly.

She didn't reply and twitched when his hand, his delightfully hard and deliciously warm hand, rested on her flat abdomen. She was wearing yoga pants and his fingers toyed with the drawstring on them as he spoke again.

"You asked me to fuck you, Selena. Hell, you begged me to fuck you."

"I did not." She croaked out.

"You did." He insisted. "And I refuse to believe that you don't remember having my cock in your mouth."

She moaned loudly as his hand slipped inside her pants and underwear and cupped her pussy firmly. She was wet and he made a soft noise of approval as he traced his fingers over the swollen lips of her pussy.

"Oh, you definitely remember." He breathed into her ear.

"Reid." She moaned as she gripped the shelving.

"Yes, sweetheart?"

"Please."

"Please what?" He pushed his fingers between her lips and rubbed at her clit.

She moaned again and widened her thighs. She tried to step back, to lean against his hard chest, but he placed his other hand in the small of her back and prevented her from moving as his fingers moved relentlessly over her clit.

"Does that feel good?" He whispered.

"Yes." She murmured.

He slid his finger down and eased it into her tight opening. "You're so wet for me, Selena. I fucking love how wet you are."

"Oh!" She gasped loudly when his fingers returned to her clit. He pinched and tugged on the swollen bud as she panted and moaned.

"Tell me the truth, sweetheart. Do you remember sucking on my cock?"

"Yes!" She suddenly cried. "I remember!"

"Good." He breathed. "I've spent all morning thinking about how hot and wet your mouth is, about how badly I want to come in your mouth and watch as you swallow it all like a good girl."

He tugged on her clit again and she made a sharp cry of need as her hands squeezed the shelving. "Please, Reid."

"You asked me to take you to my bed and make you mine. Do you remember that, Selena?" He asked as his fingers paused in their rubbing.

She nodded. She was on the knife's edge of climaxing and she waited breathlessly for Reid to touch her again. All she needed was one more tug, one more stroke of his rough fingers, and she would find the release she so desperately needed.

"I'm going to make you come all over my fingers," he breathed hotly into her ear, "and then you're going to come back to my room and I'll do what you asked. I'll take you to my bed and make you mine. I want you under me. I want you screaming my name as I make you come over and over, as I slide my hard cock deep into your tight, wet pussy, and – "

The door popped open and Mannie stuck his head into the room. "Reid, there you are. You're late for the fucking meeting, you asshole. What the hell are you – "

He stopped, his eyes widening at the sight of Reid with his hand in Selena's pants. "Well, holy shit!"

Selena, her face flaming red, yanked Reid's hand out of her pants and fled the room, pushing past Mannie and scurrying down the hall as Mannie hollered after her. "You need to be at that meeting too, Selena!"

He turned back to Reid and grinned at him.

"You have the worst fucking timing." Reid snarled.

"Sorry, dude." Mannie laughed and held his hands up apologetically. "How was I to know you were trying to bang Selena in the gun room?"

Reid glared at him and Mannie laughed again. "Try to keep it in your pants at the meeting, would you, Reid? I know it'll be difficult with Selena there but - "

"Shut up, Mannie!" Reid snapped and stalked out of the room.

Still laughing, Mannie followed him.

Chapter 10

"Welcome, everyone." Jordan smiled at the crowd of people who had gathered in the main training gym.

"I thought it would be best if I introduced myself to everyone. I'm Jordan Hart and I'm the new director of the facility. I know the last few weeks have been a difficult time but we're doing our best to get things back to normal."

He paused and smiled at the large crowd. "I'm sure you've noticed the crew who have been working outside. They'll have our new surveillance system set up tomorrow afternoon. This will help ensure that what happened here at the facility, will never happen again."

Hannah, standing near the back with Will and Selena, made an unladylike snort and Will squeezed her hand warningly as a few of the recruits glanced back at them.

"There have been a few changes to the program. We have a new group of recruits joining us in the next few days. Constance, one of our weapons instructors, will now be working solely with the new recruits. As well, Hannah will be taking over the training of the kenjutsu until our regular instructor, Chen, is back on his feet."

Hannah smiled faintly as the group of people turned to look at her. She could see Alex and Paul standing together near the side and she grimaced at the looks they were giving her. She would have to speak to them about being their sparring partner and nothing more.

Jordan clapped his hands and the crowd turned back to him. "I'm sure that over the next few weeks, you'll have plenty of questions. I want you to know that my door is always open and I'm available for questions or comments whenever you need to talk. As well, please feel free to talk to any of the instructors if I'm not available. That's it for now. Again, if you have any questions or concerns, please talk to myself or one of the instructors."

He stepped back and the crowd of people began to slowly disperse, talking quietly among themselves. Mannie joined Hannah and the others and sighed loudly. "Well, that went better than I thought."

"What did you think was going to happen?" Selena asked.

Reid appeared beside her and a blush crossed her cheeks as she inched away.

"I thought for sure there would be questions about why we allowed this attack to happen in the first place." Reid frowned. "Everyone seems remarkably calm about what happened."

"I think they're still in fucking shock." Mannie grumbled. "No one can quite believe it happened. There will be plenty of questions in the future."

"Does it matter though?" Hannah questioned. "Do you really think Jordan or the Board of Directors is going to care if the recruits or the instructors are upset? If what you and Will told me is true, they're more concerned about increasing the number of recruits to fight the vampires. If their current batch is unhappy, what do they care?"

"They'll want to keep as many people in the program as possible. Pumping out the new recruits is great but what they really need are the people who've already graduated and proven themselves capable of slaying vampires." Will replied. "With the training period accelerated, the program will need people like you and Selena and Mallorie and Ryan to help the babies during the actual hunts."

"Fuck!" Mannie suddenly snapped. "They're making a big mistake in changing the program. If they think – "

"Keep your voice down, Mannie." Selena said nervously as she glanced at the few people who were still milling about the gym. "If the babies or recruits hear you talk that way, they'll lose the little confidence they have left."

"Yeah." Mannie muttered. "I'm going to grab a bite to eat. You guys coming?"

Will and Hannah nodded and followed Mannie to the door of the gym. Reid grabbed Selena's arm and tugged her to a stop.

"Hi, Selena." He grinned at her and she gave him a nervous look.

"Hello."

"I was thinking maybe you and I could have dinner at my apartment tonight. What do you think?" He stroked her arm lightly and she cleared her throat before tugging her arm free.

"That's not a good idea, Reid."

"Sure it is. I make a mean spaghetti sauce."

"Reid, I'm sorry but what happened in your apartment was a mistake. I was drunk and I shouldn't have done what I did. I'm really embarrassed about it."

He frowned at her. "Then why did you do it, Selena?"

"I – because I was drunk." She stammered.

"Really? You weren't drunk in the gun room." He replied. "What's your excuse for that?"

She sighed with frustration. "Listen, obviously I'm attracted to you, but that doesn't mean us sleeping together is a good idea. In fact, it's a really, really bad idea."

He winced. "You sure know how to make a guy feel good, Selena."

She flushed. "I'm sorry. I'm blowing hot and cold with you and I know how that makes me look, really I do, and I don't mean to mess with you. I just – I think it's best if we stay away from each other."

He sighed angrily. "Yeah, you keep saying that. And then you show up at my apartment begging me to fuck you. You get why I might be a little confused, right?"

She stared down at the floor. "I do. I'm sorry."

"I didn't take you for a tease, Selena." He snapped.

She pressed her lips together and gave him her own look of anger. "I said I was sorry. But maybe you could take some responsibility for it as well. It wasn't me who came into the gun room and started talking dirty and sticking my hand down your pants."

"No, I guess it wasn't." He scowled at her. "You have to be drunk to do that."

"You asshole! I should have known apologizing wouldn't work. And for the record? I'm not a damn tease. I was drunk and people make stupid mistakes when they're drunk."

Her face was bright red and he could see tears welling in her eyes as she gave him another look of frustration. "I am sorry for – for leading you on like that. But trust me – it won't happen again."

"Selena, wait – "

He felt a wave of guilt at the look of shame in her eyes and snagged her arm as she moved away from him. She yanked it free and hurried out of the gym.

"Fuck! You're such a goddam idiot, Reid!" He muttered.

* * *

"Chen? Are you decent?" Andrew called through the curtain.

"Mostly." Chen replied softly.

Andrew peered around the curtain and frowned. "You're supposed to be dressed, Chen."

Chen stared silently at him. He had pulled his briefs on, struggling to do it one-handed as his anger and depression grew, and then had sat back down on the bed.

"I'm tired."

"Nonsense." Andrew said cheerfully. "Here, put your pants on."

He held the pants out, frowning again when Chen didn't move. "Come on, Chen. We've got work to do."

"Not today." Chen replied.

"Yes, today." Andrew said firmly.

Before he could stop him, Andrew had knelt at his feet and quickly slid his pants up to his knees. "There, stand up and do the rest."

Scowling at him, Chen stood and awkwardly caught his pants with his right hand. He yanked them up and fumbled with the button and zipper, his face growing progressively redder, as Andrew watched quietly.

When they were buttoned, Andrew nodded. "Good. I'm going to help you with your shirt only because it's going to be a bit painful for you."

He picked up Chen's t-shirt and smiled reassuringly when the sword instructor flinched backwards. "I don't bite, Chen."

An image of Andrew's straight white teeth nibbling at his throat flooded through Chen's mind and he bit the inside of his cheek and stared at the floor. Christ, he had to get a hold of himself. He didn't even know if the man was gay.

He is. You know he is.

He cleared his throat as Andrew tugged the shirt over his head. "Ready?" He grinned at him and Chen nodded, shuddering a little at Andrew's warm touch as he gripped his arm just above the stump.

"Did that hurt?"

"What?" Chen said hoarsely. He tried to breathe shallowly. Andrew smelled delicious and he was itching to touch the dark chest hair he could see peeking out from above his shirt. For the first time since he had woken up in the infirmary, he wasn't thinking about the loss of his hand, about what the vampire Samuel had taken from him, and he unconsciously leaned a little closer as Andrew touched his chest lightly.

"Chen?"

"Sorry, what?" He cleared his throat as Andrew gave him an odd look.

"I asked if it hurts when I touch your arm. You're shaking a little."

Chen shook his head. "No, it doesn't hurt."

"Good. Unfortunately, this probably will." Andrew said sympathetically. "Raise your arm, please."

Chen turned his head away and tried to lift his arm. It sent a bolt of pain into the end of the stump and he made a soft gasp before lowering it. "I can't."

"I know it hurts but it's a good exercise." Andrew said softly. "Try again."

Gritting his teeth, Chen lifted his arm and ignored the pain as Andrew gently pulled his stump through the arm of the t-shirt. He helped him struggle into the rest of the shirt and Chen was embarrassed to realize he was sweating and shaking by the time they were done.

He flinched back when Andrew reached out and casually smoothed his hair down for him.

"Sorry, I'm kind of touchy-feely." Andrew grinned at him. "Comes with the territory of being a physiotherapist."

He led Chen out into the main part of the infirmary. "Barb, we'll be back in a bit."

"Sounds good." Barb smiled at them as she ducked past the curtain surrounding Ryan's bed.

"Where are we going?" Chen asked.

"For a walk. I thought you'd like to get out of the infirmary." Andrew replied.

"I don't!" Chen snapped.

"That's too bad, because we're going anyway." Andrew took his right arm in a firm grip and led him toward the door. "It'll be good for you."

He ushered Chen out into the hallway. There were a few recruits walking by and they smiled nervously at Chen, their gazes shying away from his missing hand.

Chen, his face red, tried to jerk free of Andrew's firm grip. "Let go of me. I don't feel like being gawked at and I'm tired and I – "

"Master!" Hannah, Will by her side, hurried down the hall toward them. She hugged Chen firmly before kissing him on the cheek.

"What are you up to?"

"Nothing." Chen grunted as Will introduced himself to Andrew. "I'm going back to the infirmary."

"No, you're not." Andrew argued. "You're going for a walk."

"No, I'm – "

"Great! I'll come with you." Hannah linked her arm with Chen's and smiled at Will. "I'll see you back at the apartment, alright?"

Will nodded and squeezed Chen's shoulder. "I'll talk to you later, Chen."

He walked away as Hannah grinned at Chen and Andrew. "Why don't we go to your apartment and I'll make us all some tea. Douglas says tea makes everything better and I'm starting to think he's right."

Andrew blinked in surprise when Chen allowed Hannah to lead him down the hall. The sword instructor obviously had a soft spot when it came to the woman, and he moved quickly to Chen's left side and listened quietly as Hannah spoke.

"So, we started training Henry this morning."

"We?" Chen raised his eyebrow at her.

"Alex, Paul and I. I thought it would be better if we did more of a team effort with him." Hannah replied.

"Until Henry picks up on Paul's tendency to raise his sword too high." Chen said grumpily.

Hannah grinned. "Paul knows he does that and he's already cautioned Henry about it. Don't worry, master, we'll try not to screw Henry up too badly until you're back."

"What do you think of Henry's abilities?" Chen asked curiously.

Hannah shrugged. "It's his first time with one-on-one training so I think it's a little too soon to tell. I mean, he's obviously got skill or you wouldn't have chosen him to continue but – I don't know – he seems a bit timid."

"You were timid once."

"Yes, I suppose I was." Hannah stared down at the thin scars on her arms. "I got over it quickly though."

Chen didn't reply but a brief smile crossed his face as Hannah looked around him at Andrew.

"So, what do you think of our facility, Andrew?"

"It's nice." Andrew replied politely.

She laughed. "I'm imagining the New York facility is a little nicer. Are you homesick for the city yet?"

"It's different." Andrew grinned at her. "But there's something to the small city living that a man could get used to. Last night I sat outside and stared up at the stars for nearly an hour. I don't think I've seen that many stars since I was a child and lived on my grandfather's farm."

"Are you originally from New York?" Hannah asked.

"No. I grew up in a little town in Iowa and moved to New York when I was a teenager."

"That's quite the move. What prompted it?"

"Leeches overtook our farm one night and murdered my parents and grandparents."

"I'm sorry." Hannah said quietly.

"Thank you."

"How did you survive?" Chen asked abruptly.

Andrew made a small, humorless chuckle. "My grandfather was big into war re-enactments. He had a collection of various weapons and I used one of the swords he had hanging in his study to kill the leech."

"Impressive." Hannah said solemnly.

Andrew shook his head. "Lucky, that's all."

"Were you bitten?" Chen asked.

Andrew nodded. "I was. I had an uncle and an aunt who lived in New York and after my parents died, they took me in. But it didn't take long for the vampires to find me. I didn't know at the time that I smelled differently, you know?"

Hannah nodded as Andrew sighed softly. "I had a couple of close calls with the leeches. I really thought that I was going crazy and, in fact, my uncle had me put in a mental hospital for a few months. I had told the police and anyone who would listen that vampires had killed my parents and grandparents but they, of course, didn't believe me."

"They put you in a mental hospital?" Hannah gave him a horrified look.

"They did. It saved my life actually. I couldn't go out but the leeches couldn't get in either. There was a man in the hospital who knew about the vampires. He'd been bitten himself and truthfully, he had actually gone a little mad from it. Anyway, he knew about the facility in New York. They had tried to recruit him but mentally he wasn't strong enough. When they released me from the hospital, I immediately went to the facility."

He rubbed absentmindedly at his goatee. "I wasn't strong enough to be a recruit, I was just a scrawny, scared-shitless teenager, but they put me in admin and after a few years, they approached me about moving into the medical program. I became a physiotherapist and worked mostly from the New York facility but I've visited a few of the other bigger centres. Not often though. They don't like to release those of us who have been bitten and have no fighting skills, into the general public."

He grinned at Hannah and Chen. "When they asked me to come here to work with Chen, I said yes immediately. I figured it would be nice to get back to my country roots for a while."

They were at Chen's apartment and Hannah opened the door and flicked the lights on. Andrew stared around curiously as Hannah led Chen to the couch. He collapsed on it with a soft sigh and she smiled happily at him before going into the kitchen.

Andrew studied the swords hanging above the fireplace. They gleamed in the light and he touched the handle of one lightly before moving to the bookshelf. He studied the picture of Chen with a young, smiling Asian woman before glancing back at Chen.

"Is this your sister?"

Chen nodded. "How did you know?"

"You look alike." Andrew smiled at him and Chen felt another one of those small bites of lust go through his belly.

"What's her name?" Andrew asked.

"Amy."

"She's a nurse." Hannah said helpfully as she put the kettle on the small stove.

Chen glared at her and she gave him a deliberately innocent look before reaching for the tea bags in the cupboard.

"Does she know what happened?" Andrew sat down next to him on the couch, his lean thigh touching his, and Chen shifted away.

"No." He muttered.

"You should tell her."

"Tell her what exactly? That I got my arm chopped off by a vampire?" Chen snorted.

"Well, it's more like your hand that got chopped off. But unless you're planning on never seeing your sister again, you're going to have to come up with something." Andrew replied.

He studied Chen carefully. "You could tell her you lost your hand rescuing a woman from a burning building."

"Or a kitten!" Hannah piped up. "Chen loves kittens."

Chen gaped at her as Andrew laughed. "Nah, we need something more badass. I know – you can tell her you lost your hand in a motorcycle accident."

"I don't drive a motorcycle." Chen blinked at him.

"Really? I'm surprised by that. I could picture you dressed in leather and driving a motorcycle." Andrew replied.

Hannah plopped down in the armchair across from the couch. "Yeah, I could see that. But I think we need to work a kitten in there somewhere. Maybe he swerved to avoid a kitten on the road?"

"A whole pack of orphaned kittens!" Andrew leaned forward eagerly. "And even though his hand was torn off, he still managed to gather them up and take them to the animal rescue before they were smushed on the road by a nerd in a mini-van. He's badass but tender hearted."

"No one gets between the master and his pack of kittens." Hannah said solemnly.

"One," Chen said through gritted teeth, "it's called a litter of kittens, not a pack, and two – my affection for cats was meant to be a *secret*, Hannah."

She gave him another innocent look. "Was it? My bad."

She bounced up from the chair and headed to the kitchen as Andrew grinned at him. "I knew you were a cat lover the moment I met you, Chen."

"You did not." Chen snapped. "And I am not telling my sister I lost my hand rescuing a litter of kittens. That's ridiculous."

"Don't worry," Andrew replied as he took his cup of tea from Hannah with a small nod of thanks, "I'm sure we'll be able to come up with something more inventive."

Hannah laughed softly as Chen scowled and stared into his cup of tea. Weirdly, Hannah's and Andrew's joking and their casual attitude about the loss of his hand was making him feel a little better. It shouldn't have been. There was nothing funny about it, but for the first time in days he could feel the cloud of depression lifting a little. It was kind of nice, he mused inwardly, to not have others feeling sorry for him.

Andrew set his tea on the side table and reached for Chen's arm. "Since we're just sitting here, I should probably do my job."

He began to pull and massage Chen's arm gently as Chen winced.

"Does that hurt, master?" Hannah asked softly.

"A little." He grunted.

She sat down next to him and took his cup of tea from him before holding his hand. "Squeeze my hand if you need to, alright?"

He didn't reply and she kissed his cheek again before resting her head on his shoulder.

"Mom wants to see you. She asked me if you were feeling up to stopping at the farmhouse for a visit." Hannah said softly.

Chen shook his head. "I don't think that's a good – "

"That's a great idea." Andrew interrupted, ignoring Chen's dirty look. "Chen can get some fresh air and it'll do him some good to get out of the facility for a bit."

"Good." Hannah gave him a pleased look and Chen closed his eyes in defeat. "We could go this evening and see them."

She hesitated. "Shit. That's not going to work. I told Selena I would hang out with her tonight. She's been going through some stuff."

She didn't elaborate further and Andrew hesitated before clearing his throat. "I can take Chen out to the farmhouse. If you don't think your mom would mind."

Hannah shook her head. "She loves meeting new people. Thanks, Andrew."

"No problem."

Chen made a soft curse under his breath and Hannah squeezed his hand. "She misses you, Chen. She'll be upset if you don't visit her and trust me, you don't want that. You should never make a hippie angry."

Andrew snorted laughter as Chen rolled his eyes. "Your mother doesn't have a mean bone in her body."

"Tell that to the ballet teacher who told me I was too fat to continue in dance." Hannah grinned at him. "Mom ripped her a new one, and I think the woman is still cowering in fear in her dance studio to this day."

A faint smile crossed Chen's face as Hannah put her head on his shoulder again. They sat in silence as Andrew rubbed and massaged, and Chen did his best to ignore the tingles of pleasure from his warm touch.

Chapter 11

"Hannah, you don't have to hang out with me. I'm fine." Selena flopped down on her bed and stared up at the ceiling as Hannah sat down beside her.

"No, you're not. You've been upset for the last few days. Talk to me, Selena."

Selena sighed. "Reid thinks I'm a tease and honestly? He's kind of right."

"People do dumb things when they're drunk." Hannah shrugged.

"That's what I told him but I was just being defensive. I'm running hot and cold with him and it isn't fair. I just need to stay away from him."

"Why?" Hannah asked.

"I told you why." Selena replied grumpily.

"Yeah but you're obviously attracted to him. I don't get why you're torturing yourself like this. Have some fun with him."

"And then what? I sleep with Reid a few times and what happens then? He's not interested in a relationship and I
_ "

"Do you know for sure he isn't?" Hannah interrupted.

Selena rolled her eyes. "He's not."

"But you're not really interested in a relationship either." Hannah pointed out.

"I know, but – "

"But what?" Hannah said a bit impatiently. "Life is short, Selena. You and I know that better than anyone. You need to –

The door to their room opened and Mannie stuck his head in. "We've got leeches outside." He said grimly.

Hannah jumped off the bed. "Shit! Where's Will?"

They followed Mannie down the hall. "He's in the control room with Jordan, Constance and Reid."

"Control room?" Selena asked.

"Yeah, they set up this room that shows us the views of all the cameras around the perimeter of the facility." Mannie replied.

He led them through the maze of hallways to an unmarked door. Hannah blinked in surprise at the numerous computers and the large screen on the far wall. Will and the others were standing in front of it and she hurried to his side, squeezing his hand lightly as she nodded to the others.

"How many?" Mannie asked.

"We've counted twenty." Jordan replied.

"Fuck. They have to know the location of the facility." Mannie shook his head. "There's no way twenty fucking leeches would just be wandering the damn forest together."

"Maybe they're a sub group of Samuel's pack of leeches." Constance said thoughtfully. "A second group ready to go if the first one failed."

Reid leaned forward and stared at the multiple views displayed across the large screen. "I don't know. They're not actively headed toward the facility. Maybe it's just a coincidence."

"Pretty fucking big coincidence." Mannie grunted. "Besides, leeches can't stand each other. They wouldn't be spending time together unless they had a purpose."

"It doesn't matter." Jordan said suddenly.

The others stared at him in surprise as he studied the screen. "We take them out now. If it is an attack, we're not going to allow them any closer to the facility then they already are. If it's just a coincidence, then it's a few less leeches to worry about."

He turned to Constance. "Gather a team of the older recruits. I want at least twenty."

"We don't have twenty left." Constance replied.

Jordan frowned. "What about the babies?"

"No." Will said immediately. "They're not ready. Sending them out there tonight means sending them to their death."

Jordan grunted with frustration. "How many do we have who can fight?"

"I'd say about twelve." Constance replied.

Jordan hesitated and Mannie rolled his eyes. "Twelve will be enough. You forget that we have Constance and Will and Hannah."

"What's that supposed to mean?" Jordan asked tightly.

Mannie shrugged. "You have no idea what Lycans are capable of but you're about to find out."

"Hannah's not shifting." Will said quickly. "She doesn't have enough control over it yet."

Mannie frowned at him. "Will – "

"He's right. I'm more comfortable with my swords." Hannah interrupted. "I don't need to shift to kill them, you know that, Mannie."

"Yeah, I guess I fucking do." Mannie muttered.

"Um, guys?" Selena had moved closer to the screen and she glanced at them. "Where the hell are these leeches going?"

She tapped the screen and the others watched as five of the leeches broke off from the main group.

"They're heading south." Jordan grabbed a map that was lying on the desk and scanned it. "What's to the south?"

Hannah stiffened as Will groaned. "The farmhouse."

"Mom?" Hannah whispered. She turned to bolt from the room, snarling at Will when he grabbed her arm in a tight grip.

"Wait!"

"Let go of me, Will." She warned softly as her eyes began to glow.

"You're not going by yourself." He snapped at her. "Calm down, Hannah."

She growled at him as Jordan gave her a thoughtful look before tapping the map. "Constance, Reid, Selena and the recruits will go after the main group. Will, Hannah and Mannie will head toward the farmhouse."

Will shook his head. "We don't need Mannie. Hannah and I can kill five leeches easily. Keep him with the larger group."

"Two against five isn't – "

"He's right." Mannie interjected. "Trust us, Jordan. We know what we're doing."

"Very well." Jordan said coolly. "Go out and do your jobs."

* * *

"It was so kind of you to bring Chen out for a visit, Andrew. I've been anxious to see him." Natalie smiled at Andrew as she held out the pot of tea. "More tea, Chen?"

"No thank you, Natalie." Chen replied. Natalie stroked his arm affectionately before sitting down at the table across from Chen and Andrew.

"It was no problem, Mrs. Torrington." Andrew bit into a cookie. "These cookies are delicious."

"Thank you, dear, and please call me Natalie."

"Where are Jim and the twins?" Chen asked.

"Jim and Tyrone went into town to visit with Heather. Just between you and me, I'm a little worried about her. She's spending way too much time alone but we can't convince her to move out to the farmhouse. That house is much too big for one person."

"You could stay with her." Chen said.

"Yes, but I do like being at the farmhouse. Barb and I have grown quite fond of each other, and both Jim and I enjoy living so closely to Hannah."

"Luther didn't go?" Chen asked.

She shook her head. "No, I'm a bit nervous about letting him go out what with being bitten and everything. He was terribly disgruntled with me and put up a fairly convincing argument about his abilities to kill the vampires, but I worry about my boy."

"So you have three children?" Andrew asked politely.

"Oh no, dear. We just have our two girls. Hannah and her younger sister Sara. Sara was murdered by the leeches and Hannah was almost killed as well. She was

154

saved by Will and brought to the facility. We actually thought she was dead for the longest time, and then vampires broke into our home and were about to kill me to draw Hannah out. But Hannah and Chen and a few of the others from the facility arrived just in time to save us. It was all very dramatic and exciting."

Andrew grinned a little before cocking his head at her. "So the twins…"

"A couple of genius hooligans." Chen muttered.

"What?" Andrew gave him a curious look.

Natalie laughed. "Chen's quite right. They're geniuses and hooligans. After Hannah faked her death, she met up with the twins after they tried to rob her and – "

"Wait, I thought she went to the facility?" Andrew interrupted.

"No, no, that was the first time we thought she was dead." Natalie said brightly. "She faked her death a second time to save us and the others she loved from being hunted down by vampires."

"Right, of course she did." Andrew replied.

"Anyway, once we found out she was alive again and met the twins, Jim and I sort of took the boys under our wing. The poor things are orphans. Jim always wanted boys and I love teenagers so it seemed natural for us to take care of them." Natalie said cheerfully.

She took a sip of tea and caught her saucer from falling off the table when a loud boom from upstairs shook the entire house.

"What was that?" Chen started to stand and Natalie waved her hand at him.

"Oh, it's just Luther upstairs. He's taken an interest in chemistry as of late. There have been quite a few explosions from his and Tyrone's room the last few days."

She laughed softly. "Jim made them put a fire extinguisher in their room. As far as I know they haven't had to use it yet."

There was the sound of a door slamming and the heavy thud of footsteps on the stairs.

"Natalie! Hey, Natalie? Guess what I made!" Luther, his face covered in soot and his eyebrows singed, charged into the kitchen.

"Luther, dearest, your sleeve is on fire." Natalie said delicately before taking another sip of tea.

The boy's shirt sleeve was, in fact, burning and Andrew watched as the young teenager hurried to the sink and doused the fabric with water before collapsing in the chair next to Natalie. He gave Chen a wide grin.

"The kung fu master is in the house." He held his fist out to Chen and Chen bumped it lightly.

"Luther, this is Andrew. He's Chen's physiotherapist." Natalie said.

"Nice to meetcha." Luther nodded at Andrew before leaning forward and studying Chen's bandaged stump.

"You gonna get a hook or what?"

Chen rolled his eyes. "No, Luther."

"Why not? You could do some serious damage to those fuc – ", he paused and gave Natalie a quick look, "those darn leeches with a hook."

Andrew nudged Chen. "He's got a good point."

Chen glared at him as Luther nodded. "Damn right I do. It's why I'm the smart twin."

"You and Tyrone are equally intelligent." Natalie said firmly.

"Actually, what you need is a sword attached to your arm." Luther rubbed at his singed eyebrows absently. "How fucking badass would that be?"

"Language, dear."

"Sorry, Natalie." Luther leaned forward again and studied the bandage on Chen's arm. "I bet I could make something that would fit around the stump."

Chen snorted loudly and Luther shrugged. "What? I could. If I had the right materials and the proper tools, I could whip something up in no time."

"I don't need a – a prosthetic arm that ends in a sword." Chen scowled at him.

"You say that now but when you see what it looks like, you'll change your mind." Luther said confidently.

Chen grunted in reply and shifted in his chair as Natalie folded her hands in her lap and smiled at Andrew. "So, you're from New York, Andrew?"

"I am." Andrew confirmed.

"Lovely. Jim and I went to New York City once on holiday. We got lost and had the most dreadful argument in the middle of the subway."

"It's a big city. It's easy to get lost."

"It certainly is." Natalie smiled at him. "So, are you married?"

Andrew shook his head. "No, ma'am."

"Dating someone? Is there a special man in your life?" Natalie asked.

Chen choked on his tea as Andrew smiled at Natalie. "How did you know I was gay, Natalie?"

She grinned. "I'm very good at reading people, dear."

She paused and gave him a horrified look. "Oh no. Is it a secret? Are you still in the closet?"

Andrew laughed. "No, I'm not still in the closet."

"Oh good." Natalie breathed a sigh of relief. "You know, I outed a boy once from our church, Joe was his name, right in the middle of a potluck lunch. It was terrible and I felt so awful about it."

She sighed before brightening. "Although, it all worked out in the end. He actually was rather pleased that his parents finally knew, and after they got over the initial shock they were very accepting of him. But still, you would think after that experience I would know better, wouldn't you?"

Andrew laughed again. "It's not a problem, Natalie."

"So, are you dating anyone?" She suddenly asked again.

Andrew shook his head. "I am not."

"What a shame. You're such a handsome and well-spoken man." Natalie replied. "Chen's single as well. Did you know that?"

Chen, his face bright red, coughed and choked on a mouthful of tea. Andrew pounded him on the back as Natalie passed him a napkin.

"Natalie – settin' up the kung fu master on a date." Luther grinned widely.

"I'm a natural matchmaker. It used to drive Hannah and Sara crazy when they were younger. I was always trying to set them up with different boys from our church." Natalie laughed. "In fact, I set up Joe with a lovely young man named Joshua. And the last I heard, they were still together."

"So why aren't you puttin' your skills to good use with me and my wolf girl?" Luther asked indignantly.

Natalie patted his hand. "One – you're much too young for her and two – she's in love with Ryan."

Chen, his face still bright red, stood up abruptly. "Excuse me, I have to use the restroom."

He left the kitchen as Natalie smiled at Andrew. "Would you like more tea, Andrew?"

"No, thank you." Andrew glanced at his watch. "I should get Chen back to the facility. I imagine he's getting pretty tired and – "

He stopped as there was a knock on the front door.

"Jim probably forgot his keys again. Be a dear and let him and your brother in please, Luther." Natalie squeezed Luther's arm and he nodded before leaving the kitchen.

"So, how is Chen doing with his physiotherapy?" Natalie asked.

"We haven't really started yet." Andrew replied. "Tomorrow morning I'm going to have him start – "

There was a startled yell from the hallway and a loud thud. Natalie and Andrew both stood and Natalie gave a soft gasp of surprise when Luther, his hand clapped over his arm and bright blood pouring out from between his fingers, ran into the kitchen.

"Natalie, get out!" He shouted and shoved her toward the back door of the kitchen. "Go, right now!"

"Luther? What's wrong? Why are you bleeding?" Natalie grabbed at his arm as there was a low chuckle from the hallway. The hair on the back of Andrew's neck stood up and he backed toward Natalie and Luther as a leech, his dark hair slicked back and his eyes glowing a soft yellow, peered into the kitchen.

"Hello, snacks!" He grinned at them as two more vampires crowded up behind him.

* * *

The vampires watched the two humans walk hand-in-hand through the forest. The vampire at the front, a squat man with short, greasy hair and pock-marked skin, held his hand up as the vampires behind him began to salivate. When the humans were less than ten feet away he stepped out into the moonlight and grinned at them as the other vampires crowded up behind him.

"Hello, humans."

The man stared at them. "Hello, motherfuckers."

The vampire frowned. "Watch your tongue, maggot."

The man dropped the woman's hand and took a step closer. "What are you going to do if I don't?"

The vampire shot forward and grasped the collar of the man's jacket, yanking him forward. "Rip it from your mouth, you impudent little – "

He stopped and cocked his head at the man before looking downward. A wooden stake was buried in his chest and as his skin began to blacken he gave a short, hoarse scream of fear. He burst into ash and blood and the man grimaced before wiping his face with his shirt sleeve.

The other vampires stared at him in shock as the woman laughed bitterly.

"That surprised them. Didn't it, Mannie?"

Mannie grinned at Mallorie. "I like to keep them on their toes."

Mallorie pulled two stakes from a holder around her waist and gripped them firmly. "Who's next?"

The vampires hissed loudly and a female leech, her eyes bright red and her dark hair tied back in a ponytail, arched her eyebrows at them. "There are only two of you and many of us."

"Two?" Mannie glanced behind him. "Who said there was only two of us?"

The vampires gave each other uneasy looks as a blond man and a small, dark-haired woman, both of them carrying guns, joined Mannie and Mallorie.

"Fuck, I hate leeches." The blond man shook his head as a low growling started to the left of them. Constance, in her wolf form and her eyes glowing bright green, stepped into the light and grinned at the vampires.

The female vampire hissed again before turning to the others. "Kill them."

The vampires surged forward as more humans, all of them armed heavily, appeared out of the darkness.

As a leech darted toward Mannie, he grinned wildly and shouted, "I love this fucking job!"

* * *

Luther tore open a drawer and pulled out a butcher knife. "Natalie! Run!" He shouted before shoving her again toward the back door. Natalie stumbled from the kitchen into the darkness of the yard.

Her heart beating fiercely, she glanced around uncertainly before taking a step back toward the door.

"Going somewhere?" A vampire appeared out of the darkness to smile benignly at her.

"Stay away from me." Natalie whispered.

"Oh, I can't do that." The vampire grinned. "Not when I'm so very thirsty."

He took a step forward as Natalie backed toward the door. "Don't be afraid. It will only hurt for a – "

Natalie made a harsh noise of surprise and disgust when there was a soft whooshing sound and the vampire's head slid from his body. As his head tumbled to the ground and his body crumpled, she sobbed with relief at the sight of Hannah standing behind him.

Will, in his wolf form, loped to her side and Hannah glanced at him briefly. "Is the other one dead?"

Will chuffed softly as Natalie rushed forward and grabbed Hannah's arm. "The others! There are three more in the kitchen!"

"Stay behind me, mom." Hannah said grimly.

Chapter 12

The three vampires crowded into the kitchen as Luther and Andrew backed away.

"Which one do you want?" The tallest vampire asked.

"That one." The vampire next to him pointed at Luther as the third one frowned.

"I don't want to share."

"Too bad." The tall vampire shoved at his companion irritably and Andrew shouted with fear and surprise when the leech moved quickly across the room and pushed him up against the wall. He punched at the vampire as, behind him, the remaining two vampires leaped at Luther. The young teenager cursed loudly and one of the vampires screamed thinly.

Luther had sliced across his throat with the butcher knife and the vampire clapped his hand to his neck before glaring at the boy. "You'll pay for that, you insolent little shit!"

He picked up Luther with one hand and threw him across the kitchen. Luther landed in a crumpled heap on the floor, the butcher knife sliding across the tile floor, and the two vampires grinned at each other and fell on him.

Andrew screamed as the vampire pinning him to the wall gripped his hair with an icy cold hand and yanked his head back. He studied the veins in Andrew's throat as saliva began to drip from his mouth. "Go ahead and scream, I don't – "

He suddenly twitched, his hand tightening in Andrew's hair, as blood began to flow from his mouth. Andrew cried out and threw his arms over his face when the vampire exploded, showering him in ash and blood.

Chen, holding the fireplace poker, the end of it drenched in the leech's blood, stared anxiously at Andrew.

"Andrew! Are you alright? Were you bitten?"

"No." Andrew wiped the blood from his face as Chen turned around.

"Stay behind me." He said quietly as he raised the fireplace poker. The other two vampires, one of them holding a struggling, cursing Luther down with a knee across his chest, hissed loudly at them.

The other stood and took a few steps closer to Chen and Andrew. "A man with only one hand believes he can defeat me?"

Chen didn't reply and the vampire grinned and shot across the room. He knocked the poker from Chen's hand and wrapped his hand around his neck. He lifted him from the floor and grabbed Chen's stump with his other, squeezing and twisting viciously. A grin crossed his face when Chen screamed hoarsely and blood bloomed on the bandage. As blood began to drip on to the floor, the vampire slammed him against the counter. Andrew scrambled forward and punched the vampire in the side as Chen made a soft, choking noise. The vampire hissed at Andrew but didn't release his grip on Chen's neck and arm.

"Get away from him!" Andrew shouted and punched him again.

With an irritated sigh, the vampire let go of Chen's arm and shoved Andrew in the chest. The slender man was knocked off his feet, his head banging painfully on the tile floor.

"There, that's better." The vampire said cheerfully. He turned toward Chen, his eyes lighting up as Chen's struggles grew weaker. "I'll have to eat quickly, you're losing an awful lot of – "

The door to the kitchen banged open and a tall, dark-haired woman rushed into the kitchen. She was carrying a long sword and the vampire dropped Chen and began to back away.

"Is that – a sword?" His frown turned into a soft gasp of surprise when the woman, moving more quickly than any human he'd seen before, lunged forward and thrust her sword deep into his chest.

Luther cursed again and tried to push the leech off of him. The vampire was drinking greedily from his neck, and he stiffened and lifted his head from Luther's neck when he felt the hot breath of the Lycan stir his hair.

"No." The leech whimpered as the Lycan grinned at him.

"Please, no, don't – "

The Lycan sank his teeth into his head, the vampire screamed pitifully as his skull cracked under the pressure of the Lycan's massive jaws, and ripped the leech's head from his body. He dropped the head to the floor and howled triumphantly as the vampire disintegrated into ash and blood.

Luther scrambled to his feet. His eyes were round with panic and he shouted hoarsely at Hannah. "Natalie! She's outside and there might be others!"

"She's fine." Hannah said quickly as Luther staggered toward the door. "Luther, she's okay, don't – "

Natalie stepped into the kitchen and Luther gave a hoarse shout of relief before throwing himself at her. She wrapped her arms around him and pressed kisses against his forehead and cheeks.

"I'm okay, honey. I'm okay."

"Are you sure?" Luther asked anxiously.

"Yes, dearest, I'm fine." Natalie stroked his hair before leading him to one of the chairs. "Sit down, Luther."

She grabbed a dishtowel and pressed it against his bleeding arm before kissing the top of his head. "Just stay still, dear."

Luther nodded and leaned his head against her stomach. He closed his eyes as Natalie stroked his head and the back of his neck and made soothing sounds of comfort.

"Master! Master, can you hear me?" Hannah was kneeling next to Chen and she helped him sit up as he coughed wretchedly.

"Fuck! You're really bleeding!" There was an edge of panic in her voice.

"Andrew?" Chen rasped before taking a ragged breath. "Where's Andrew?"

"I'm right here."

Andrew, his face pale and blood trickling down his temple, knelt beside him. He had a handful of dishtowels in his hand and he gave Chen a grim look. "I'm sorry, this is going to hurt like a bitch."

Hannah flinched when Andrew pressed the dishtowels against the bleeding stump and Chen screamed hoarsely. The towels were almost immediately soaked through and Andrew lifted his gaze to Hannah.

"My belt. Take it off – quickly!"

Hannah unbuckled his belt and pulled it free as Andrew smiled reassuringly at Chen. "Wrap the belt around his upper arm and pull it tight." He didn't take his gaze from Chen's pale face.

"You'll have to hold it in place." Andrew instructed as he reached out and smoothed Chen's hair back. "I'm going to lift your arm over your head. Ready?"

Chen nodded and Hannah made a soft noise of distress when Chen screamed again.

"It's okay, I know it hurts." Andrew soothed quietly. He glanced at Hannah in alarm. "Hannah? Are you alright?"

Her eyes were glowing bright green and she was making low snarling noises under her breath as hair began to grow on her cheeks. She was staring wide-eyed at Chen, and Andrew swallowed nervously.

There was a soft pop and then a naked Will was kneeling next to them. He cupped Hannah's face and made her look at him. "It's okay, Hannah."

"Chen." She whispered. "He's dying, Will. He's dying and I – "

"He's not dying." Will said calmly. "We'll get him to the infirmary and Barb will take care of him. Take some deep breaths, honey. If you shift, it's not going to help. We need you to help us get Chen back to the facility."

Hannah turned her gaze back to Chen. He stared steadily at her, but his face was pale and his body was beginning to tremble violently. She took a shaky breath as the front door slammed. Will, a growl rising in his chest, stood up as Luther staggered to his feet and stood protectively in front of Natalie.

Jim, holding Reuben in his arms, sauntered into the kitchen. "Nat? We're – "

He stopped, making a small grunt of pain when Tyrone ran into his back, and stared wide-eyed at the blood and ash on the floor as Tyrone peered around him.

"What the fuck?" Tyrone said softly.

"Language, dear." Natalie replied calmly before bursting into tears.

* * *

"Selena! Behind you!" Mallorie screamed.

Selena whirled around and fired her gun at the vampire. It just grazed his shoulder and he twitched before grinning at her. She cursed loudly and raised her gun to fire again as a sword sliced the vampire in half. Alex, sweating profusely, stabbed the fallen vampire in the chest.

"Thanks." Selena panted.

"Don't mention it." He ran toward a vampire attacking Paul as Selena scanned the forest.

They were winning. There were less than five vampires left and she watched as Constance, her dark fur gleaming in the moonlight, leaped on to the back of a vampire trying to crawl away and tore its head off.

There was muffled shout and Selena twisted around to see a vampire grab Reid and lift him in the air.

"Reid!" She screamed as the vampire threw Reid as easily as a ragdoll into a large tree. There was a sharp crack and the blond man bellowed with pain.

Reid stared up at the vampire towering over him. His gun had been knocked from his hand and he groped frantically for it as the vampire reached for him.

"Fool!" The vampire hissed. "Do you really think you can defeat me? I – "

A gun pressed against his temple and the leech turned to see Selena grinning manically at him. "Fuck you, leech."

She pulled the trigger and the vampire's head exploded in a spray of blood and brains.

Selena hauled Reid to his feet. "Are you alright?"

"I think my arm's broken." His face was ashen and he cradled his arm against his side as another vampire landed with a thud in front of them.

Selena raised her gun and fired. The vampire laughed at the dry click and clapped his hands together delightedly. "Poor baby. Is your gun empty? Not so tough now, are you?"

Before he could reach for them, Mannie was standing behind him. He shoved a long wooden stake into his back and grunted triumphantly when the vampire exploded.

"You two okay?"

"Reid's broken his arm." Selena slipped her arm around Reid's waist as Mannie scanned the forest.

He studied the bloody, sweating group of humans who were gathering together. Nothing remained of the vampires and Mannie nodded to the others. "Good job, everyone. Let's get back."

He smiled at Selena and Reid. "Come on, Reid. Let's get you to the infirmary."

* * *

"How is he?" Hannah asked anxiously as she nearly ran in to the infirmary. Jordan had insisted on a debriefing when the group had returned to the facility and she had spent the entire time worrying about Chen. Will and Selena were with her and Will rubbed her back soothingly as Selena peered behind each of the drawn curtains. She disappeared behind the third one as Hannah continued to stare nervously at Barb.

"He's okay. He lost quite a bit of blood but he'll live." Barb gave her a tired smile as she washed her hands. "It didn't take long to re-suture and I've given him some morphine for the pain. He's pretty drowsy at the moment."

"I'll stay with him." Hannah started forward as Barb shook her head.

"Andrew's with him and besides, Chen isn't going to remember much of tonight. You should check on your mom. She's upset."

Will frowned. "Is Luther okay?"

"Oh, he's fine." Barb replied. "The vampire sliced his arm open and he lost some more blood when he was bitten but he's young and healthy. He'll bounce back quickly. It was scary for Nat though and she was pretty upset when I was suturing Luther's arm."

Barb scrubbed her hand across her face. "I still need to set Reid's broken arm, Paul's got a pretty nasty cut to the abdomen and Leanne was bitten and needs the wound cleaned and disinfected."

She sighed heavily. "We really need to have more than just me. I'll have to talk to Jordan about bringing in a larger medical team. The facility isn't the same now, is it? More recruits, and talk of more hunts. If Richard were alive, he would..."

She trailed off and Will squeezed her arm gently. "You're doing a great job."

She smiled faintly. "Thanks, Will."

She hugged Hannah briefly before giving her a light push. "Go on. Go see your mom."

* * *

Selena sat on the edge of the bed and stared worriedly at Reid. The blond man's eyes were closed and he was pale with dark circles under his eyes. She stroked his left arm gently and his eyes popped open.

"Hi, Reid. How are you feeling?"

"I feel great." He grinned at her. "Barb gave me morphine."

She smiled as he took her hand and squeezed it. "How are you?"

"I'm fine."

"Thanks for saving my life, sweetheart."

"You're welcome."

"I was thinking," he said conversationally, "that after Barb sets my arm you should climb in to this hospital bed and I'll show you how grateful I am."

She laughed. "That's not a great idea, Reid."

"Sure it is. Even with only one good arm, I'll rock your world."

She laughed again. "That's the morphine talking."

He snorted loudly and glanced at his broken arm. "Trust me, sweetheart, I've got moves in the sack you've only dreamed about."

"I'm sure you do, but after Barb sets your arm you're going to need some rest. Once that morphine wears off, it's going to hurt like hell."

"I think you're turning me down because you're afraid you'll have too much fun, and get a little too attached to this smoking hot body of mine." Reid grinned at her.

She rolled her eyes. "If anyone gets too attached, it'll be you. You're not the only one with moves."

Reid snickered before stroking her hand lightly. "Don't worry, Selena. I know exactly what this is."

"And what is this?" She asked softly.

"We're just two people having some adult fun together. There's nothing wrong with that.

Before she could reply, Barb hurried through the gap in the curtains. She was pushing a small white cart that had an x-ray film balanced on top and she smiled at Reid. "The break is bad but, all things considered, pretty clean. I'm going to set the bone and then we'll cast it. How's the morphine holding up?"

"It's super!" Reid said so enthusiastically that both Selena and Barb laughed.

"Yes, well, enjoy it while it lasts." Barb said dryly. "Do you want Selena to leave while I set your arm?"

"Nope." Reid winked at Barb. "After you set my arm, Selena's going to crawl into the bed with me and I'm going to rock her world."

"Reid!" Selena's face turned bright red.

"Sorry, Reid. The infirmary is a sex-free zone." Barb said firmly before grinning at Selena.

"What?" Reid replied indignantly. "That's ridiculous. Besides, Selena won't be able to resist jumping my bones so if you hear any strange noises behind the curtain just ignore them."

"Reid, be quiet." Selena gave him a pointed look before smiling nervously at Barb. "He's just high on the morphine. I don't want to sleep with him."

"Sure you don't." Barb winked at her before patting Reid's leg. "Are you ready, Reid?"

"Ready, Freddie!" Reid wiggled his eyebrows at her before squeezing Selena's hand. "You're going to stay with me, right?"

"Yes." Selena replied softly. "I'll stay with you."

* * *

Chen groaned softly. His arm was throbbing, his head was swimming and he was terribly thirsty. Keeping his eyes closed, he cleared his throat painfully and croaked Barb's name.

"Chen? What's wrong?" Andrew's deep voice spoke in his ear and a wide ribbon of relief washed over him. The fight in the farmhouse had ended in a blur and he couldn't remember if Andrew had lived or not.

"Thirsty." He croaked again.

"Okay. Hold on. I'm going to raise the bed." Andrew's warm hand stroked across his forehead and Chen swallowed down the nausea when there was a soft whirring noise and the upper half of the bed began to rise.

"Okay?" Andrew asked worriedly.

"Yeah. Just a little nauseous."

"That's probably from the morphine. Take small sips of water, okay?"

A straw was held to his lips and he took a few sips of the cold water. It felt wonderful against his parched throat and he made a low noise of protest when Andrew took the cup away.

"Sorry." He soothed his hand across Chen's forehead again. "You can have some more in about ten minutes."

Chen nodded and stared blearily at Andrew. "Are you okay?"

"Yes." Andrew smiled at him. "Thanks to you. Do you remember what happened?"

"Not all of it. I remember killing the vampire that was attacking you."

"Not bad for a man with a missing hand." Andrew said quietly.

Chen closed his eyes. "Before I would have easily killed all three of them."

Andrew touched his shoulder hesitantly. "You saved my life, Chen."

"What happened after that?" Chen asked wearily.

"Well, the second vampire grabbed you by the throat and by your arm. I panicked and started punching him because, you know, that's effective technique against a leech."

Chen smiled faintly and Andrew grinned at him. "Then Hannah and Will showed up and killed the leeches."

"Chen?" Andrew squeezed his arm and Chen opened his eyes.

"Is Hannah a Lycan?"

"Yes."

Andrew didn't reply and Chen frowned at him. "What?"

"Nothing. I just – it seems strange that a Lycan would learn to use swords."

"She wasn't always a Lycan. When the vampires attached the facility she managed to kill Samuel, the head vampire, but he stabbed her in the chest. Will turned her to save her life."

"Wow." Andrew breathed lightly.

"They didn't tell you she was a Lycan before you came here?"

"No. I knew that they had three Lycans as instructors but I didn't know she was one."

"How did you find out?" Chen suddenly asked.

"Hannah was kind of freaking out after she killed the leeches. She thought you were dying and her eyes were glowing and I think she was about to shift. She doesn't seem to have much control over it." Andrew replied.

"She doesn't. Not yet, anyway. Will is teaching her how to control the shift." Chen cleared his throat. "Can I have some more water?"

Andrew held the straw to his mouth and Chen took a few sips before sighing softly. "How much has this set me back?"

"Not as much as you think. Your sutures were torn when the leech grabbed your arm but it shouldn't take long to start healing again."

"Right."

"It'll be okay, Chen. I promise." Andrew hesitated and then gently rubbed Chen's chest. "You should try and get some rest, alright?"

"Yeah." Chen closed his eyes. "Are you leaving now?" His cheeks reddened slightly.

"Only if you want me to."

"I don't."

"Then I'll stay." Andrew replied quickly. "Get some sleep, Chen. I'll be right here."

Chapter 13

"Reid, let me in." Selena knocked on his apartment door for a third time and waited patiently.

After a few minutes, the door opened a crack. "What, Selena?'

"Let me in."

"I'm tired and in pain. Can we talk later?"

"No." She shoved on the door and he sighed irritably and opened it. She blinked at him. He was shirtless and wearing just a pair of gym shorts. His usual clean-shaven face was covered in blond stubble and his short hair was sticking up everywhere.

"God, Reid."

"What?" He glared at her as she looked around the apartment.

"You haven't left your apartment in three days."

He shrugged, wincing a little, before cradling his arm against his chest.

"So."

"So, everyone wants to sign your cast."

He rolled his eyes and walked back toward the bed. "I'm going back to bed."

"No, you're not. You're going to shave, have a shower and go to the cafeteria with me to get something to eat." She said firmly.

"Like hell I am."

"Like hell you're not." She took his arm and dragged him toward the small bathroom. "Get in there, Reid."

"I'm right-handed, Selena. I'll cut my own throat if I try and shave with my left hand." He scowled.

"I'll help you." She put the lid of the toilet seat down and pushed him into a sitting position before filling the sink with hot water.

He realized he was too tired to argue plus his face really was itchy as hell. He scratched at it as she rummaged through the medicine cabinet for his razor and shaving cream. She put some shaving cream in her hand and tilted his head back with her other one before slathering the cream on his face and neck.

After rinsing her hands, she picked up the razor and grinned at him. "Ready?"

"Have you done this before?" He gave her a suspicious look.

"No, but how hard can it be?"

"Great." He grunted. "I'll be back in the infirmary having my face sewn back together."

"Oh please." She scoffed. "If I can shave my girlie bits without drawing blood, I can shave your face."

His eyes dropped to her crotch and she blushed a little before tugging lightly on his hair. "Lift your head and hold still."

He closed his eyes and breathed in her sweet scent as she carefully shaved his face. As she worked she hummed softly to herself, and he only winced a little when she placed the razor on his throat.

"Hold still." She reminded him firmly.

"Right."

She shaved his throat with careful concentration before shaving his upper lip and chin. When she was finished, she wiped his face with a warm, wet cloth and he couldn't stop his groan of appreciation.

She touched his smooth face with her soft fingers. "There, much better."

"Thanks."

"You're welcome. I'll be right back, don't move."

He waited patiently as she left the bathroom and eyed the black garbage bag and duct tape she returned with in surprise. "What's that for?"

"Have you never had a cast before, Reid?"

He shook his head and she laughed softly. "I would have thought you'd have broken all sorts of bones as a kid. You seem like the daredevil type to me."

"I was lucky, I guess."

"This is probably going to hurt a little." She warned as she tucked the garbage bag over his cast. Using the duct tape, she wrapped the bag around the top of his cast until it provided a water proof seal.

"There, now you can have a shower without getting your cast wet."

"Yeah, because it's so easy to shower with a garbage bag on your hand."

"Don't be such a big baby." She sighed.

He eyed her ass as she bent and turned the knobs to the shower. She adjusted the temperature until the water was hot and steam began to fill the small bathroom. "Okay, clothes off and in the shower."

"I can't, Selena." He protested. "I can barely get my own pants off. My left hand is fucking useless."

She sighed loudly. "Oh for the love of God. Stand up."

He stood up and grunted in surprise when she unceremoniously yanked his shorts to his ankles. He wasn't wearing underwear and he blushed when she eyed his cock.

"Do you always sexually harass men when they're hurt and helpless?" He asked.

She laughed. "Whatever. You've been asking me to ride your dick for weeks, but now suddenly you're going to play shy?"

"This is different." He muttered.

"No, it isn't. Now get in the shower. You smell, Reid."

He glared at her and she shrugged. "What? You do."

Grumbling under his breath he stood in the shower, carefully maneuvering his garbage bag covered-arm so that the water didn't directly hit it. He held his head under the hot spray and had to admit that it did feel good.

"Wash up." Selena called to him.

"Why are you still in the bathroom?" He didn't open his eyes.

"I'm waiting for you to actually use the soap."

"Water will have to do." He grunted.

He heard her sigh irritably and then blinked in surprise when, after a moment, the shower door opened and Selena squeezed in beside him. She was wearing just her sports bra and panties and he watched as she reached for the shampoo.

"Most people shower naked, Selena."

"Yes, well, you don't need to see me naked."

"You're seeing me naked." He pointed out.

"It's not a competition. Tilt your head back." She had poured shampoo into her hand and she stood behind him and began to wash his hair. He groaned as her strong hands kneaded his scalp and he closed his eyes in bliss.

She finished washing his hair too quickly and tapped him on the back. "Duck under the spray."

He ducked his head obediently and she rinsed his hair before reaching for the soap. Lathering it between her fingers she quickly washed his back, ass and legs before pressing closer to him and lathering her hands with more soap.

The feel of her warm, wet, skin made his dick spring to attention, despite the throbbing pain in his right arm, and he gritted his teeth as she cleaned his left arm. She reached around him carefully and washed his chest and abdomen with quick, efficient strokes. He made a harsh groan when, after a moment's hesitation, she moved her hands to his crotch.

"I'm sorry. Did I hurt your arm?" She whispered.

"No." He croaked out. "It's fine."

He stared at the shower wall as her soft, soapy hands cupped his balls. She cleaned them gently before moving her hands to his cock. He was rock-hard and he could feel her breath speeding up against his wet back as she stroked him slowly back and forth.

After nearly five minutes of torturous touching, he cleared his throat. "I'm starting to think you wanted me to shower just so you could molest me."

"I'm trying to be nice. This has nothing to do with wanting to touch your dick, Reid." She snorted.

"No? Because you've been *washing* my dick for five minutes now and I'm pretty sure it's as clean as it's going to get."

Her hand tightened around him and he nearly embarrassed himself by coming right there in the shower. She dropped her hand and he turned around quickly, ignoring the pain in his right arm. The water had soaked through her white panties and bra and he stared at the outline of her dark nipples against the fabric of her bra before his eyes dropped to her pussy.

She cleared her throat nervously. "Eyes up here, buddy."

He lifted his gaze to her face, grinning at the hot blush that covered it. "I didn't say you needed to stop."

"It's time to rinse." She said firmly.

"I'm going to need your help for that too." He replied innocently and she glared at him before pushing him back under the spray of water.

"Hold still."

"Whatever you want, sweetheart."

Selena rolled her eyes but secretly she was happy to see some of his old swagger coming back. When he had opened the apartment door, she had been a little scared by how pale and drawn he looked. If an accidental handjob was what it took to get the old Reid back, then so be it.

Accidental? Please, girl. You were enjoying it as much as he was. I bet he'd really perk up if you gave him a blowjob. Why don't you test that theory out?

Lust unfurled in her belly, hot and deliciously sweet, as the image of her on her knees in front of Reid, his large cock sliding in and out of her mouth, flooded through her.

She shoved the image out of her head and tamped the desire down to a more manageable level as she quickly rinsed the soap from Reid's body. She hesitated briefly and, sending a silent prayer for strength, began to rinse his hard cock.

He inhaled sharply and his hips jerked toward her. She bit her lip as her fingers wrapped around his cock like they had a mind of their own and rubbed him firmly.

"Fuck." He muttered. "I'm going to come all over you if you keep doing that, sweetheart."

"Sorry." She whispered. She reached around him, he groaned when his cock rubbed against her smooth stomach, and shut the water off before hurrying out of the shower. She tucked the towel around her body before using a second towel to dry Reid's back and chest. She wrapped the towel around his waist and carefully removed the garbage bag from his arm before urging him toward the door.

"Go sit on the couch, I'll be out in a minute."

He nodded and left the bathroom as she quickly stripped out of her wet panties and bra. There was a t-shirt hanging on the back of the bathroom door and after a brief look at her pants and shirt, she slipped into his t-shirt instead.

She was being silly but she wanted to wear his shirt, wanted to smell him on her skin after she left him, and she smoothed it down nervously before joining him in the living room. He was sitting on the couch with his eyes closed and she touched his shoulder gingerly.

"Reid?"

"Yeah?"

"Do you want to go to the cafeteria and get something to eat?"

"I really don't." He sighed. "I'm sorry, Selena, but I'd rather just stay here."

"That's fine. I'll make you something to eat."

"You don't have to do that." He protested.

"I don't mind." She squeezed his shoulder and headed into the kitchen.

* * *

"Are you feeling better?" Selena sat next to Reid on the couch. She had helped him into a pair of shorts and they had eaten a quick supper, she had been dismayed at how little he actually ate, before she had sent him back to the couch to relax as she cleaned up the dishes.

"Yeah. The Tylenol is helping a little." He replied. He was back to being pensive and withdrawn, and she rested her hand on his arm.

"Reid, if the pain is that bad you need to see Barb. It was a really bad break and you might need something a little stronger than Tylenol."

"It's fine." He said dismissively.

"No, it isn't." She argued. "You're not yourself and if it's because of the pain then you need to – "

"It's not the pain." He snapped at her.

"Then what's your problem?" She snapped back.

"I'm useless, okay? For the next six weeks I'm going to have to sit here in the damn facility while you and everyone else goes hunting. Do you know how ridiculous I feel? It's fucking killing me that you're going to be out hunting without me around to prot – "

He stopped and breathed harshly through his nose. "I can't even be an effective teacher right now because I can't shoot worth shit with my left hand. How am I supposed to teach them if I can't even – "

He stopped again and slammed his hand against the couch. "I'm a complete fucking waste of space and it's driving me crazy."

"You're not useless. There's plenty of stuff you can still do and besides, it's only for six weeks."

"It might as well be six years." He muttered.

She could barely keep the grin from her face at his brow drew down in a childish scowl.

"You're not useless." She repeated.

"I am." He snapped. "Listen, you should go. I'm tired and I – "

"Nope. I'm not leaving until I convince you that I'm right and you're wrong." Selena replied.

"I'm really not in the mood for games, sweetheart." He growled. "Please, just – "

He stopped as she jumped up from the couch. Despite what he had said, he really didn't want her to leave and he swallowed his disappointment as she disappeared into the bathroom.

She returned after only a moment, still dressed in his shirt, and he jerked in surprise when she straddled him.

"What are you doing?"

"Showing you you're not useless."

She had a condom in her hand and he gave her a confused look. "Selena, I'm not sure what – "

She reached between them and slid her hand into his shorts. She stroked his cock and his breath hissed out as he immediately hardened.

"Selena – "

"Be quiet, Reid. We're going to fuck, and you're going to make me come. Got it?"

"This isn't that romantic, sweetheart."

"Oh, I'm sorry." She said tartly as she placed the condom on the arm of the couch. "I didn't think you did romance. We're just two people having some adult fun together, right?"

"Right." He gritted out as her soft hand continued to stroke him.

"Good." She suddenly stripped off his shirt and he stared at her small breasts. Their nipples were already hard and swollen, and he licked his lips as she ran her fingers through his hair and tugged lightly.

"You just going to look at them or put your mouth to good use?"

Without replying, he leaned forward and took one nipple into his mouth. He traced it with his tongue before sucking hard and she moaned softly as her hand tightened in his hair. He cupped her other breast with his left hand, pinching and pulling lightly on her nipple as she arched her back and urged him to continue.

Her sweet pussy was practically screaming his name and he slid his left hand between her spread thighs and stroked the small, neat patch of dark hair at the top of it before sliding his fingers down. She moaned again, her legs squeezing his thighs, as he rubbed and stroked her clit until it swelled under his touch.

"I'm sorry." She suddenly muttered. "I can't wait."

"Fine with me, sweetheart." He rasped.

He raised his hips so she could ease his shorts down his legs and he kicked them off impatiently as she tore open the condom wrapper. She rolled it down over his cock and gave him a brief smile before lifting herself up and guiding his cock to her entrance. She slid the head of his cock into her warmth and they both moaned loudly. She pushed experimentally and then bit at her bottom lip as she hesitated.

"You're so thick." She moaned. "I'm not sure I can - "

She broke off as Reid reached between her legs and rubbed her clit again. He was rewarded with her loud cry of pleasure and a surge of wetness and he rubbed the moisture over his cock.

"Try again." He whispered.

She nodded and pushed downward. This time he slid smoothly into her warmth and he groaned. Her warmth and the way her pussy squeezed him so tightly was bringing him dangerously close to the edge.

She began to move and his hand squeezed her waist. "Wait, please."

She stopped immediately and gave him a worried look. "Is something wrong? Did I do something or – "

He shook his head. "No. You feel amazing. Too fucking amazing. I need a minute or I'm going to embarrass myself."

A small grin crossed her face and she stroked his face softly. "You're bigger than anyone I've been with."

"You're great for my ego." He groaned. Her pussy was making small fluttering movements around his cock and he gritted his teeth. "Please stop doing that, sweetheart."

"Stop doing what?" She was panting lightly, her eyes closed and her hands gripping his left arm as she stretched around him.

Her pussy fluttered again and he cursed under his breath. "That! Stop doing that!"

"I can't help it." She grinned at him.

"I don't believe you." He groaned again.

"Would I lie to you?" She bounced experimentally on his lap.

He gave her a pleading look. "Mercy, Selena. Please, for the love of God, just give me one more minute."

She shook her head. "Time's up, handsome."

Being careful not to touch his injured right arm, she braced her hands on his hard abdomen and thrust her small body up and down. He cried out, his left hand squeezing the couch cushion as Selena made a small gasping noise of pleasure before beginning to shake.

"I can't – I can't stop!" A low, breathy moan tore from her throat as she threw her head back and rode his cock with a wild, almost reckless, abandonment. After only a few minutes she was coming, her pussy tightening exquisitely around his throbbing cock, and he made a low, hoarse howl as his orgasm tore through him. Shaking wildly, he thrust his hips into her repeatedly until his arm screamed in protest, and he collapsed back against the couch with another hoarse groan.

Selena touched his face gingerly. "Reid? Are you okay?"

He nodded but didn't open his eyes as she stroked his left arm and his chest with her soft hands. "Are you sure? Is your arm really hurting now?"

There was more than a hint of worry in her voice and although his arm was throbbing like a son of a bitch, he shook his head. "No, it's fine."

"What's wrong?"

"Nothing."

"There's something wrong, tell me." She insisted. "Is it – was it something I did? I mean, I – "

His eyes shot open and he frowned at her. "Fuck, no. You were incredible."

She blushed prettily. "Then what's going on with you?"

He muttered another curse under his breath. "Let's just say I usually make a better – *longer* - first impression in the bedroom."

She smiled. "It was perfect, Reid."

He kissed her lightly on the mouth. "Will you stay with me tonight, Selena?"

"I will."

Chapter 14

"You're too heavy footed, Henry." Paul frowned as Henry, panting heavily, circled around a grinning Hannah.

"You want to stay on the balls of your feet." Paul continued. "Don't stomp around your opponent."

"Okay, right." Henry replied.

Hannah raised the wooden bokotu and gave him a short bow. "Try again, Henry."

He nodded determinedly and attacked her with gusto. She parried his strike and danced backwards as Paul studied the two of them closely.

The wooden blades made heavy thuds as they clashed and Henry lunged forward, groaning loudly when Hannah knocked the bokotu from his hand and kicked his legs out from under him. He collapsed on the mats, his face red, and Hannah held her hand out to him. She hauled him to his feet, clapping him on the arm as he gave her a nod of thanks.

"Good, much better." Paul said approvingly.

"Not really." Henry muttered.

"It's true." Hannah smiled at him. "You were much lighter on your feet that round. It takes time to – "

She paused as the door opened and Chen, followed by Andrew, entered the room.

"Hello, master." She bowed as Paul and Henry did the same.

"How are you feeling, master?" Paul asked as Andrew sat down on the long wooden bench against the wall.

"Fine, thank you, Paul." Chen said softly. He held his bandaged arm against his side and looked around the room as Hannah smiled at him.

"It's good to see you in here."

Chen nodded before studying her and Henry. "Show me your training."

"Yes, master."

Hannah bowed to him again and Henry, clearing his throat nervously, bowed as well before turning to Hannah.

"Are you ready?" She asked softly.

"Yes." Henry raised his bokotu and he and Hannah began to fight as Chen watched closely. After only a few moments, Chen frowned and raised his arm.

"Stop."

Hannah stopped immediately, backing away from Henry and lowering her bokotu, as Henry gave Chen an uncertain look.

"How many times has she knocked the bokotu from your hand?" Chen asked Henry.

"A lot." He admitted.

"Move your hand higher on the handle." Chen advised. "It will give you both a tighter grip and better control."

"Yes, sir." Henry replied politely. He repositioned his hand, giving Chen another nervous look and Chen nodded briefly.

"Better. Begin again."

He watched the two of them fight as the door to the training room opened and Natalie slipped into the room. She sat down next to Andrew and squeezed his arm affectionately.

"Hello, Andrew. How are you?"

"I'm good. How are you doing?"

"Oh, much better." Nat smiled at him.

"Have you gone back to the farmhouse?"

Natalie shook her head. "No, they told us it was too dangerous. We've actually been staying here in the facility."

"That's probably a wise idea."

"I guess." She sighed. "I didn't realize I had a touch of claustrophobia until we started living here. Jim said we should go to Heather's and stay with her, but the boys don't want to go and I feel like it's too far away from Hannah. I've been practicing deep breathing techniques and trying not to think about how deep we are under the ground."

She shuddered a bit before giving Hannah an affectionate look. Chen had stopped them again and Natalie smiled happily when he took the bokotu from Henry and began to swing it in a slow, deliberate arc.

"It's so good to see Chen in here. Did you have to force him into the room?" She asked.

"Surprisingly, no." Andrew replied. "It was his idea to come to the training room when we were going on our walk. I think he just wanted to see the room but I'm glad there's a training session going on. I think it's good for him."

"Oh, I think so too." Natalie agreed immediately. "Hannah's told us what a wonderful teacher he is and he really seems to have a love for it. You can see that easily."

"You're not kidding." Andrew smiled. Chen's face, usually so solemn, was flushed with excitement as he talked with Henry and swung the bokotu again. His eyes dropped to Chen's ass and he felt a sharp bite of lust in his stomach.

"Did you come here to watch Hannah train?" He forced himself to look away from Chen and blushed when he realized Natalie was grinning at him.

"No." She said cheerfully. "I was actually heading to the kitchen and took a wrong turn. I'm forever getting lost. I peeked into this room and saw Hannah, and figured I'd get her to lead me to the kitchen when she was done."

She laughed and crossed one leg over the other. "Jim and the twins were engaged in a rather spirited game of Scrabble when I left and I doubt they'll even notice I'm gone. Although," she paused and gave Andrew another grin, "why Jim even bothers playing Scrabble with them, I'll never know. He's not a dumb man, far from it in fact, but the boys are just brilliant. They're going to destroy him at it."

"I said no, Hannah." Chen's voice, raised in anger, washed over them.

Hannah raised her eyebrows at him. "It'll be easier and faster to show Henry the proper technique you're describing if you and I just fight."

"I am not fighting today." Chen said grimly.

"Why not?" Hannah persisted.

"You know why. Drop it, Hannah."

"You are more than capable of fighting with one hand, master."

"I said drop it." Chen said warningly.

"Are you afraid that I will beat you, master?" Hannah said tauntingly. "Afraid that your student is better than you?"

"Oh dear." Natalie whispered as Chen's face turned bright red. He turned toward Paul and Henry.

"Leave this room. Both of you."

"Yes, master." Paul bowed and hurried toward the door as Henry trailed after him.

The door shut and Andrew held his breath as Chen turned toward Hannah. He had never seen the Asian man so angry but Hannah simply gave him a cool look and held her bokotu loosely.

"You dare to speak so disrespectfully to me in front of my students? You may no longer be my student but I am still your master." Chen said in a low voice. His accent had thickened to the point where Andrew could barely understand him.

"I meant no disrespect, master." Hannah replied.

"Did you not?"

"No." She smiled impudently at Chen. "Speaking the truth is not being disrespectful."

Chen's face reddened further and Natalie reached out and gripped Andrew's hand tightly as Chen bowed his head and took a deep breath. His hand tightened on the bokotu and he raised it in front of him before staring disdainfully at Hannah.

"Begin."

A small grin crossed her face and Natalie gasped loudly when she attacked Chen fiercely. Chen, his face serene, battled back and Natalie and Andrew watched silently as the two of them moved quickly about the room, their bokotus clashing repeatedly.

"Goodness, it's like a dance, isn't it?" Natalie breathed.

Andrew nodded in stunned silence. He had assumed that Chen was good but he was unprepared for the fluid, silky movement of the man's body as he thrust and slashed the wooden sword at Hannah. Hannah showed him no mercy as she darted and lunged and swung repeatedly at him.

"I don't think this is a very good idea." Natalie suddenly whispered. "Chen's going to get hurt. Maybe we should stop them."

Andrew cringed when Hannah pushed past Chen's sword and knocked him to the floor. The Asian man winced as Hannah, panting lightly, backed away.

"Do you yield, master?" She asked insolently as Chen climbed to his feet.

He snorted angrily and raised his sword. "Again."

She made a harsh bark of laughter and rushed him again. Her eyes were glowing a bright green and she stepped back nimbly as Chen's sword swept past her throat.

"Not fast enough, master." She taunted.

Chen didn't reply and she winked at him as she attacked. Natalie squeezed Andrew's hand again and made a ducking motion as Chen and Hannah swept past them.

"Oh my goodness," she muttered, "I really think this is a very bad idea. I don't – "

She gasped again as Chen rushed Hannah. He blocked her bokotu with his own before mimicking her earlier move with Henry and kicking her legs out from under her. She landed on the floor with a heavy thud and made a loud growl of anger when Chen stepped on her wrist, pinning her bokotu to the ground, and held his own to her throat.

"Do you yield?" He said softly.

She reached for his leg with her free hand and made a hoarse howl of pain when Chen ground her wrist into the mat with his foot and jabbed the wooden bokotu into her throat.

"Do you yield?" He repeated.

"Yes!" She snapped at him.

He smiled with satisfaction and lifted his foot from her wrist before dropping his bokotu. Hannah sat up and rubbed at her wrist as Chen held his hand out to her. After a moment, she took it and he helped her to her feet.

She held his hand for a moment. "Welcome back, master."

He gave her a cool, assessing look. "Speak to me in that manner again, and I will not be so easy on you the next time. Do you understand?"

She flushed and bowed. "Yes, master. Forgive me."

He nodded and then gave a grunt of surprise when Hannah hugged him and kissed his smooth cheek. He pushed her away lightly and she grinned and took his bokotu from him, hanging them neatly on the wall before crossing the room and plopping down beside Natalie.

"Hi, mom."

"Hello, dear."

"What did you think of our fight?" She rested her head on Natalie's shoulder.

"I think you were amazing, dearest, but Chen still wiped the floor with you even with only one hand. He's really quite a remarkable fighter, isn't he?"

Andrew snorted laughter as Hannah raised her head and gave her a mock scowl. "You're supposed to be rooting for me to win, mom."

Natalie just shrugged as Chen joined them. He sat down on the bench next to Andrew and Natalie reached across and patted his leg. "Are you alright, Chen?"

Chen was sweating and his face had paled but he nodded and gave Natalie a faint smile. "I'm fine."

Hannah's face dropped and she stood and hurried over to Chen, crouching in front of him and studying him anxiously. "I'm sorry, master. Is your arm okay?"

"Now you're worried about me?" He raised one eyebrow at her and she gave him a small grin.

"I didn't think you wanted me to go easy on you."

"I didn't." He said gruffly.

Andrew touched his arm lightly. "Let's go back to your apartment, Chen. I want to massage your arm and check the sutures. I think you've had enough exercise for one day."

As the two of them left the room, Natalie smiled fondly at Hannah. "You look tired, honey."

"Will and I have been going out every night so I can practice shifting. I haven't been getting a lot of sleep."

"How much?" Natalie asked curiously.

"A couple hours every night."

"What?" Natalie frowned at her and Hannah shrugged.

"Lycans don't need much sleep."

"How is it going?" Natalie smoothed Hannah's hair back from her face.

"Not very well. If I'm not angry, I still can't shift without, - well - never mind," Hannah blushed and looked away, "and I don't feel like I have any control over it. Will's worried. He says he isn't and that I'm doing fine but I know that isn't true."

"You'll catch on to it, dearest."

"I hope so." Hannah said quietly.

"You will." Natalie said firmly.

"How are you doing?" Hannah asked suddenly. "Dad said you were feeling a little claustrophobic."

"I'm getting used to it." Natalie smiled at her and Hannah hugged her impulsively.

"I'm so sorry, mom. I wish I had never dragged you into this crazy life and I – "

"Nonsense!" Natalie interrupted. "This is the most excitement your father and I have had in years, and knowing that you're alive and safe is all that matters to us. Besides, if we hadn't been dragged into this new weird world of yours, we would never have met the twins or Will and Chen and the rest of your friends. We love you, Hannah, and you have nothing to apologize for."

"I love you too, mom." Hannah hugged her again and Natalie squeezed her tightly in return.

"Now, why don't you come back to the apartment with me for a bit? Your father is playing Scrabble with the boys and it'll be a hoot to watch him get his ass kicked."

Hannah laughed and nodded. "I'd like that."

* * *

"Chen? Are you alright?" Andrew paused, his hands gripping Chen's forearm just below his elbow.

Chen nodded without opening his eyes and Andrew rubbed his arm gently. "Are you sure?"

"Yes." Chen said irritably.

He was lying. His arm was aching, although not as bad as he feared, but worse than that – he could feel a small trickle of hope. He had resigned himself to never using the sword again and his victory over Hannah earlier had ignited a small flickering flame of possibility.

She let you win.

No, she hadn't. He knew Hannah had gone after him with everything she had. She hadn't held back, despite his mind trying to convince him otherwise, and he was grateful to her for her lack of mercy. For the first time since he'd woken in the infirmary, he felt like himself again and a small part of him hated her for it. He wanted to wallow in his self-pity for a while longer, wanted to –

"Chen?"

He opened his eyes. Andrew had leaned forward until his face was only inches away and Chen's gaze dropped automatically to his mouth. God, he had a nice mouth. He wondered briefly what it would be like to kiss that mouth, to slide his tongue between Andrew's lips and –

He made a muffled noise of surprise when Andrew pressed his mouth against his. They were warm and firm and, after a few seconds, he kissed him back. Andrew moaned, a low hoarse sound that sent a thrill through Chen's body and when he parted his lips, Chen slid his tongue into his mouth. He touched Andrew's tongue with his own before kissing him harder, urging Andrew to open his mouth wider. Andrew's hand tightened on his arm and he moaned again, sliding his tongue along Chen's before he pulled away abruptly.

Panting, he gave Chen an embarrassed look. "I'm sorry. I shouldn't have done that. It's just that watching you fight was, honestly, really hot."

Chen grinned and Andrew blushed before looking down at his hands. "But I shouldn't have done that."

"Why not?" Chen asked quietly.

"I don't usually throw myself at someone without knowing that they're, you know, interested in me."

"I'm interested." Chen replied immediately.

A small grin crossed Andrew's face. "It's all kinds of inappropriate. I'm your therapist and it's probably not a good idea for us to – "

Chen gripped the back of his neck and pulled him forward, kissing him hard on the mouth as Andrew slid his arms around his waist and held him tightly. The two men kissed deeply and Andrew gasped loudly when Chen nipped at his bottom lip.

"I like inappropriate." Chen muttered against his mouth before trailing a path of kisses down Andrew's neck.

"Me too." He gasped. "But your arm – you probably should get some rest after fighting Hannah and – "

"I'm not tired." Chen slid his hand under Andrew's t-shirt and stroked the hard contours of his chest.

Andrew shivered lightly before cupping Chen's face. "Chen, are you sure? I don't want to pressure you."

Chen grinned at him. "I've wanted you since the day I met you. Join me in my bed, Andrew."

He bent his head and licked and sucked at Andrew's neck, sliding his tongue along the rough stubble as Andrew inhaled sharply.

"Fuck," Andrew muttered, "you're making it very difficult to say no, Chen."

"Good." Chen stood and held out his hand.

Andrew grasped his hand and Chen, another small, pleased grin on his face, led him toward his bed.

Chapter 15

"I'm telling mom you're giving Reuben bacon." Hannah threatened.

Jim gave her a wounded look. "You'd rat me out like that? I thought we had an agreement."

"You know he's chunky enough." Hannah replied as Reuben danced excitedly around her dad's feet.

"How's Chen feeling?" Jim asked as her mother joined them from the bedroom.

"How's breakfast?"

"Delicious, Nat, thank you." Jim patted her gently on the butt as she walked by.

"The bacon is perfect." Hannah grinned at her dad as he gave her a pointed look.

"Yes, well, I'm sure Reuben is enjoying it too." Her mother responded dryly.

"So how is Chen doing?" Jim cleared his throat loudly.

"Really good." Hannah replied happily. "In the last week he's been to the training room every single day and he almost always takes over Henry's training halfway through. Plus, he's been practicing with Paul and Alex and I."

"That's wonderful!" Natalie sat down beside her before taking a drink of orange juice.

"Yes. He seems much happier."

"That might have something to do with dating Andrew." Natalie said delicately.

Hannah laughed. "How did you know they're dating, mom? I know about it, but the last time I checked you didn't have a Lycan's sense of smell."

Natalie shrugged. "It's obvious, dear."

Hannah glanced at her dad who shrugged. "I had no idea."

"Anyway, whatever the reason, he's doing much better and I'm very proud of him." Hannah replied.

She suddenly frowned. "Where are the twins? It's not like them to miss breakfast."

Natalie gave Hannah an odd look. "Didn't they tell you?"

"Tell me what?"

"They've been recruited."

"What?" Hannah stared at her mother in shock.

Natalie sighed and nodded. "Yes. A couple days after the incident at the farmhouse, Jordan stopped by the apartment and spoke to the boys about joining the recruit program. They were all for it and they're starting training this morning with the other new recruits."

"They're fifteen fucking years old!" Hannah suddenly shouted and Natalie winced as she slammed her fists into the top of the island. "They are way too fucking young to be in the recruit program! Why the fuck did you let them sign up?"

She glared at her father as her eyes began to glow.

"Calm down, Hannah!" Jim barked as Natalie reached out and took his hand. "They're not our kids so technically we couldn't stop them from joining. We tried to convince them not to but we couldn't outright forbid it. They would have just joined anyway."

He gave Natalie a bitter look. "Jordan is quite the salesman. He talked about how they have real talent for killing vampires, kissed their genius little asses, and told them they could go far in the program if they applied themselves."

"That fucking asshole!" Hannah stood up and her mother gasped loudly when she slammed her fists into the island again and a wide crack appeared in the granite.

"Hannah – "

"I'm going to kill him." She snapped as her teeth lengthened into fangs.

"Sit down, Hannah!" Jim snapped at her. "You need to calm down, right now."

Ignoring him, her entire body rippling and a low hoarse growl erupting from her throat, Hannah turned and ran from the apartment. The door slammed shut behind her and Natalie gave Jim a frightened look.

"Honey? What do we do?"

Jim stood and hurried to the door. "We find Will."

* * *

"Line up, babies!" Mannie shouted over the excited babble of the new recruits.

"Move! I haven't got all day!" He hollered irritably and the dozen recruits scrambled to form a line as Will and Constance entered the main training room.

"My name is Mannie and this is Constance and Will. From this moment forward, your asses belong to us. Do you get me?"

There were a few muttered replies and Mannie rolled his eyes and shouted, "DO YOU GET ME?"

"We get you, sir!" The recruits shouted back in unison.

"Good! First up – "

"Luther? Tyrone? What the hell are you doing in here?" Will interrupted. He stared in surprise at the twins as they gave him matching grins.

"We're recruits now, wolf boy." Luther replied before wiggling his eyebrows at Constance. "Hey, hottie. You been missin' Luther?"

"Watch your fucking mouth." Mannie growled at him.

"Who said you could be recruits?" Will couldn't hide his disbelief.

"That Jordan guy." Tyrone replied. "He asked us to join."

"Hell, he *begged* us to join." Luther snickered. He reached out and slapped Constance on the ass. "How about later, you and I – "

He shouted in surprise when Constance whipped around and knocked him off his feet. She glared down at him. "Fifty push-ups, now."

"C'mon now, don't be like that." Luther protested.

She booted him lightly in the ass. "Seventy-five. And if you slap my ass again, I'll break your arm. Clear?"

"Clear." Luther muttered as Tyrone laughed loudly.

"Keep laughing and you'll be joining him." Constance said softly. Tyrone shut his mouth with a snap.

"Will? Where are you going?" Mannie called as Will turned and stomped toward the door.

"To have a little conversation with that asshole Jordan." Will replied angrily.

* * *

Jordan stared at the computer screen in front of him before scrubbing his hand across his face. He picked up his cup of coffee, sipping delicately at the hot liquid, before reaching into his top drawer for a file. As he pulled the file free, the door to his office burst open and Hannah ran into the room.

She was snarling at him and a thin thread of fear went through him at the sight of the large, sharp fangs protruding from her mouth. He swallowed down his fear and smiled politely.

"Good morning, Hannah."

"The twins aren't joining the recruit program." She growled.

He raised his eyebrow at her. "Are you their legal guardian, Hannah?"

"You know I'm not." She snapped.

"Then I'm afraid you have no say over their decision to join the recruit program."

"They didn't decide to join." She spat. "You talked them into it."

"I merely suggested they consider joining. They're extremely talented young men and we could use them in the program."

"They're fifteen years old, you idiot!"

"Watch your mouth, Hannah!" Jordan said sharply. "I am well aware of their age just like you're well aware of their unique abilities when it comes to killing vampires. That, combined with their intelligence, will take them far in the program. Who knows what they'll accomplish. They could be the head of a facility by the time they're thirty or – "

"They could be dead in six months!" Hannah shouted. "They're too young to join the program and you know it! Are you that fucking desperate for recruits?"

"Frankly, this is none of your business." Jordan said firmly. "You're not their mother or their guardian and you'd be wise to watch your mouth. You and your boyfriend are on thin ice with the Board of Directors as it is and – "

"If you think that I'm going to let you bring the twins into this fucking miserable excuse for a life, you're in for a surprise." Hannah snarled at him.

"You can't stop me." Jordan said simply.

"Do you really believe that?" Hannah asked silkily as hair sprouted on her face and her nails began to lengthen into claws.

"Control yourself, Hannah." Jordan replied. He tried to sound firm but even he could hear the fear in his voice and he took a shaky step back when Hannah grinned fiercely.

"Take the twins out of the program or you'll regret it." She warned.

"Are you threatening me?" Jordan asked. "I'll kick both you and Will out of the facility if you are. Do you hear me? I won't put up with your bullshit."

"Take the twins out of the program." She said softly.

"No." Jordan said quietly.

With a howl of rage, Hannah shifted fully, her clothes tearing apart to land in a heap at her feet. Snarling and baring her fangs, she crouched down as Jordan backed away.

"Don't do this, Hannah."

She howled again, the sound deafening in the small office, and Jordan reached into the top drawer of his desk and pulled out a gun. He pointed it at Hannah as the door to his office was thrown open. Will, his face grim, barreled into the room and threw himself at Hannah just as she leapt for Jordan. Will's large body hit her like a freight train and she made a high yelp of pain and surprise as she was driven into the wall. The plaster cracked and Jordan winced as Hannah's head bounced off the wall before she slid to the ground in a heap. Whining softly, she stared dazedly at Will as her paws scrabbled uselessly against the floor.

Will stroked the thick fur on her side soothingly as he crouched over her. "I'm so sorry, honey. Take deep breaths."

She whined again before shaking her head and Will winced when blood flew from her mouth. She shifted with a soft pop and he yanked his shirt off and wrapped it around her naked body before lifting her into her arms.

"She tried to attack me, Will." Jordan said quietly. "She's a liability and she can't stay."

Will glanced over his shoulder. His eyes were glowing with anger and he bared his teeth at the older man as

Jordan's hand tightened on the gun. Before he could say anything else, Will strode jerkily from the room.

* * *

"How is she?" Douglas peered around Will into the dim apartment.

"Fine." Will grunted. "I had Bev look at her. I broke a couple of her ribs but she's healing and sleeping."

"Good. Can I come in?"

Will hesitated before stepping back. "Keep your voice down. She needs more rest."

Douglas nodded and sat down at the island. Hanna was lying motionless on the bed and Douglas sighed softly before turning to Will.

"Jordan's called a meeting in half an hour for the instructors."

"Has he? I didn't get the invitation." Will replied irritably.

"I believe he's going to tell us that he's kicking Hannah out of the program."

Will snarled under his breath. "There's no fucking way I'm letting him kick her out."

"You'll be fired as well, Will. You know that."

"I don't care." Will snapped. "That asshole has fifteen year old boys joining the program. Since when did we start letting children into the program, Douglas?"

Douglas shrugged. "The rumour I've heard is that Jordan was told by the Board of Directors to approach the twins. You have to admit that for their age they are rather remarkable at killing vampires."

"It doesn't mean they should be in the program." Will raked his hand through his hair before standing and pacing back and forth in the small kitchen. "Honestly, I'm not sure I even want to stay if we're going to be allowing children to fight our fucking battles."

"The twins are not your average teenagers." Douglas pointed out gently. "Besides, you and Hannah aren't their guardians and you have no say over what they do or don't do. It would be better for you to train them and keep an eye on them, don't you think?"

Will shrugged before rubbing wearily at his forehead. "Fuck, Douglas, I don't know what to do."

Douglas glanced at Hannah before lowering his voice. "Did she really try and attack Jordan?"

Will nodded. "Yes. If I hadn't shown up when I did she would have torn his throat out. If Jordan hadn't shot her first."

Douglas sighed as Will dropped on to the stool across from him. "What do I do, Douglas? She," he hesitated, "she's not learning to control it as well as I had hoped. I haven't said anything to her, just told her that she needs more time, but she still can't shift without being angry nor can she control the urge to shift when she's upset. Have you seen others struggle like this?"

Douglas gave him a careful look. "Truthfully, I have not met that many humans who were turned. The few that I knew did well in learning to control it."

Will sighed loudly and Douglas patted his hand before standing and placing the kettle on the stove. "I'll make us some tea."

Will smiled faintly. "Tea doesn't solve everything, Douglas."

"No, I suppose not, but it does help clear the head." Douglas replied.

Will watched silently as Douglas made the tea and nodded his thanks when the old Lycan placed a mug in front of him. He stared at the dark liquid as Douglas sat down and sipped some tea.

"You know," he said thoughtfully, "perhaps the problem is that there is too much going on for Hannah to fully concentrate on learning to control the shift. She's worried about Chen, about her parents, and now about the twins. Perhaps what she needs is to be taken away from it for a little while."

"She'll never agree to it, Douglas." Will replied.

"Then you must convince her." Douglas said firmly. "Remind her that her parents and Chen are perfectly safe in the facility. The twins won't be going out hunting anytime soon so they're in no danger either. Hell, this facility is the safest place for them at the moment."

"I can try." Will said moodily.

Douglas frowned at him. "You must do more than try, Will. Jordan may be willing to hold off on kicking Hannah out of the program if you take her away for a month or two and teach her to control it. At the meeting tonight, I'll speak to Jordan and convince him to wait until you and Hannah come back. You can take Hannah deep into the woods and spend the next few weeks teaching her how to manage her Lycan side. She's a bright girl – this will work."

"And if it doesn't?" Will suddenly asked hoarsely. "If she becomes one of the half-breed Lycans that can never be trusted, then what? She won't be welcome in the human world or the Lycan one."

"That's not going to happen." Douglas said firmly. He reached out and squeezed Will's hand. "This will work. I know it will."

* * *

Jordan stared at the instructors gathered in his office. "No doubt, you've all heard that Hannah attacked me earlier today."

When there was no reply, he cleared his throat and continued. "I've made the decision to remove Hannah from the program. Once our meeting is finished, I'll be speaking with the Board of Directors about my decision."

Mannie swore under his breath before glaring at Jordan. "What about Will?"

"What about him?" Jordan raised his eyebrows. "He's still employed."

Mannie snorted. "If you kick Hannah from the program, he'll leave."

"Well, that's obviously his own personal choice. I'll do my best to convince him to stay but he's free to go if that's what he wants."

Douglas leaned forward. "Jordan, I've spoken with Will and suggested that he take Hannah away from the facility for a month or two. It's impossible for Hannah to learn to control the shift with so much happening around her. Give her a second chance and I guarantee you that when she returns, she'll be in full control of her Lycan side."

Jordan hesitated before shaking his head. "I can't do that, Douglas. I appreciate how skilled Hannah is and I know she's one of our best in the program but the situation has changed. If she lost her temper and attacked and killed one of the recruits or, hell, one of you, it's my ass on the line. I can't take the chance, I'm sorry."

"Give her a chance." Douglas implored. "You can understand why she was so upset about the twins. Hell, we all are."

Mannie grunted. "Three quarters of the new recruits are barely out of their teens. That's too young, Jordan."

Jordan sighed harshly. "What do you want me to say? The Board chose the recruits, not me. And I'm sorry but I can't allow Hannah to stay in the program. End of discussion."

Chen, his face pale but composed, stood and walked toward the door.

Jordan frowned at him. "Chen, where are you going?"

"I quit, Jordan. I'll pack my things and leave the facility by tomorrow morning."

Jordan's mouth dropped open. "You what? Chen, you can't quit."

Chen smiled at him. "I can and I am. If you're kicking Hannah out of the program, I'm quitting."

Jordan gave him a grim look. "You're making a mistake, Chen."

"You're the one making a mistake." Chen replied softly.

Mannie stood up. "I quit too."

Jordan stared in disbelief as Reid, his right arm still enclosed in a thick cast, stood as well. "Fuck it. I quit, Jordan."

"Don't be ridiculous!" Jordan snapped as a small smile crossed Douglas' face. "The three of you cannot quit just because – "

"Four." Constance rose to her feet and gave Jordan a sweet smile. "I quit, Jordan."

Douglas stood with an easy grace. "Consider this my resignation, Jordan."

"For fuck's sake!" Jordan shouted. "Have you all lost your damn minds?"

Douglas shrugged. "Give Hannah a second chance and we'll stay. All of us."

"This is blackmail!" Jordan shouted again.

"It's not blackmail." Mannie said cheerily. "We've all just had the sudden urge to pursue other career options. I'm sure the Board of Directors will understand."

Jordan glared at the group of instructors. His face was bright red and he was gripping the armrests on his chair hard enough to turn his knuckles white.

"Fine!" He suddenly snapped. "I'll give Hannah one more chance. But if this doesn't work - if she attacks and kills someone at this facility - I swear to God, I'll take all of you down with me. Do you hear me?"

Douglas nodded. "I'll speak to Will and let him know you've had a change of heart."

"Get out!" Jordan roared. "All of you out of my fucking office, right now!"

* * *

"Promise me you'll be careful." Natalie said softly.

"I will, mom." Hannah smiled wanly at her as she hugged Jim.

"Is this really necessary?" Natalie gave Will a plaintive look and the Lycan nodded.

"It is. I'm sorry, Natalie."

The twins, their faces uncharacteristically somber, leaned against a tree and stared into the woods as Hannah approached them.

She hugged Luther tightly and kissed his cheek. "Be good, Luther, I love you."

"Yeah." He sighed.

She hugged him again before turning to Tyrone. "You too, Tyrone. Stay out of trouble."

Tyrone nodded, his throat working compulsively, and Hannah pulled him into her embrace. "I love you, honey. I'll be back soon."

"I'm sorry, Hannah. This is our fault." He whispered into her ear.

"It isn't, honey. Just promise me that you'll work hard and listen to Mannie and Constance, okay?"

"Okay."

"Good." She kissed his cheek and turned to embrace Selena.

Selena hugged her tightly. "I'll see you soon, Hannah."

"You bet. I love you."

"I love you too." Selena replied before stepping back.

Chen was standing behind her and Hannah smiled faintly at him. "Hello, master."

"Hello, Hannah."

She hesitated and then hugged him firmly. He returned her hug and she placed her mouth to his ear.

"I'm afraid, master." She breathed lightly.

His arm tightened around her and he stared solemnly at her. "You have nothing to fear. This is no different than learning the sword."

"It's completely different." She protested.

"It is not." He replied calmly. "You will master this just as you mastered the sword. Do you understand?"

"Yes, master." She smiled briefly and hugged him again before taking Will's hand.

He adjusted the large pack strapped to his back and gave her a confident smile. With one last look at the others gathered at the edge of the forest, the two of them disappeared into the trees.

Chapter 16

"We're lost, Gary."

"We are not lost, Jill."

"Yes, we are." The petite blonde woman glared at the driver.

Gary sighed as Jill crossed her arms and stared woodenly out the windshield. "It's not my fault. These small towns all look the same. Besides, you're the one who forgot the GPS."

"Oh, so now this is my fault? I wasn't the one who had the brilliant idea to take a shortcut." She said frostily.

"Oh for God's sake, Jill, we - "

"There's a gas station. Stop there and we'll ask for directions." She interrupted as she pointed to the dimly-glowing gas sign about twenty feet ahead of them.

"Let's just go a little further. I'm pretty sure that - "

"Stop the car, Gary!"

"Fine!" He grunted irritably and pulled into the gas station. He parked in front of the small building and stared at its grungy windows and flickering 'open' sign. "Is the damn place even open?"

"Of course it's open." Jill snapped.

She exited the car, slamming the door so hard the car rocked. Gary sighed again and stepped out of the car. He stretched tiredly before scanning the area curiously. There were two ancient gas pumps in front of the store and a smaller building - a faded restroom sign tacked to the front - to the left of it. He squinted in the growing dark at the building that loomed behind the station. It was a house, the paint faded and peeling and the front porch sagging dangerously, and a shiver of apprehension slid down his spine. About twenty feet behind the house was an old barn. Like the house, it was old and tired-looking and surrounded by overgrown bushes. Vines covered nearly half of the building, creeping and crawling up the sides of the rotting wood, and he cleared his throat nervously.

"Jill, wait!" He called softly.

"What?" She gave him an impatient look as she reached for the door of the gas station.

"I think we should keep moving."

"Don't be ridiculous, Gary. We have no idea where we are, I'm thirsty and I have to pee. Let's just get the damn directions, okay?"

Without waiting for his answer, she pulled open the door and disappeared into the building. He took another look around - his skin was crawling with goose bumps and he had a sinking feeling in the pit of his stomach - before following her.

"Evening."

The man sitting behind the corner was the perfect stereotype of a small town gas attendant. From the trucker's cap perched on his head to the large beer belly pushing out the dirty and stained white t-shirt he was wearing, Gary could almost hear banjo music playing.

He forced himself to smile at the man. "Hello."

He hurried down the aisle toward Jill as the man stood up from his stool and peered out the grimy window at their car. "That your car out there?"

Considering they were the only two people in the place, Gary thought it to be an extraordinarily stupid question but he bit back his smartass reply and nodded briefly. "It is."

"Pretty fancy." The man scratched at the stubble on his cheek. "You folks from the city?"

"We are." Gary took Jill's arm in a tight grip and squeezed warningly.

She looked up from the cooler in front of her and frowned. "What?"

"We should get going. We have a long drive."

"Yes, I know. But maybe you could swallow your pride first and find out how the hell to get back to the main highway? What do you think, Gary?"

Anger flared inside of him and he tamped it down grimly. Now was not the time to get into a screaming match with his wife. It had been a mistake to take this road trip, a mistake to think that some time alone would glue the fractured pieces of their marriage back together. Although in all fairness, up until tonight it had been working – sort of. They had been on the road for nearly four days and everything was going smoothly. Hell, they'd even had sex last night for the first time in eight months – laughing and giggling when the cheap motel bed had groaned and squealed in protest. Jill was putting effort into repairing the damage she had done, and he could almost forget the affairs she had first vehemently denied and then begged forgiveness for. Almost.

Now, he gave her a grim smile and tugged on her arm again. "Time to go, honey."

He prayed she would take the hint, that she would see past his polite exterior and pick up on his odd sense of unease that was growing by the minute. Eight years ago she would have known immediately but they had drifted apart over the years. He supposed it was more his fault than hers. His need to prove to his father that he wasn't a failure had driven him into a career that demanded every ounce of his attention, and a part of him understood why Jill had found comfort in other men's arms.

"Go where?" She rubbed the tips of her fingers over her eyebrows, a gesture he used to found endearing but now irritated the shit out of him, and gave him a brittle smile. "Going to try taking yet another shortcut, *honey*?"

The bell tinkled over the door and a man walked into the store. He was wearing a plaid jacket and a cowboy hat, and Gary's apprehension grew when he strolled to the counter and leaned against it. Ignoring Gary completely, he scanned Jill up and down, a small grin crossing his face.

"You get the pump fixed, Judd?" The man behind the counter asked.

Judd shook his head and scratched at his chest. "Nah. The damn thing is fucked. We're gonna have to buy a new one."

He continued to stare at Jill, the grin on his face growing, and Gary took her arm in a firm grip and pulled her toward the door.

"Gary? That hurts!" She squealed at him.

"Let's go, Jill!" He muttered under his breath. The fear was flowing through him now, hot and unpleasant and utterly ridiculous, and he could no longer Ignore Its relentless call.

As he nearly dragged his wife toward the door, he uttered a harsh curse when she ripped free of his grip and, rubbing her arm and giving him a petulant look, hurried to the counter.

"Excuse me? We're wondering if you could tell us how to get back to the main highway?" She smiled at the two men standing at the counter as Gary moved to her side.

"You lost?"

"We are. Obviously." There was a note of impatience in Jill's voice and another pulse of fear flooded through Gary's chest when the man named Judd frowned at her.

"We're fine, actually." Gary said hurriedly. He wedged his body between Jill and Judd and nodded to the men. "Thanks anyway."

"We're not fine!" Jill protested angrily. "We have no idea where we are."

She peered around Gary's body. "Could you help us?"

Judd gave her another slow perusal and Gary watched as Jill's look of anger faded and she gave him her own look of apprehension. She had finally picked up on the weird vibe that was emitting from the two men and she reached for Gary's hand.

He held it tightly before smiling at the two men. "Thanks but I think we're good."

"Now hold on," the man behind the counter said lazily, "you ain't never gonna find your way back to the highway without directions."

"We've got it handled, thanks." Gary started toward the door and swallowed down his fear when Judd's large hand clamped down on his arm.

"You think we ain't smart enough to help?" He asked quietly.

"No, no. Of course not." Gary said hurriedly.

"You know what the problem is with the city folk, Billy?" Without releasing Gary's arm, Judd turned to the man behind the counter. "They think we're stupid. They think we ain't nothing but a couple of lazy, uneducated hicks."

"That's not true." Gary replied. "We're just in a bit of a hurry so – "

"They think they're better than us." Judd continued softly. "And it pisses me off."

Billy snorted laughter. "Everything pisses you off, Judd."

"Let go of my arm." Gary said suddenly. "Let go of my arm right now or I'll –"

"You'll what?" Judd raised his eyebrows. "You think because you go to the gym every day and lift some weights that you're tough?"

Gary took a quick look a Jill. Her eyes were huge and the colour had faded from her skin leaving her pale and washed out.

"I'm going to ask you once more to let go of my arm, you ignorant redneck." He said quietly. "I'm not –"

Jill yelped in surprise when Judd hissed loudly and, with a smooth, hard gesture, tore Gary's arm from his body. Blood splattered across the counter and Billy yodeled loud laughter as Jill stared blankly at the bright red liquid splashing on to the grimy floor.

Judd bent his head and opened his mouth, lapping at the spray of blood from the gushing stump as Gary turned his head slowly toward her.

"Gary?" She whispered as his hand tightened around hers.

"Jill?" His face was white and his eyes round with shock as he stared at her. "Jill – run."

She whimpered his name again as Billy hopped over the counter with surprising ease for a man his size. He grinned at her, his fangs glistening in the fluorescent lights and a soft, moaning gasp escaped her lips.

"Run." Gary whispered weakly before releasing her hand. With the last of his strength he gave her a hard shove and Jill stumbled backward, her hands clutching at the hem of her t-shirt as she backed up against the door.

Gary turned back to Judd. The man's face was covered in his blood and he grinned at him as Gary sank to his knees. His vision was darkening and he blinked in confusion at the vampire standing above him.

Judd licked his lips before sucking at the blood on his fingers. "City folks taste awful." He told Billy conversationally. "I think it's all that damn tofu they eat."

Billy snorted as he moved slowly toward Jill. "Just because they're from the city, don't mean they eat tofu. Christ, Judd, you *are* an ignorant redneck."

"Fuck you." Judd said without malice before grabbing Gary's hair and yanking his head back. "You still with me, Gary?"

The dying man stared blankly at him and Judd reached out and sliced his throat open with one dirty fingernail. Blood trickled out of his throat and Judd frowned.

"Well, shit. There ain't nothin' left."

"Of course there ain't! You let most of it drip on to the floor, you jackass!" Billy smiled at Jill as she reached behind her for the door handle.

Judd eyed her thirstily. "We can share her."

"No fucking way. She ain't very big and it's not my fault you lost your temper and wasted half your meal." Billy snapped.

He grinned in delight when Jill clawed open the door and, with a loud shriek, tumbled out into the darkness.

"I love it when they run, Judd." He sauntered slowly out of the store.

* * *

Jill, her heart thudding painfully in her chest, yanked viciously on the door handle to the car. It was locked and she screamed shrilly. Gary had the keys in his pocket and she pulled uselessly again as the door to the store opened and Billy peeked his head out.

"Hey there, princess. Having trouble getting into your car?" He grinned.

She screamed again and fled across the parking lot, darting around the store and running toward the house and barn. Panic clawing at her insides, her breath tearing in and out of her chest, she fled past the house and bolted for the dilapidated barn. She stumbled in the dark, falling to her knees and tearing her jeans. Blood was dripping down her leg and she whimpered in pain before climbing to her feet and staggering forward. She could hear nothing but the sound of her own ragged breathing and her heartbeat thundering in her ears, and she eased open the door of the barn and slipped inside.

Gasping and sobbing, she ran forward and barked harshly in pain when she ran into something smooth and metal. It was a car and she stared blankly at it for a moment before trying the driver door. It was locked and she bit back her sob of fear as she glanced behind her at the barn door. It stayed closed and she took a few deep breaths before staring around her. Her breath caught in her throat in a ragged moan and she clamped her hand over her mouth. The barn was filled with cars and she realized with sudden, horrifying clarity what it meant.

Billy was going to hunt her down. He was going to hunt her and hurt her and when she was dead like Gary, he would simply drive their car into the barn and park it with the others. There were at least a dozen cars in the barn and as she hurried deeper into the barn, she glanced into the window of a mini-van. A child's stuffed animal was lying on the back seat and she moaned loudly as the door to the barn opened.

"Come out, come out wherever you are, princess." Billy's voice, mocking and full of black humour, drifted to her and she dropped to her knees behind the van. Arms shaking madly, her hair hanging in her face, she crawled silently across the dirt floor. Her bloody knee left small prints in the dirt and she wondered briefly how long it would take for the vampire to smell her.

She crawled faster as Billy, whistling cheerfully, shut the barn door with a loud bang. She leaned against a car, trying to slow her breathing and the pounding of her heart as she listened to Billy's footsteps grow closer.

Her mind jabbering useless half-formed thoughts, she flattened her body to the ground and slid on her belly under the car. Tears streaming down her cheeks, she held her breath and listened carefully. There was no sound at all and the sudden silence frightened her more badly than the vampire's whistling.

She screamed hoarsely when an ice cold hand wrapped around her ankle and she clawed frantically at the dirt. She screamed again when one perfectly manicured fingernail peeled back sending a throbbing bolt of pain through her hand, as Billy dragged her easily out from under the car. He lifted her to her feet and chuckled when she kicked at his shins.

"You're a feisty one, aren't you?" He crooned before wrapping his hand in her hair and whipping her head back.

"Please don't! Please, please, please - "

"Shh, now. I don't want to listen to you no more." He grinned at her. "Keep that pretty mouth of yours shut or I'll —"

She screamed again when he was pulled away from her, his hand taking a fistful of her hair with it. She fell to the ground and stared dazedly at the large dark-haired man standing above her. He was holding Billy by the throat, and the vampire hissed and snarled at him as a look of distaste crossed the man's face.

"You're pathetic." He said softly.

Jill watched wide-eyed as the man's nails lengthened and he sliced across the throat of the struggling, writhing vampire in his grip. Billy's eyes widened in surprise and he clutched at his neck as he made a harsh, gargling noise of protest.

The man sneered at him before wrapping his hand around Billy's hair and ripping his head from his body. As the vampire's body burst into ash, the dark-haired man dusted his hands off before crouching and holding out his hand. "Stand up, lovely one."

She scooted backwards on her butt and a brief look of irritation crossed the man's face before he snagged her by the wrist and lifted her easily to her feet. He stroked her cheek soothingly and smiled down at her.

"There, there. It's alright now." His voice was deep and thick with a German accent.

There were another dozen men behind him, each of them just as powerful and large as the one standing before her, and she gave them a dazed look of incomprehension. They were wearing dark suits and red ties, and she moaned in terror when the one holding her wrist smiled again and his fangs flashed in the dim light.

"Please don't hurt me." She whimpered.

"Shh. What's your name, lovely?" The man asked.

"J-Jill." She stammered. "My – my husband, Gary, they – they killed him back in the store."

"That's unfortunate." He glanced at the pile of ash at his feet before staring at the cars. He kept a firm grip on Jill's wrist as he turned and spoke to the men behind him in German.

They nodded and he spoke again before returning his dark gaze to Jill. "Don't be frightened."

"You – you're a vampire too." She whispered.

"I am." He confirmed.

"Vampires aren't real." She moaned.

"Oh I can assure you that they are." The man replied. "I am standing before you, am I not?"

"Why are you helping me? Why did you kill Billy?"

"Billy? Was that his name? Ridiculous." The man snorted loudly. "I helped you because I hate to see a beautiful woman such as yourself being treated so poorly by an absolute pig of a vampire."

"You're a good vampire?" She whispered as she stared up at him. His eyes were a striking shade of blue and she stared at them in fascination as he drew her up against his body. He brushed her hair back from her neck and licked his lips as he stared at the vein pulsing just below the skin.

"That's right, my lovely." He murmured. "I'm a very good vampire. Close your eyes. I know you're tired."

"I am." She sighed. "I'm so very tired."

"But of course you are." He stroked her hair lightly as he bent his head to her neck. "Everything will be just fine."

"Do you promise?" She whispered.

"I promise." His mouth latched on to her soft skin and she made a low moan that was a combination of pain and desire. As his fangs broke through her skin and he suckled eagerly, she clutched helplessly at his back, her nails digging into his suit jacket.

The other vampires watched silently as their leader drank the woman dry. When he was finished he dropped her body to the ground and pulled a handkerchief from his pocket. He wiped the blood from his lips before placing it back in his pocket.

"Brothers, I know it's been a long journey and you are thirsty and tired. We will stake our claim to this place and begin our new lives."

One of the vampires stepped forward and bowed briefly. "Forgive me, Olof, but are you sure this is where you want to begin again? It is a small town and it will be more difficult to blend in."

Olof shook his head. "You are wrong, Lars. It is the perfect place for us. Besides, I have no desire to "blend in" with the humans. We will take what is rightfully ours and when we have bled this town dry, we'll move on to the next."

The door to the barn swung open and Judd ran into the barn. He skittered to a stop and stared suspiciously at the men in dark suits.

"Who the fuck are you? Where's Billy?"

"I'm sorry to say your oafish friend Billy got exactly what he deserved." Olof pointed to the pile of ash at his feet before glancing at the others. "Bring him to me alive."

Judd, his eyes widening in fear, turned and shot toward the door. The vampire was quick but not quick enough and the other vampires easily surrounded him, grinning and hissing as they closed in on him. As Judd screamed hoarsely, Olof smiled to himself.

"Yes, this place will do rather nicely."

Chapter 17

Two months later

The Lycan picked his way carefully through the trees. His fur rippled in the wind and he lifted his snout to the sky and inhaled deeply before continuing forward. There was a low growl that turned into a whine of happiness and the wolf grinned at the gray Lycan that emerged from the trees to his left. The gray wolf brushed up against him, nudging his shoulder in a friendly way before turning and loping away. The second wolf followed and it was only a few minutes before they had reached a clearing in the trees. A large camouflage-coloured tent was erected at the edge of it, and two camping chairs and a crackling fire contained by a ring of large stones were in the middle of the clearing. The Lycan watched as the gray wolf shifted to his human form.

"Hello, Douglas." Will ducked naked into the tent and Douglas waited patiently until he returned. He had pulled on a pair of pants and he dropped a second pair in front of the wolf. With a soft pop, Douglas shifted and nodded his thanks before pulling the pants on. They were too big and he held them up with one hand as the two men embraced.

"It's good to see you, Will."

"You too." Will grinned at him before crouching next to the fire. "Can I make you some tea?"

Douglas laughed. "I'd like that."

He sat down in one of the chairs as Will set a large metal rack over the fire before pouring water from a jug into a pot. He set the pot on the rack to boil as he rummaged through a bag and produced a mug and a plastic baggie of tea bags. He dropped a tea bag into the mug before sitting down next to Douglas.

"You look good, old man."

"Thanks. So do you." Douglas glanced curiously around the campsite. "Where is Hannah?"

"She's out hunting."

"How is it going?" Douglas asked.

"Good. Really good, actually." Will gave him a pleased look. "She has much better control over the shift now and her emotions don't affect her Lycan side like they were before."

"That's great news." Douglas shifted in his chair. "Will you be coming home soon?"

Will hesitated. "I've been talking to Hannah about it but she – "

There was a soft bark and the dark brown wolf loped into the campsite. She rubbed her head affectionately against Douglas' knee and he stroked the fur on her back lightly.

"Hello, Hannah."

She barked again and sat down, her large tail sweeping back and forth, as she stared brightly at the old Lycan.

Douglas waited patiently and when she didn't shift, glanced at Will. Will cleared his throat.

"Hannah, you should shift so we can talk with Douglas."

She made a chuffing sound of displeasure and Will frowned at her. "You're being rude, honey."

She chuffed again before standing and disappearing into the tent. After a few moments, she emerged from the tent in her human form and wearing one of Will's shirts. Douglas stood and hugged her firmly and she patted his back before kissing his weathered cheek.

"Hi, Douglas. What are you doing here?"

The old Lycan shrugged. "Just thought I'd come by and see how it was going."

"Really good." Hannah sat on Will's lap. "Isn't it, Will?"

"It is. I was just telling Douglas how well you're doing at controlling the shift."

She smiled happily. "You were right, Douglas. I just needed to get away from all the shit that was going on."

She jumped up and poured the boiling water from the pot into the mug before handing it to Douglas. He gave her a nod of thanks as she returned to Will's lap. She kissed his temple affectionately and wrapped her arm around his shoulders.

Douglas waited a few moments and when Hannah didn't say anything, he cleared his throat. "Your mom and dad said to say hi and they miss you."

Hannah smiled. "Tell them I said hello and that I love them."

"Selena and the twins were asking about you as well."

"Were they? That's nice." Hannah said absently as she raised her head and inhaled deeply.

"They're wondering when you're coming home."

Hannah didn't reply, she was staring over Will's shoulder into the trees, and she cocked her head as a faint smile crossed her face. "Do you want rabbit for dinner tonight, my love?"

"Douglas asked you a question, honey." He said gently.

She forced her gaze back to the old Lycan. "I'm sorry. What did you say, Douglas?"

"People are wondering when you're coming back home."

She laughed bitterly. "Home? The facility is hardly a home."

"You know what I mean, Hannah." He replied quietly.

She sighed and looked into the forest again. "I don't know. When I'm confident I have full control over it, I guess."

"You seem to have control over it now." He pointed out.

She shrugged and stroked Will's thick hair. "I can use some more practice. Tell him, Will."

"Douglas is right, Hannah. You've done very well, and I'm confident that you'll be fine at the facility."

She sighed loudly. "Well, I'm glad you're confident in my abilities."

"Hannah – "

She stood up abruptly and gave them a strained smile. "I'm going to go for a run. Douglas, it was good to see you."

She ran to the edge of the clearing and they watched as she turned her back to them and pulled Will's shirt over her head. She shifted with a soft pop and, without looking at them, disappeared into the trees.

"How much time does she spend in her Lycan form, Will?"

"Nearly all of it." Will admitted. "We sleep and we mate in our human forms and that's about it."

"That's dangerous for her."

"You think I don't know that?" Will stood and paced back and forth. "What would you have me do? Over the last month or so she has grown increasingly fond of staying in her Lycan form."

"She's losing her human side, Will. She didn't even ask about her parents nor did she show interest in her friends."

"I know!" Will nearly shouted. "I've tried to talk to her about it but for the first time since I met her, she's happy,

Douglas. Truly happy. I find it difficult to take that away from her."

"I know it's hard." Douglas replied. "But you must remind her that she is not only Lycan. She is still human, and she has responsibilities and people who love and miss her."

Will sighed and dropped into the chair as Douglas gave him a sympathetic look. "I understand wanting to make your mate happy, I really do, but do you believe that this is what will make her happiest in the long run?"

"No." Will said quietly.

"Hannah's been through a terrible time. It's understandable why being in her Lycan form and living out here in the woods with her mate is so appealing to her, but that doesn't mean it's the right thing to do. You need to convince her to come back to the human world."

"Yeah, I know." Will sighed again.

The two Lycans sat in silence for a few minutes before Douglas set down his untouched mug of tea. "I should get back. I'll tell the others that you're doing well and will return soon, alright?"

Will nodded and Douglas clasped his shoulder, squeezing gently. "Take care, Will. I'll see you and Hannah soon."

* * *

"They're not ready, Jordan."

"It's been two months. They're ready."

Mannie raked his hand through his hair before glancing at Reid. "Tell him they're not ready."

"They're not." Reid confirmed. "They need a few more weeks."

Constance rolled her eyes. "Try a few more months."

"The Board of Directors feels that, based on the results from their latest round of tests, they're ready to go hunting."

"Ready? Fuck, Jordan! A month with me and Constance and a month with Reid and you think they're ready? In the old days they would have trained with us for months before even graduating to the weapons level. Half of them still can't hit the target seven times out of ten and you think they're ready." Mannie shouted.

"Not me – the Board of Directors." Jordan replied calmly.

Mannie snorted angrily. "Tell me, Jordan –do you have any control over what happens in this facility or are you just the Board of Directors monkey?"

"Mannie!" Constance said sharply as Jordan flushed a bright red.

"Richard would never have allowed the Board of Directors to run over him like this." Mannie snapped.

Jordan cleared his throat as his face continued to burn a bright red. "Yes, well, Richard started the program using his considerable wealth and he had a certain sway over the Board that I, unfortunately, do not."

Mannie snorted again and Jordan sighed loudly. "For what it's worth – I agree with you. I don't think they're ready either but the Board is pushing for this. Ultimately they have the final say."

"Maybe you could find your balls and tell the Board they'll be sending their batch of fresh-faced recruits to their deaths." Reid retorted.

When Jordan glared at him, Reid shrugged. "Just a suggestion."

"If I balk at sending the recruits out, if I tell the Board that I'm flat out refusing to do it, all that will happen is they'll demote me and bring someone new in. And the new person might not be nearly as easy-going as I am." Jordan replied with a brittle smile.

He pushed a few buttons on his computer and pointed to the large screen on the wall of his office. A map had appeared and he tapped a spot that had been marked with a small red 'x'. "There's been a pod of vampires spotted moving around in this area. It's fairly remote which is a little odd. There's a gas station about ten miles away and a few scattered farmhouses but that's it. It's odd to have a group of vampires in an area with few humans to feed on. The Board is concerned that another uprising is already beginning, or that this pod is a part of the initial uprising. We have no idea how many followers Samuel had, and we all know how odd it is for vampires to be in close proximity with each other."

"I'm starting to wonder about that." Constance said softly.

Jordan glanced at her. "What do you mean?"

She shrugged. "I'm just saying that it seems like more and more vampires are banding together. When Will and I hunted together as teenagers, it was always lone vampires. Occasionally there would be two of them together, but that was extremely rare. Now, it's starting to be rare to see a leech alone."

Reid rubbed at his smooth jaw. "If you think about it, the bloodsuckers hunting together makes sense. They're less vulnerable to attack and they can take down more humans at one time. I'm surprised it's taken them this long to realize it."

"They're fucking idiots and they can't stand the sight of each other." Mannie shook his head. "Even if they've had the brilliant idea of hunting as a pack, it'll never last. They can't go more than a few days without turning on each other."

"Samuel managed to build himself an army." Jordan pointed out.

"The average vampire isn't capable of doing what Samuel did." Mannie countered.

"Regardless, we're sending a hunting team for this pod. After what happened, the Board is extremely nervous about vampires who have banded together."

"Jordan –"

"The decision has been made, Mannie." Jordan interrupted. He regarded the three of them solemnly. "I've selected a few older recruits to go as well – Selena, Leanne, and Alex. Mannie and Constance will be the team leads and I've emailed you the list of recruits the Board wants on the hunt."

"I'm going as well." Reid replied.

"Not this time." Jordan answered. "You just had your cast removed and – "

"Two weeks ago. My arm is fine." Reid protested.

Jordan shook his head. "We'll give it another week or two before we send you hunting."

"I'm going on this hunt, Jordan." Reid snapped.

"No, you're not. We don't need you on this one."

"Fuck!" Reid swore loudly and stomped from the room, slamming the door behind him as Jordan raised his eyebrows at Mannie.

"Any idea what that was about?"

"Nope, not a clue." Mannie lied. "When's the hunt?"

"Tomorrow night. You and Constance can brief the recruits today and get them set up with their weapons. If you have any questions, come see me."

Mannie and Constance left Jordan's office and Constance gave Mannie a curious look as they walked down the hallway. "What's up with Reid?"

"Selena." He replied briefly.

"Oh. I thought that was just a casual thing."

"It is. Just like you and Ryan are a casual thing." Mannie grinned. "Hey, how old is Ryan again?"

"You know how old he is." Constance scowled at him.

"You'd better be careful, Connie, they're going to start calling you cougar instead of Lycan." Mannie laughed.

"Call me Connie again and I'll wear your guts for garters." Constance replied tartly as she raised her hand and lengthened her fingernails into sharp claws.

"God, you know it turns me on when you threaten me like that." Mannie grinned again and Constance rolled her eyes before slapping him lightly on the back.

"Seriously though, Mannie, I'm worried about the hunt. I don't think – "

"I'm going with you." Reid stepped out from an adjoining hallway.

"Sorry, buddy. You heard Jordan."

"Fuck Jordan! I'm going on the hunt." Reid snarled.

"Listen, he's right. Your arm could use another week or so." Mannie replied before slapping Reid on the back. "Don't worry, man. Selena will be just fine. She can take care of herself."

Reid snorted angrily. "I know that! I'm just anxious to be out hunting again. It has nothing to do with Selena."

Mannie laughed as Constance made a noise of disbelief.

"What? It's true." Reid scowled at them. "This has absolutely nothing to do with Selena."

"What has nothing to do with me?" Selena had come up behind them and Reid flushed a dull red before shaking his head.

"Nothing.'

"It's obviously not nothing." Selena answered. "What's going on?"

"There's been a hunt scheduled for tomorrow night. You're going on it and Reid isn't. He thinks you can't take care of yourself and is trying to worm his way in on the hunt." Mannie said cheerfully.

"Shut up, Mannie!" Reid said through gritted teeth.

"I can take care of myself." Selena frowned at him.

"I know." Reid said hastily. "It's just been a while since I've hunted, that's all. I'm anxious to get back in the game."

Selena gave him an appraising look. "Good. Because I don't need a babysitter, Reid."

"I never said you did." He said defensively.

There was a moment of silence that Mannie broke. "Well, this is fucking awkward as shit."

Selena shrugged. "I'm leaving. Douglas is back and I want to hear how Hannah is doing."

She marched down the hallway and when she had disappeared, Reid blew his breath out in exasperation. "Thanks a lot, Mannie."

"What did I do?" Mannie protested.

"Just do me a favour and keep your mouth shut around Selena, okay?" Reid sighed.

He walked away before Mannie could reply and Constance smiled briefly. "He really likes her."

"You think?" Mannie laughed. "Selena has him wrapped around her little finger and she doesn't even know it."

* * *

Selena collapsed against the bed, panting harshly and her body shuddering, as Reid rolled off of her. He lay on his side next to her and propped his head up with one arm.

"Hey." He grinned smugly at her as he traced small circles on her flat abdomen with his fingertips.

"Stop looking so smug." She pinched his cheek affectionately as his grin widened.

"What? Can I help it that I'm so damn good in bed?"

"Yes, you keep mentioning that." She said dryly.

"And proving it – over and over. Let's not forget about that." He nuzzled his face into her neck and cupped her small breast.

She shivered delicately and he placed a soft kiss below her ear. "Maybe I should prove it again."

She smiled in the dark before stilling his roving hand. "I should probably go back to my room."

"It's still early." He nipped at her collarbone.

"I know but I need to get some sleep. I need to be well-rested for the hunt tomorrow night."

He stiffened against her and she turned to face him when he eased away from her.

"What's wrong?"

"Nothing."

She rubbed her thumb across his cheekbone. "Tell me."

"I'm worried about you."

"I told you I don't need a babysitter."

"I know." He said irritably. "But that doesn't mean I can't worry about you. Wouldn't you be worried if I was going on the hunt and you weren't?"

She stared silently at him and disappointment churned in his belly. "Forget it."

He started to turn away and she pushed her naked body against his. "Reid, wait."

He stopped but stared over her shoulder at the wall as she rubbed his chest. She could see the hurt on his face and she pressed her mouth against his. He resisted at first but she licked at his lips with her soft tongue until he groaned and opened his mouth. They kissed deeply and he squeezed her firm ass as she rubbed her pelvis against him.

When they broke apart, she smiled at him and brushed her hand through his hair. "Yes, I'd be worried. But, I also know that you can take care of yourself, just like I can."

He didn't reply and she smiled reassuringly at him. "I'll be fine, Reid. I will."

"I know." He murmured.

She squeezed him lightly but when she started to slide from the bed he wrapped his arms around her and pulled her into his embrace.

"Don't go." He whispered. "Stay the night with me, Selena. Please."

She nodded. "Alright."

He sighed with relief and kissed her forehead as she stared up at him.

"I sleep better in your bed with you than alone in my own." She admitted quietly.

She waited for his smart ass remark but he only smiled at her and kissed her forehead again. "Good night, sweetheart."

"Good night, Reid."

Chapter 18

Will stared at the ceiling of the tent as a particularly strong gust of wind rattled the canvas. He shifted into a more comfortable position, pulling the blankets to the middle of his chest and tucking his hands behind his head, as he listened for Hannah.

It was another ten minutes before she trotted into camp. He listened to her sniffing around the edges of the tent before she shifted and ducked into the tent. She smiled at him as she straddled his hips and stroked his chest.

"You didn't run for very long."

He shrugged. "I was tired."

"How tired?" She leaned down and kissed the line of his jaw, making a growling noise of happiness when he shivered under her.

"We need to talk, honey."

"Do we?"

"Yes. About going back to the facility."

She sighed loudly before nipping at his throat. "Fine, but we talk after. I need you, Will."

"Hannah – "

"After." She whispered before pressing her mouth against his.

He groaned and she flattened her naked body against his, rubbing herself against him as she kissed him with light fluttering kisses.

His cock was hardening against her and he made a low growl of need before sliding his hand to the back of her neck and pushing his tongue between her lips. He kissed her deeply, claiming her mouth, as she pulled the blanket down and rubbed her wet pussy against his erection.

"I love you, Will." She breathed into his ear.

"I love you too." He sucked on her bottom lip as his hands stroked her breasts and flat stomach.

Her eyes were glowing and she made a soft growl of satisfaction before lifting herself and sliding her warm core down over him. They both moaned with pleasure and she gave him a naughty grin before reaching for his arms. She pinned them above his head and began to ride him with a fast and wild pace that had him on the verge of coming.

"Wait!" He muttered as she ran her teeth along the sensitive spot on his neck.

"For what?" She grinned at him and he growled warningly.

She growled back, her eyes flashing, and squeezed her muscles around his aching cock.

"Fuck! Hannah, don't do that!" He moaned.

She leaned over him and licked his collarbone with the tip of her warm tongue. "All mine."

"Yes." He agreed before easily breaking free of her grip and sitting up.

She arched her back and urged his head to her breasts. He kissed the tip of each nipple and she tugged sharply on his hair. "Don't tease, Will."

He sucked her nipple into his mouth and nipped it lightly with his teeth. She moaned and clutched at his head as she rode him frantically.

"Oh, Will!" She cried out before her entire body froze and she howled with pleasure.

He buried his face in her warm neck as her tight core pulsed around him, and gave into the blinding urge to come. She clung to him as he muttered her name and sucked roughly on her throat.

She collapsed against him and he kissed her repeatedly before easing her on to the pile of blankets that made their bed. He pulled the top blanket over their naked bodies as Hannah pushed her hair back from her face.

"That was super." She grinned enthusiastically at him and he laughed.

"Glad you enjoyed it."

She kissed him before turning on to her side. "Good night, my love."

"Hey." He grabbed her arm and swung her gently back to face him. "No going to sleep. We need to talk, remember?"

"I'm tired." She pouted at him. "Can't we talk in the morning?"

"No, honey. You can't keep avoiding this conversation."

"I'm not avoiding. I'm just tired." She gave him a small smile. "The morning, alright?"

"No."

Her nostrils flared and her eyes flashed green before she sighed heavily and sat up. "Fine. You want to talk about the facility – let's talk."

"It's time to go back." Will said gently.

"I'm not ready yet."

"You are. We both know it." He rubbed her back as she stared at her hands.

"I still don't have full control over it and if I screw up one more time, Jordan will kick me out. Is that what you want, Will?"

"You do have control over it now. You've done really well and you're ready to go back." Will replied.

She sighed harshly. "You don't know that. Anything could happen. It's safer for me and others to be away from them."

Will sat up and put his arm around her waist. "Honey, we can't stay out here forever."

"Why not?" She asked suddenly. "Why can't we stay here in the forest – just you and I?"

He gave her a startled look. "You can't mean that."

"I do." She said firmly. "These last couple of months have been the happiest months of my life, Will. We're Lycans and being in the wild, hunting and mating, is what we're meant to do. Can you not feel that?"

She cupped his face and kissed him lightly. "This is what you want too. Don't try and deny it, my love."

"What about your mom and dad? What about Chen and Selena and the twins?"

"What about them?" She asked harshly. "They aren't Lycan, Will. They don't know what it's like to try and constantly suppress their true nature. I can't live among the humans anymore. I'm not like them."

"This isn't your true nature, Hannah." Will frowned. "You are human."

"I am Lycan!" She snarled at him.

He shook his head. "No, you are not. I am Lycan. You are a human that has been turned."

"There's no difference." She snapped.

"There is." He insisted. "I'm not saying it makes you weak. I'm saying it makes you different and your human side cannot be forgotten."

"I haven't forgotten it." She protested.

"You have. What you're suggesting we do is madness. Have you forgotten about the leeches? You wanted your vengeance for Sara. Have you forgotten that?"

"No, I have not!" She growled loudly. "But how many leeches am I expected to kill? How long must I live this wretched life before I have killed enough to make up for the loss of my sister? I helped stop the vampire uprising, I killed Samuel and had my life changed forever because of it. Haven't I done enough, Will? Am I expected to spend my entire life doing nothing but destroying them?"

"No, I just – "

She grabbed his arm and squeezed it tightly. "I want children. I want to live with you and our babies and raise them without fear. I'm tired, Will. I want to live in the light instead of dying in the darkness. I want a normal life!"

Will gave her a look of sadness. "It's too late for that, Hannah."

She bared her fangs at him. "It isn't! This could be our life, Will. There are too many vampires to defeat. There will always be more, and we'll do nothing but spend our entire lives fighting a useless battle."

"It's not useless."

"It is." She insisted. "Open your eyes, Will. Please! We are never going to win. Why shouldn't we live the rest of our lives in happiness? Why must we punish ourselves?"

"I never thought I would see you admit defeat, Hannah."

"I'm not!" She glared at him. "I'm being realistic and maybe a bit selfish. But is it really that wrong or selfish of me to want a normal life?"

"No." Will shook his head. "I get it, Hannah, I really do."

"Do you?" She asked sadly. "I don't think so or you wouldn't be fighting me on this."

"You think this is what will make you happiest," Will pulled her into his embrace, "but it isn't. Please believe me. The last year of your life has been awful, I know, and I understand the appeal of leaving it all behind but you'll regret it."

"You don't know that." She sighed.

"I do." He replied. "You have a family and friends who love you and you love them. Stop using the excuse that you're a Lycan to escape the life you now have. It won't work."

She didn't reply and he kissed her temple. "I love you, Hannah."

"I love you too." She whispered.

"We have to go back. We'll pack up tomorrow and – "

"No." She interrupted. "Not tomorrow, Will. Please."

"Hannah – "

"Just a few more days and then we'll go back. I promise."

He sighed and she stared up at him, her eyes swimming with tears. "Please, Will."

He nodded and brushed away the tears that were spilling down her cheeks. "It's the right thing to do, honey."

She nodded and turned away, lying on her side and closing her eyes wearily. "Good night, Will."

He gave her a troubled look before curling up behind her and wrapping his arm around her waist. "Good night, honey. I love you."

* * *

"That one counts as mine!" Luther hooted loudly and danced away as Tyrone glared at him.

"Fuck you, Luther! It does not!" He turned and stabbed a hissing, drooling vampire in the chest with the large, sharp stake he held. "I stabbed him first!"

"Yeah, but I finished him off, ya dink!" Luther ducked as the head of a vampire came flying toward him. It exploded in mid-air and Luther grinned at a panting, blood-covered Alex.

"Nice move, Alex!"

"Thanks." Alex ran toward a group of vampires who were closing in on Selena and two female recruits named Liz and Valerie. The three of them were firing rapidly but it was easy to tell that only Selena's were finding their mark.

As Alex chopped the head off the closest vampire, a blur of dark fur and loud growling blew past Luther and leaped on to the vampire about to attack him.

The vampire screeched in fear, her hands beating at the Lycan that was snarling and biting into her body, before trying in vain to rip the wolf's head from its body. The Lycan snarled angrily and sunk its teeth into her neck. The leech screamed again, the sound trailing off as the wolf tore her head from her body. Blood spurted out in a thick spray and Luther danced backward as the Lycan howled in triumph.

"Nicely done, hottie!" He gave the Lycan a short bow. "You need Luther to give you a bath? Clean that blood from your smokin' hot body?"

Constance chuffed and turned away, her tail twitching, as Tyrone shouted loudly, "Stephanie, watch out!"

The dark-haired girl turned, her eyes widening as the vampire lunged at her. He knocked her to the ground and tore the stake from her hand before laughing and yanking her head back by her long hair. He plunged his fangs into her throat, drinking thirstily as Stephanie screamed shrilly into the night air.

Tyrone, his lime green board shorts glowing in the darkness, sprinted toward them. He hit the vampire with a heavy thud, knocking him from the woman, and the creature and the boy struggled briefly on the hard ground before Luther threw his body on to the vampire. Working together, the twins quickly pinned the struggling vampire to the ground, the muscles in their thin arms straining, as the vampire hissed and spit Stephanie's blood at them.

"Quick, Luther! He's fucking strong!" Tyrone shouted.

"Don't get your damn panties in a bunch!" Luther shouted back as he ripped a stake from the belt around his waist.

He plunged the stake into the vampire's chest and the vampire's eyes widened in shock and dismay as his skin began to blacken.

"Get back! He's gonna blow!" Luther hollered.

He and Tyrone scrambled back as the vampire burst into ash.

"Nice." Tyrone held up his fist and Luther bumped it before they staggered to their feet and ran to Stephanie.

"Steph? You okay?" Tyrone hauled her to her feet and she nodded before touching the holes on her neck.

"I think so."

"Atta girl!" He slapped her on the ass and she jumped before glaring at him.

He grinned impudently at her and draped his arm across her shoulders. "Maybe you should stop by my room after all this is over and we'll debrief."

"TYRONE!"

Tyrone flinched as Mannie, standing in a pile of ash and carrying bloody stakes in both hands, shouted at him.

"This is not a fucking social event! Do you get me, you fucking moron?"

"I get you, sir!" Tyrone hollered immediately. He dropped his arm from around Stephanie's shoulders and the three of them jogged toward the remaining vampires. The six leeches had been herded into a group and they hissed at the humans that were slowly surrounding them. One of them, his eyes rolling with fear, darted forward in a useless attempt to break through the circle of humans. He made a soft gagging noise as Leanne, her red hair pulled back in a high ponytail, stabbed him through the throat with the knife in her left hand.

Her face pale, she plunged the stake in her right hand into his chest and yanked both weapons free before stepping back. The vampire dropped to the ground, blood pouring from his throat and chest before bursting apart.

Working quickly, the humans killed the remaining leeches. When they were dead and the forest around them was silent, Mannie gave them a pleased look.

"Good job, babies. Let's get - "

A strangled noise of surprise interrupted him and his eyes widened in horror. The others turned to look behind them. A vampire had dropped from the trees above them and wrapped its hands around Leanne's throat. It dragged the redhead backwards, hissing and snarling at the humans, as Leanne struggled in its grip.

"Let her go!" Mannie warned.

The vampire screamed laughter and tore Leanne's throat open with its sharp nails.

"NO!" Selena screamed.

She ran toward Leanne and the leech. As the leech dropped Leanne to the ground, she raised her gun and fired. It struck the vampire in the shoulder and it gave a shrill scream of surprise and fear as Selena fired again. This bullet found its mark and the vampire stared at its chest as a blue light began to throb in its veins. It staggered back, touching its skin with soft wonderment, before bursting apart.

Selena fell to her knees beside Leanne and clamped her hands across the gaping wound in her throat. Blood poured between her fingers and she stared helplessly at Mannie as the rest of the group crowded around them.

"Mannie! Help me!" Selena gasped.

Mannie yanked off his shirt and pressed it against Leanne's throat. The redhead's face was paling and she made a soft gurgling noise as Selena, her hands dripping in blood, brushed the woman's hair back.

"It's okay, Leanne. You'll be okay."

Blood was soaking through Mannie's shirt and he swore under his breath as Leanne clutched weakly at Selena's arm.

Selena took her hand and squeezed it firmly. "Stay still, honey. It'll be alright."

She choked back a sob as Leanne made one last gasping gurgle and died. Mannie, his face grim and his hand trembling lightly, reached out and closed her eyes as Selena began to cry softly.

The others stood in shocked silence, staring down at the dead woman as Mannie squeezed Selena's shoulder.

"Why so sad, humans?"

Mannie stiffened and the entire group turned to see the very large vampire standing behind them. He was wearing a dark suit and red tie and his dark hair was long and pulled into a neat ponytail at the base of his neck.

He straightened the cuffs on his jacket and smiled at them before glancing at the dead woman. "Lost one of your own, have you?"

Selena glanced at Mannie. The vampire had a thick German accent and he seemed unconcerned about the large group of humans and Lycan standing in front of him. In fact, a small smile crossed his face when Constance, growling loudly, began to stalk toward him.

"A Lycan. They're so puny here, are they not, Lars?"

"Ja, Olof." A second vampire, his dark hair was cut short and his eyes were the same startling blue as Olof's, appeared next to him.

"Fan out." Mannie murmured.

The recruits, glancing nervously at each other, did as he asked.

"We watched you destroying the others. Not bad work for humans." Olof said admiringly.

"Thanks." Mannie grinned at him before plucking the stake from the holder around his waist. "Glad you approve."

As Constance crept closer, there was a soft whispery noise and more vampires descended from the sky. They landed with a soft thud and Selena swallowed nervously as she quickly counted them. All together there were thirteen of the large vampires and when a red one with freckle-covered skin casually ambled toward her, she drew her weapon and shot him in the chest.

The vampire grimaced as blue light began to appear through his pale skin. He bent over, one hand held against his chest and the other rubbing at his temple, as the other vampires watched silently.

After only a moment or so, he straightened and Selena's eyes widened when the pulsing light faded and disappeared. He smiled at her as he unbuttoned first his suit jacket and then his shirt before using his long nails to dig in the hole in his chest. He pulled the spent bullet out, glancing disinterestedly at it before dropping it to the ground and buttoning his shirt.

"Klaus?" Olof said quietly.

"Es geht mir gut, Olof." The vampire replied. "Sie vermisste mein Herz."

Olof smiled at Selena. "You should always be certain to aim for the heart, my lovely."

"Fuck you!" Selena spat and fired her gun again. Olof dodged the bullet easily before turning to his companions.

"I want them. Bring them to me alive."

"Was ist mit der Wölfin?" Lars asked.

Olof turned his cold eyes to the growling, snarling, Constance. "Kill her."

Chapter 19

"Good morning."

Will sat down in the chair next to Hannah and placed his hand on her knee. She smiled at him in the bright sunshine and he studied the dark circles under her eyes and the pallor of her skin.

"Are you alright?"

She nodded. "I didn't sleep well."

"We have to go back, Hannah."

"I know." She stared off into the distance and sighed softly. "I meant what I said, Will. I'll go back in a couple of days. I just – I need a little more time to enjoy the peacefulness and the – the rightness of being out here with you. Is that so awful?"

"Of course it isn't." Will squeezed her knee lightly. "And we can always go camping anytime you want."

She gave him a small, bitter, smile. "It's too late for a normal life, remember?"

"Hannah, I – "

He stopped as a familiar scent drifted to them on the wind.

"Why is Douglas back?" Hannah asked.

"I don't know." Will began to build up the fire as Hannah ducked into the tent to get dressed.

When the old wolf loped into the campsite, Will tossed him a pair of pants. Douglas shifted and pulled the pants on as Hannah emerged from the tent. She took one look at his pale, drawn face and hurried toward him.

"Douglas? What's wrong?"

"There was a hunt last night. No one has returned."

"What?" Will frowned at him. "No one?"

Douglas shook his head. "Jordan is sending out a team to search for their bodies."

"Why is he so certain they're dead?" Hannah asked immediately. "They may still be alive."

"Maybe. But why have they not called in? Even if only a few of the babies escaped, they all know the protocol. You call in and confirm your status."

"The babies?" Hannah whispered. "Douglas – who went on the hunt last night?"

Douglas gave her a grim look. "Mannie and Constance were the team leaders. Selena, Leanne and Alex were there as well."

"The babies?" Hannah whispered again. "What babies did they send?"

Douglas' face was so pale that Will reached out and placed a steadying hand on his arm. He was afraid the old Lycan was going to pass out.

"There was a group of eight recruits sent on the hunt. The twins were a part of the group."

"Shit!" Will cursed as Hannah took a staggering step backward.

"No." She whispered. "No."

"Why the hell would Jordan send them on a hunt?" Will asked. "They're not ready."

"Mannie and the others tried to tell him that but he insisted."

"I'll kill him." Will muttered.

Douglas shook his head. "I don't think Jordan wanted to send them either. Mannie said that Jordan admitted he didn't think they were ready but the Board disagreed. He said if he refused to send them on the hunt, the Board would simply dismiss him and bring someone else in."

Hannah, her face pale, took a deep breath. "We have to go back, Will. We have to go back right now."

"Of course." He kissed her firmly on the forehead. "We'll find them, honey."

* * *

Natalie opened the door of the apartment and stared in numb surprise at the woman standing in front of her.

"Hannah?"

"Hi, mom."

Natalie's face was pale and her eyes were puffy and red, but a smile broke out on her face and she gathered Hannah into her embrace and hugged her tightly.

"I've missed you." She whispered.

"I've missed you too." Hannah kissed her cheek before moving toward her dad. He hugged her as Natalie wrapped her arms around Will and hugged him firmly before ushering him into the apartment.

"I'm so glad you're back." Natalie sighed. She took Jim's hand and squeezed it as Hannah and Will sat down at the island.

"Tea. I'll make us some tea." Natalie said distractedly.

"How did you know to come back?" Jim asked.

"Douglas hiked to our campsite." Will replied.

"Dear Douglas." Natalie said fondly as she pulled mugs out of the cupboard. "He's such a sweet man. He came to tell us as soon as he heard the news that the twins and the others were – were…"

Her breath hitched in her throat and she turned away quickly as Jim stood and took the mugs from her trembling hands.

"They'll be alright, Nat. They're smart boys." He said quietly.

Natalie shook her head. "They're dead. I know they're dead. I can feel it, Jim, and so can you."

"They're not dead!" Jim said fiercely. "They're still alive, Nat. You can't give up hope like that. We thought Hannah was dead twice now, and she's always come back to us. The boys will too."

She shook her head again and wiped her streaming eyes with a tissue as Jim gave Will and Hannah a helpless look.

"They're not dead." He repeated.

"We'll find them, dad." Hannah said quietly.

"Are you going with the search party?" Jim asked.

Will nodded. "Yes. We just got back but Hannah wanted to see the both of you before we join the others in Jordan's office. Douglas said they're meeting in about ten minutes."

"I want to come with you." Jim sat down beside them as Hannah shook her head.

"No."

Her father scowled at her. "I'm not some student you can tell what to do, Hannah. I'm your father and those boys are," he hesitated, his voice cracking, "special to your mother and I. I'm going with you and you can't stop me."

"You'll slow us down, dad." Hannah reached out and grasped his hand. "You have no training, no skills for killing vampires, and I can't be watching out for you. You know that I'm right."

He sighed loudly as Natalie leaned against him and kissed the top of his head. "Hannah – "

"We'll find the boys." Hannah interrupted before standing. "We should go, Will. I don't want to be late to the meeting."

With a final kiss to her mother's pale cheek, the two of them left the apartment.

Will captured her hand and gave her a grave look as they hurried down the hall. "Honey, the odds of the twins or any of them still being alive is – "

"I know." She interrupted. She stopped in the hallway and gave him a look of such smoking anger that he recoiled. "The twins are dead. Selena is dead. Mannie and Constance - the babies - they're all dead, and I'm going to find the fucking leeches who did it and kill every last one of them."

Her eyes glowing, she bared her fangs at him before turning and striding down the hallway.

* * *

Jordan stared solemnly at the others gathered in his office. "The five of you need to understand that the Board is considering this a body recovery, not a rescue mission."

"Big fucking surprise." Reid said bitterly.

Jordan gave him a look of compassion. "Do you really believe they're alive?"

Reid didn't reply and Chen leaned forward. "When are we leaving?"

"As soon as we're finished here." Jordan replied. "Are you sure you're good to go?"

"I'm fine." Chen answered shortly.

Jordan nodded and turned to face the image on the wall behind him. "This," he tapped a red x on the map, "is the area of the hunt. We're assuming their bodies will be in a five mile radius."

"What if they didn't kill them but turned them?" Chen asked quietly.

"All of you know as well as I do that vampires rarely turn humans, unless they are looking to increase their numbers or suspect the human has information they want. Since we've crushed the vampire uprising, I think it's safe to assume that our team was killed not turned." Jordan answered.

"Didn't you tell us the Board isn't so sure we've ended the uprising?" Reid asked.

Before Jordan could reply, there was a brief knock on the door and Will and Hannah stepped into the room.

"Hannah." A small smile crossed Chen's face and he crossed the room quickly to hug her tightly.

"Hello, master."

"It is good to see you." Chen smiled warmly at her and Hannah gave him a faint smile in return.

"Hi, Paul." Hannah squeezed the young man's shoulder and he nodded to her as Jordan regarded her steadily.

"Hello, Jordan." Hannah took a deep breath and faced the older man squarely as Will stepped to her side.

"Welcome back, Hannah." He studied her carefully. "Did it work?"

"Yes. I have control over it."

He continued to study her, his head cocked to the side, before nodding. "Good. Have a seat."

Hannah sat down. She was surprised by Jordan's quick acceptance and she gave Will a look of confusion. He shrugged slightly as he pulled up a chair next to hers.

"I'm assuming you and Will are going with the others?" Jordan asked.

"Yes." Will confirmed. He rested his big hand on Hannah's knee, stroking small circles, as she gnawed on her bottom lip and jiggled her other leg restlessly.

"We should get going. We're losing the light." She blurted out.

"As soon as we're finished here, the team will leave. Now that you've returned, Will – you're team leader. I was just telling the others that the Board considers this a body recovery, not a rescue mission."

When neither Will nor Hannah responded, he turned back to the map. "We suspect the bodies are within a five mile radius of the hunt. There isn't much in the area so there's little worry that other humans will catch you when you're removing the bodies. That being said, I'm expecting you to move quickly and quietly. We don't need a bunch of civilians on some damn nature trek stumbling on to you."

He turned and gave them all a grave look. "You go in, you find the bodies, and you bring them back. No hunting. Do you understand?"

They nodded and he rubbed at his forehead before frowning. "And for God's sake, keep your eyes open for more leeches. It had to be a much larger group than Intel suspected, to have killed our entire team."

"Or more powerful." Chen said quietly.

"Powerful enough to kill a Lycan?" Will asked.

His face pale and his voice strained, he continued. "Constance was a skilled hunter, Chen. She'd been killing leeches since she was a teenager. It would have to be very powerful leeches to kill her. It's more likely that it's a large pod of them. If there were enough of them, they could have overpowered her."

"You don't know she's dead!" Ryan suddenly shouted.

The others jerked in surprise as he jumped up and knocked his chair backwards before stalking toward Will.

"Constance *is* a skilled killer, not *was*. Stop acting like she's fucking dead when you don't know if she is or not, you asshole!"

He was standing over Will now, his face red and his fists clenched, and Will squeezed Hannah's leg when she growled warningly at Ryan.

He glared at her. "What? You want a piece of me, Hannah? You think your stupid swords are faster than my gun? Is that it?"

Mallorie stood and hurried over. "Ryan, knock it off."

"Stay out of this, Mallorie." Ryan said without looking at her. "No one asked for your opinion."

"Ryan – "

"It's fine, Mallorie." Hannah stood and gave Ryan a look of sympathy. "I'm sorry, Ryan. I know you love her."

Ryan's shoulders slumped and he took a deep breath before backing away. Hannah stood and touched his shoulder gently. He jerked away from her and shook his head. "I'm fine. Let's just go, already."

As the others filed out of Jordan's office, he touched Will's arm. "Can you stay behind for a moment, Will?"

Will nodded and squeezed Hannah's hand. "I'll be right there."

"If this is about me, then I want to stay." Hannah said.

"It isn't." Jordan replied.

She stared suspiciously at him before leaving the office.

"Does she have control over it?" Jordan asked when the door was shut firmly behind her.

"I thought you said it wasn't about her." Will frowned.

"I lied."

Will snorted in disgust. "Yes, she has control over it. If she didn't, she would have turned and killed you the moment we found out the twins were dead."

Jordan winced. "If I'd had a choice, I would never have recruited them. You know that."

"Yeah, I know." Will muttered. "Hannah's learned to control the shift. You don't have to worry, Jordan."

"Good." Jordan replied.

Will started toward the door, stopping when Jordan cleared his throat. "One more thing, Will. This is a body recovery mission only. No hunting. I know people are upset and I understand why, but I can't have them going off searching for the leeches who did this. You're the team leader, I'm expecting you to keep your team under control."

"They'll want their revenge." Will said quietly.

"I know. And they'll have it - just not tonight." Jordan answered.

"Why?"

"The Board doesn't want another hunt so soon after this one. They're worried about more losses."

Will shook his head angrily. "What the fuck is going on with the Board, Jordan? Do they even care that their "losses" are human beings? That the teenagers they recruited are dead?"

"They're worried, Will." Jordan said quietly. "They're certain that a second uprising will happen sooner than later. They're convinced that the vampires are becoming bolder and more willing to work together to achieve what they desire most. If that happens..."

He trailed off and Will sighed loudly. "We've always stopped them before, Jordan. And we did it without using *children* in our battles."

"I don't know what to tell you, Will." Jordan said. "If I refuse, the Board will just find someone else to – "

"Yeah, I know." Will interrupted. "I need to go – it's getting late."

"Good luck." Jordan held his hand out and after a moment Will shook it firmly.

Chapter 20

Will held his hand up and the others stopped immediately, staring into the woods that surrounded them. Although the sun hadn't set yet, the entire group was uneasy and on edge, and they waited as Will sniffed the air.

"What?" Reid finally asked with a touch of impatience.

"Blood." Will replied. He stared briefly at Hannah. He had been smelling leech blood and ash for the last half hour but he had picked up a new scent. One that was making his stomach roll with fear and anger. The blood was Lycan and by the look on Hannah's face, he knew she could smell it too. She turned to study Ryan and he frowned at her.

"Why are you looking at me like that?"

"Nothing." She replied quickly. She pulled her swords free and gripped them tightly as Will spoke.

"We're getting close. Remember, we find their bodies and bring them home. I know we're all upset and it's about to get a hell of a lot worse, but we need to focus. Understand?"

The others nodded and Will gave them a grim look before continuing on. They had discovered the van of the missing group parked next to an abandoned house only a few miles away. They had parked and hiked into the woods, the smell of blood and ash growing stronger to Will and Hannah by the minute.

"Look!" Paul darted forward and the others followed him. A campfire with lawn chairs scattered around it could be seen through the trees and Hannah scanned the area anxiously as Reid kicked at the cold ashes in the campfire.

"Obviously this is where they set up the hunt." Reid frowned.

"Fuck!" Paul shouted. He ducked behind a large tree and dropped to his knees as the others followed them.

"Oh, Leanne." Hannah whispered.

Leanne was lying motionless on the ground with her throat torn open. Paul groaned and closed her eyes as Reid looked at Will.

"Where are the other bodies?"

"Maybe they ran deeper into the woods. The leeches hunted them down and killed them." Will replied distractedly. He was inhaling repeatedly, turning in a slow circle, as the others studied the trees.

"All of them?" Reid frowned again. "They all ran after Leanne was killed? You know as well as I do that Mannie would never run. Neither would Selena."

Chen studied the large dark stains on the ground. The wind was blowing firmly and he rubbed his fingers together. "There's blood on the ground and ash in the air."

Mallorie, holding two wooden stakes, shook her head. "There has to be – "

A low whine interrupted her and she gave the others a tentative look. ""Did you hear that?"

"Yes." Hannah said. Will's face was pale as the two of them sprinted toward a large fallen log that was to the right of Mallorie.

They leaped over the log and Hannah cried out in dismay as Will made a hoarse bark of pain and sorrow.

"Constance?" Ryan whispered. He stumbled toward the log and peered over it.

"Constance!" He screamed her name and dropped his gun before sliding clumsily over the log. Bits of moss and bark scattered on to the fallen wolf's body and, trembling badly, Ryan dropped to the ground and gathered the bloody and battered animal into his arms.

"Can you hear me, honey?" He whispered.

There was a soft pop as Constance shifted to her human form. Hannah moaned loudly at the sight of her mangled chest and Will dropped to his knees beside Ryan and Constance, touching the Lycan's arm lightly as Ryan bit back a harsh sobbing cry.

"Jesus." Reid whispered. His face completely white, he gripped Chen's arm and squeezed tightly. "Why isn't she healing?"

"Her wounds are too deep." Chen replied. He swallowed thickly as Ryan stroked Constance's hair.

"Ryan?" Constance voice was barely audible.

"Yeah, baby. It's me. I'm here." Ryan kissed her mouth and shifted her closer.

She gasped weakly with pain and he flinched. "I'm sorry, baby. I'm so sorry."

"Will, we need to get her back to Barb." Hannah said quietly. Feeling sick to her stomach, she stared at Constance's chest. The Lycan had been ripped open from her sternum to her navel, and Hannah could see bone and exposed muscle and nerves. Blood was oozing out of the wound and the ground around her was soaked black. The Lycan had to be in incredible pain and Hannah had no idea how she had survived this long.

Will leaned closer to Constance. "Constance? Ryan and I are going to move you. It's going to hurt. We'll try to – "

"Too late." Constance breathed.

"Don't say that." Ryan kissed her again. "Just close your eyes, baby, and concentrate on healing, okay? We'll get you back to the facility and after a few weeks of rest you'll be good as new."

Constance smiled wearily, blood was smeared across her teeth, and shook her head. "I love you, Ryan." She drew in a ragged breath. "Should have said it earlier, I'm sorry."

"I love you too." Ryan replied quickly. "Now stop talking. You need to conserve your strength for the trip home, okay?"

"Too late." She repeated and Ryan, tears beginning to drip down his cheeks, scowled angrily at her.

"It's not too late! Just try, baby. You have to try, okay? Try for me."

Constance closed her eyes, her breathing was harsh and laboured in the quiet air, as Will gave Hannah a helpless look. She reached out and took his hand as Chen spoke.

"Who did this to you, Constance?"

"What does it matter?" Mallorie snapped. "Leave her alone!"

"We need to know." Chen said quietly. "Does this look like vampires to you, Will?"

"No." Will admitted. "The wound is odd for leeches."

Constance's eyes flew open and she made a harsh, barking cough, her back arching as Ryan struggled to hold her still. Blood flew from her mouth in a thick spray and she howled hoarsely with pain before collapsing in Ryan's arms.

Gasping for air, her eyes rolled wildly to Will. She reached out and clutched at his arm, pulling him closer.

"The others!" She gasped.

"Are they dead?" Will asked.

Hannah's heart knocked fiercely in her chest when Constance shook her head weakly.

"Alive." She breathed. "Leeches."

"Leeches did this?" Will squeezed her hand as Constance coughed again.

"Yes." Her breath was whistling in and out of her throat and Ryan stroked her face soothingly as she continued to stare at Will.

"So strong, Will. Tried to – to save them but too strong."

"It's alright, Constance." Will soothed. "Did the leeches take the others?"

She nodded again, her eyes were starting to close, and Will squeezed her hand. "Constance, look at me, honey. Look at me!"

She blinked wearily and Will squeezed her hand again. "Do you know where they took them?"

She shook her head and Ryan pushed Will away. "Enough."

"Ryan, we need – "

"Honey?"

Will stopped and stared up at Hannah. She was standing over him, tears sliding down her cheeks, and holding her hand out to him. He took it, his throat squeezing painfully, and allowed her to lead him away from Ryan and the dying Lycan.

"Hannah, we have to – "

"She's dying, Will." Hannah said softly. "Give her time with her loved one."

His face twisted and as Hannah wrapped her arms around him and drew her into his embrace he turned to stare at Ryan and Constance. Ryan was still holding her in his arms and he rubbed her cheekbone tenderly with his thumb as she stared up at him. He leaned down and kissed her mouth before whispering in her ear.

A whine slipped from Will's throat and he turned and buried his face in Hannah's neck, breathing deeply, as she rubbed his back. After a few moments, she led him to the others and they stood quietly in a circle.

After nearly five minutes, Ryan uttered a single sobbing cry. Paul, his face pale, moved around the fallen log and crouched next to Ryan.

"I'm sorry, man."

Ryan eased Constance to the ground and kissed her tenderly on the mouth. He brushed her hair back before pulling his jacket off. He covered her head and upper body with his jacket and stared numbly at her body.

Paul squeezed his arm. "We need to take Leanne and Constance back to the facility. Reid, Will and I will carry Constance, okay? You can help Hannah and Mallorie with Leanne."

Ryan shook his hand off and staggered to his feet. He climbed over the log and picked up his gun from the ground.

"Ryan? What are you doing?" Reid asked cautiously.

"I'm going to find the leeches who did this to her and kill them." He replied calmly.

He stalked toward Hannah and Will, studying them with bloodshot eyes. "I know you can smell them."

Hannah glanced at Will. "Ryan, it's not – "

"Shut up." Ryan said with the same eerie calmness. He stared up at Will. "You're going to lead me to them."

"It's not that easy." Hannah said quietly. "The scents are mixed up and – "

"Not for him." Ryan pointed at Will. "Tell her."

Will didn't reply and Hannah frowned at him. "Will, can you track them?"

Without waiting for his reply, she moved away from him and lifted her head. She inhaled deeply for a few moments, her eyes closed and her body tense, before she suddenly twitched.

"I can smell the twins." She whispered.

"Hannah – "

"I can smell them!" She rushed back to Will and clutched at his arm. "It's faint and it's fading in and out, but I can smell them. We need to go."

"We can't." Will replied. "It's too dangerous. We have no idea how many leeches we're dealing with, and the smart thing to do is go back to the facility and get more people."

"Who? More babies?" Ryan said bitterly. "Do you think they're going to be able to help? By the time we get back here, the scent will have faded completely."

"He's right." Reid broke in. "We need to move now."

Will glared at him. "Reid, this is madness. You know it is. Don't let your feelings for Selena cloud your judgment."

"Lead us to them, Will." Reid said firmly.

"I can't!" Will nearly shouted. "I won't put everyone else in danger on the off chance that the rest of them are still alive. Do you honestly believe that the leeches haven't killed them by now?"

"I can smell the twins!" Hannah protested.

"That doesn't mean they're alive." Will replied.

Hannah winced and Will grimaced. "I'm sorry, honey. You know I'm right."

"You might not be." Hannah reached up and cupped his face. "What if the twins and Selena are still alive? What if Mannie is alive? Can you really just leave knowing that they're going to die because we didn't go after them?"

"Hannah, the vampires killed Constance. Do you have any idea how powerful they'd have to be to kill a Lycan?"

"If there were a lot of them, they could have overpowered her." Paul said.

"Either way, it's too dangerous." Will snapped. "I can't let -

"Mannie and Selena would come after us." Hannah said softly. "You know they would."

Will stared at her and she returned his look calmly. "We can't leave them out here."

"Fuck!" Will suddenly shouted. He tore away from Hannah and, growling loudly, punched his fist against a tree. He stood with his back to them, growling continuously, as his body swelled.

Reid gave the others a nervous look. "Will – "

"Give him a minute." Hannah interrupted.

They waited quietly until Will took a deep breath and turned back to them. "Hannah and I will follow the scent. Everyone else goes back to the facility."

"No fucking way!" Ryan retorted.

"You'll take Constance and Leanne back," Will continued as if Ryan hadn't spoken, "and update Jordan. I'll call in when we find the others and give you the location. You can come back with the cavalry and we'll kill the leeches and rescue our people."

"I'm coming with you and Hannah." Reid stepped toward them.

"So am I." Ryan stared at the blood on his hands. "You can't stop me."

"Both of you will slow us down. We'll track and move faster without you." Will replied. "If the others are still alive, we need to move quickly."

"Oh and us driving all the way back to the fucking facility, is moving quickly?" Reid shouted.

"We don't have enough people." Will scowled. "We can't rescue anyone if we're being slaughtered ourselves. Now stop wasting more fucking time and get back to the facility. I'll call Chen on his cell when we find the others."

There was a moment of silence and Will bared his teeth at them. "Get moving!"

Chen squeezed Hannah's arm. "Be careful."

"I will, master." Hannah took a deep breath and followed Will into the forest.

* * *

Christ, his head hurt. The pounding was like a damn steel drum and he couldn't imagine how it would feel to open his eyes. He had drank too much again and his mother was going to kill him. She hated when he snuck out with his friends to party, especially on a school night. His arms were aching and he tried to move them, groaning loudly when they refused to cooperate and something harsh and heavy bit into his wrists. What was going on? Why was his bed so uncomfortable? He groaned again and forced his eyes open a crack. The light was dim and he breathed a sigh of relief. Maybe it wasn't a school day and his mother was showing mercy on him. Maybe he'd –

"Mannie, wake up."

He grunted and tried to drift back into sleep. The pounding in his head wouldn't stop and he felt like he'd taken a brick to the head. God, he had to stop drinking. If he kept this up, his liver would be failing by the time he was twenty-five. His mother kept telling him that –

"Mannie! Open your eyes. C'mon, wake up now."

"I'm up." He muttered. "Jesus Christ, ma, I'm up."

"Mannie!"

"Fuck!" He forced his eyes open and cursed again as nausea rolled through him.

"Fuck me sideways." He groaned as he quickly closed his eyes again. "Ma, get me some aspirin, for the love of God."

There was no reply and he turned his head and squinted blearily at the figure beside him. "Ma?"

"Mannie, snap out of it." His mother whispered.

He blinked in confusion. His mother was a bleached blonde, always had been, so why was her hair so dark? Why was she wearing leather pants and a t-shirt stained with blood?

He shook his head, crying out at the pain, and grimly tamped down his urge to vomit as the room swayed alarmingly. He blinked repeatedly until his eyes finally focused, and studied the woman next to him.

"Selena?"

"Oh thank God." She breathed. "How do you feel?"

"Like shit. How do I look?" He grunted.

"Like shit." She gave a breathless laugh of relief. "You've been unconscious for most of the day. I thought you were in a coma or something."

He stretched his neck, grimacing when it cracked loudly. "What happened?"

"One of the leeches threw you headfirst into a tree. You're lucky he didn't break your neck or give you brain damage."

"Jury's still out on the brain damage." A voice replied.

Mannie craned his head to the left and stared at Tyrone. The twin winked at him. "Selena's right, dude, you look like shit."

"Thanks. Where's your brother?"

"Right here." Tyrone leaned back and Mannie stared at Luther. Unlike his brother who seemed as cocky and defiant as ever, Luther was pale and subdued.

"You okay, Luther?" Mannie squinted at him.

Luther nodded and Tyrone gave his brother a look of sympathy before shifting on the hard ground. They were lined up in a neat row against the wall. The boy's hands were tied behind his back with thick rope and the rope was attached to an iron loop driven into the wall behind him. Mannie tried to move his own hands, grunting with frustration and pain when the rope wrapped around his wrists didn't budge.

"Don't bother." Alex said bitterly. "We've been trying all day to loosen them."

Mannie studied their surroundings. They were sitting on the floor of what looked like a dilapidated barn and his heart sped up when he realized that other than the twins, Stephanie was the only other baby in the barn.

"Where are the other babies?"

Stephanie started to cry and Selena made a soothing noise under her breath. "It's okay, Steph. It'll be okay."

"Selena, where are the others?" Mannie repeated.

"Dead, probably." Tyrone said. The cocky look had faded from his face and he stared dejectedly at Mannie. "After they brought us here, they took Liz and Valerie, A.J., Derek and Zach."

"Took them where?"

"We don't know." Alex replied grimly. "Somewhere into the woods, I guess. We heard Liz screaming."

"That was last night," Selena said, "and we haven't seen the babies or the vampires since."

"Fuck!" Mannie shook his head and winced as another bolt of pain shot across his temples. "Christ, that hurts."

"You've got a concussion, I'm pretty sure." Selena said gravely.

"Yeah." He muttered. He paused as a thought struck him. "Constance? Where's Constance?"

Selena didn't reply and Mannie glanced at Tyrone. He was staring at his brother and Mannie nudged him with his foot. "Tyrone? What about Constance?"

"She's dead." Luther said bluntly.

"We don't know that, man." Tyrone said immediately. "She might have survived."

"She had four of those leeches attacking her when the rest of them dragged us away. You know she's dead, Tyrone."

"Luther – "

"Leave me alone, Tyrone." Luther said wearily. He closed his eyes and leaned his head against the wall as Tyrone gave Mannie a worried look.

"What time is it?" Mannie asked.

"Don't know. But the sun will be setting soon." Tyrone replied.

"Mannie, these vampires – they aren't, I mean, they're nothing like we've seen before." Selena said urgently. "They're so strong. I don't know if you remember this but I shot one of them in the chest and the ultraviolet light didn't kill him. They captured all of us in less than five minutes."

"What language were they speaking? Does anyone know?" Mannie asked suddenly.

"German." Tyrone replied. "When Selena shot the leech, the biggest one asked if he was okay and he said he was fine and that it missed his heart."

"You understand German?" Mannie asked.

"Yeah. Doesn't everyone?" Tyrone asked. "Luther and I learned it when we were seven. We also know French, Spanish and Latin."

"Of course you do." Mannie sighed. He cocked his head and squinted across the darkening barn. "Wait - who the fuck is that?"

There was a man strung from the ceiling by heavy, silver chains around his wrists. His head was down and his long, greasy hair obscured his face. His feet just brushed the ground and he swayed lightly back and forth.

"No idea." Tyrone shrugged. "He was here when they brought us in and he ain't said a fucking word. I think he might be dead."

"He ain't dead, ya fucking idiot." Luther snapped. "He's breathing, ain't he?"

Mannie waited for Tyrone to snap back but instead the twin gave him a look of quiet relief before shrugging again. "Yeah, you're right."

"Of course I am. I'm the fucking smart one." Luther snapped again.

Some of the tension disappeared from Tyrone's body and he leaned against the wall. Mannie had an idea that Luther's uncharacteristic depression had been worrying his twin more than the prospect of being a leech's lunch did. Not that he blamed him. It had been more than a little weird to see Luther acting so subdued and quiet.

"We need to get out of here before the sun goes down completely and the leeches come back." Mannie pulled at the rope around his wrists, wincing as it dug into his skin again.

"I told you, it's pointless." Alex said morosely. "They're too tight."

"Well, there has to be something we can use to cut them or loosen them." Mannie said irritably. His head was aching and throbbing, his vision was blurry and he could hardly control the urge to vomit.

A soft chuckling made the hair on the back of his neck stand up and he and the others stared across the barn at the chained man. He lifted his head and Stephanie gasped in surprise when he grinned at them and revealed long, sharp fangs.

Mannie stared in shock at the leech. He had never seen one so emaciated before. The leech's skin was stretched tightly over his face, giving it a skull-like appearance, and large clumps of hair had fallen out of his scalp. His eyes had turned a deep red and he licked his lips hungrily before grimacing. He turned his head and spit out a tooth before licking the blood from his mouth.

"Yer all gonna die." He announced in a dry and dusty voice.

"Fuck you, leech." Luther spat at him.

The vampire cackled laughter that turned into a dry, hacking cough. Mannie winced when a second tooth flew out of the vampire's mouth and landed on the floor in front of him.

"No need to be like that, boy. What's your name?" The vampire grinned at him and Luther gave him a look of disgust.

"My name's Judd." The vampire continued when Luther didn't reply. "It's nice to meet ya." He cackled laughter again and muttered something that Mannie couldn't hear.

"Why are you in here, Judd?" Mannie asked cautiously.

Judd squinted at him. "I'm a prisoner just like you."

"Why?"

"I don't know. I've begged them to kill me like they killed old Billy. Begged 'em hundreds of time, but they won't do it. They just laugh at me."

He gave Mannie a desperate, haunted look. "I'm so hungry. Do you understand how hungry I am?"

"I do." Mannie said lightly. The vampire had gone insane, whether it was from lack of blood or being kept prisoner by his own kind he didn't know, and he made his voice soft and gentle.

"How long have you been in here?"

Judd stared at the floor in thought. "I don't rightly know. A couple months, maybe?"

"Where did the other leeches – vampires – come from?" Mannie asked.

"I don't know. They just showed up one night. Me and Billy, that was my partner at the store, we was talking to some fancy city folk. Well, talking might not be right." The vampire giggled loudly. "I was drinking from the husband and Billy was chasing after the wife. She'd tried to run. They usually do. We always catch 'em though. I didn't like it so much but Billy loved it when they ran. He loved to chase 'em. He would have loved these new guys if they hadn't killed him."

"Did you and Billy do this a lot?" Mannie asked.

"Oh yeah. We had a real nice thing going. We ran the gas station out front and when humans showed up for gas or food or to take a piss, we just ate our fill. It was so easy." Judd said dreamily.

He licked his dry, cracked lips. "I ain't had nothin' to eat since the husband. What was his name again?"

"Judd, how many of the other vampires are there?"

"Barry? No, that ain't right. Larry, maybe. Jesus, that don't sound right either." Judd said tiredly. "What the fuck was the husband's name? If Billy was here, he'd know."

"Judd? How many, big guy?" Mannie repeated softly.

"Thirteen. Thirteen of the big bastards. They are big, ain't they? Poor old Billy didn't have a chance. I didn't either. I tried to run but they're so quick. They're from Europe I think. England, maybe. I ain't never been to Europe but they got that English accent."

"Oh my God. They're from Germany, you fucking moron." Luther rolled his eyes and Mannie glared at him.

"Be quiet, Luther!"

"How many other people have these vampires taken?" Mannie stared at Judd.

Judd shrugged. "I don't know. Plenty. They took over our scam. They mind the store and pick up the humans that come in. They're smarter than us. They got a guy that takes the cars and strips 'em down and sells 'em for parts."

They do it to hide the evidence." He explained carefully. "That's awful smart, huh? Me and Billy – we ain't never thought of that. We just hid 'em here in the barn." He paused and gave Mannie a sly look. "They ain't as nice as old Billy and I were, though."

"What do you mean?"

Judd didn't reply. He was staring off into space and he scowled lightly. "Harry? Maybe his name was Harry."

"Judd! Concentrate!" Mannie said harshly. "What do the vampires do to the humans?"

"They hunt them." Judd said dreamily. "They release them into the woods and then they hunt them. They say the human's blood is sweeter when they're being hunted. Somethin' about the adrenaline, maybe?"

He gave Mannie and the others a chilling smile. "The sun will be down soon. They'll come in and they'll choose more of you for the hunt. You'll be dead before the sun rises."

Chapter 21

"Chen, I don't like this." Reid muttered.

Chen shrugged. "Will is right. We would have slowed them down and we have to assume that it's a large pod of vampires. We're going to need more people."

"We don't have more people." Reid replied.

"The babies are better than nothing."

"Fuck." Reid muttered again.

They had carried the bodies to the large mini-van and loaded them carefully into the back seat. They were headed back to the facility, Paul was driving and Mallorie was sitting shotgun. He and Chen were sitting in the first row of seats and Ryan, his face pale, was sitting in the middle row of seats staring blankly out the window. One arm was slung over the seat and his hand was resting on Constance's arm. He stroked it gently as Reid leaned forward and tapped Paul on the shoulder.

"Drive faster."

"I'm driving fast enough." Paul snapped. "If we get pulled over for speeding, are you doing to explain to the cop why we have two bodies in the back seat?"

"We're in the middle of nowhere." Reid pointed out. "I hardly doubt that a cop is going to – "

There was a sudden, loud bang and Paul cursed and yanked on the wheel when the van careened toward the ditch. The mini-van skidded and swayed, and Mallorie shouted in pain when her head thumped against the side of the door frame with a hard thud.

Paul, still cursing loudly, struggled to gain control of the mini-van. After a few seconds, he straightened it out and guided the vehicle to the side of the road. He parked and stared at Chen and Reid through the rear view mirror.

"What the fuck was that?"

"Blown tire from the sounds of it." Reid slid across the seat and pulled the sliding door open before jumping nimbly to the ground. He headed to the back of the mini-van as the others, with the exception of Ryan, followed him.

Reid kicked at the shredded back tire as Paul squatted next to it. "Well, it's completely useless."

"C'mon," Reid motioned to him, "we'll grab the spare and get it changed."

Paul nodded and followed him to the back of the mini-van. He opened the back door and lifted out the bottom, staring at the empty space.

"Where the hell is the spare?"

Reid sighed loudly. "I have no fucking idea."

He pulled his cell phone out and frowned at it before pushing a couple of buttons. He held it up in the air and cursed lightly.

"I have no service. How about you?"

Paul yanked his phone from his jacket pocket and gave it a quick glance. "Nope."

"Fuck me. Can this day get any fucking worse?" Reid grumbled.

He leaned around the mini-van. "Chen, we've got a problem. There's no fucking spare. Does anyone have cell service?"

Chen and Mallorie joined them and both shook their heads after checking their cell phones.

"Son of a bitch!" Reid slammed the door shut on the mini-van. "Now what?"

The sun had set and Chen checked his watch in the growing gloom. "There was a gas station a mile or so back. We'll use their phone to call Jordan and get some help."

"And what if Will and Hannah are trying to call you?" Reid asked.

"Maybe we'll have better service at the gas station. Either way, we need to get moving."

Mallorie ducked her head into the vehicle. "Ryan? Sweetie, we need to go back to the gas station."

"I'm not leaving her." Ryan said quietly. He was still sitting on the seat, one hand stroking Constance's cold arm.

"Ryan – " Mallorie started to protest and Chen shook his head.

"Leave him." He said quietly before leaning in beside her. "We won't be long, Ryan. Alright?"

Ryan nodded distractedly as he leaned over the seat. He pulled his jacket down and studied Constance's pale face as Mallorie eased the door shut and the others walked quickly down the road.

They had hiked less than half a mile before Reid slowed to a stop. "We shouldn't have left Ryan alone, Chen."

"He'll be fine." Chen said quietly. "He's tough."

Reid shook his head. "You don't need me. I'm going to hike back and wait with Ryan. He's just a goddamn kid."

"Alright. Be careful." Chen studied the dark sky and touched the sword that was belted around his waist, before holding his hand out to Reid.

Reid shook it firmly. "You too. I'll see you soon."

* * *

Ryan pulled the flashlight from his pocket and shone it on Constance's face. He studied her pale features carefully before leaning over the seat and kissing her mouth. Her lips were cold and he closed his eyes and rested his forehead against hers before whispering, "I'll see you soon, baby."

He slid out of the van, shutting the door gently behind him, and pulled his gun out as he walked around the side of the mini-van and leaned against it. He turned and stared into the window, shining his light on Constance's face as he pressed the gun against his temple.

"I love you, baby." He whispered.

He closed his eyes and took a deep breath, his finger tightening on the trigger. After a moment, he burst into tears and lowered the gun, sliding down the side of the van to sit on the cold pavement. He continued to cry, loud wracking sobs that shook his body, as he placed his gun on the road and buried his face in his arms.

"Why so sad, young man?"

His heart jerked in his chest and he grabbed his gun and scrambled to his feet at the sound of the strange voice. He shone his flashlight into the dark and blinked at the two men standing at the front of the van. They were dressed in matching dark suits and red ties, and the younger of them shook the crease from the front of his pants as the other gave him a sympathetic look.

"Why do you cry so bitterly, my young friend?"

"Who are you?" Ryan raised his gun and pointed it at them.

"There's no need for that." The man had a thick accent and he gave his friend a brief smile before turning back to Ryan. "We won't harm you."

"Who are you?" Ryan repeated without lowering his gun.

He frowned in confusion when the younger man gave his companion an irritable look and spoke in a gruff voice. "Genug geredet, Otto. Nehmen sie das Gewehr."

"Alles zu seiner Zeit, mein Freund. Alles zu seiner Zeit." The man replied calmly.

Ryan took a step forward. "I don't know who the fuck you are or what the fuck you're saying, but you're going to walk away. Do you hear me? Unless you want a bullet in your head, just walk the fuck away."

"My name is Otto and this is Simon. What's your name?" The first man said in a friendly voice.

Ryan took another step toward them. "Are you even listening to me, Otto?"

Simon sighed loudly as Otto smiled.

"Ich habe versucht net zu sein, Simon."

With blinding speed, Otto shot forward and grabbed Ryan's wrist, twisting it harshly. Ryan screamed in pain but hung on to the gun grimly as he punched the larger man in the side with his left hand.

The man didn't even flinch and he twisted again, snapping Ryan's wrist before slamming the younger man against the side of the mini-van. The metal groaned in protest as the man drove Ryan's body into it, smashing his head against the thick side window and shattering the glass.

The gun dropped from Ryan's hand and he stared dazedly at the man holding him against the van. Otto grinned, his fangs gleaming and Ryan moaned softly as Otto peered over his shoulder into the van.

"Die Wölfin!" He said in surprise before staring at Ryan again.

"How do you know the she-wolf? Tell me." He shook him roughly and Ryan curled his lip at him.

"Fuck you!"

Otto laughed and glanced at Simon who was leaning against the van with a bored look on his face.

"Such spirit. I like it. I really should save him for the hunt, Olof will be displeased to lose such a fine warrior as this one, but I am so very hungry."

He smiled cheerfully at Ryan. "Tell me how you know the she-wolf or I will rip off your – oh, how do you say it in English – testicles? Yes, testicles. I will rip them from your body and make you eat them."

"She was my girlfriend."

Simon laughed heartily. "Was würde eine Wölfin mit einem mickrigen Menschen Du wollen?"

Otto grinned. "My friend wants to know what a Lycan was doing with one as puny as you."

"I've got a really big dick." Ryan spat impudently and Otto laughed loudly.

"Ich mag diesen Mensch, Simon."

Simon snorted and rolled his eyes as Otto grinned again at Ryan. "I was just telling my friend that I liked you. Not enough to let you go but perhaps enough to turn you. What do you think? Would you like to live forever, human?"

He shouted in surprise and pain when Ryan whipped his head forward with surprising speed and smashed his forehead against the bridge of his nose. It broke with a sickening crack and the vampire shouted again and dropped Ryan to the ground before staggering back. He cupped his gushing nose and stared in surprise at the blood on his hand before baring his fangs at Ryan.

"We killed your Lycan lover, foolish boy. And now we're going to kill you."

"You bastard!" Ryan howled in anger and shot to his feet. He threw himself at the vampire and Otto grabbed him by the throat and tossed him easily into the ditch. He sighed loudly and dusted off his jacket before pulling out a handkerchief from his pocket and pressing it against his nose.

"Humans are so annoying." He started toward the ditch, stopping when Simon spoke.

"Wo ist das Gewehr?"

Otto turned and stared at the ground behind him. "His gun?"

There was a sharp whistle and he turned to see Ryan standing in the ditch pointing his gun at him. Before he could dodge out of the way, Ryan fired and Otto felt a sharp biting pain in his chest. He looked down and grimaced, ripping at the blackened fabric of his shirt to peer at the light pulsing through his veins.

His skin was burning and he moaned in pain before falling to his knees.

"Otto?" Simon said alarm.

He held his hand up and took a few deep breaths, waiting patiently for the burning to dissipate. When it finally did, he climbed to his feet and smiled at the stunned human standing in the ditch. "You missed. You need to have better aim, my friend."

He flew forward and knocked Ryan off his feet. The man landed face first in the ditch, the gun landing a few feet away, and he shrieked with pain when his broken wrist got caught under him and grated across the hard ground. Otto lifted him to his feet and shook him like a ragdoll as Simon, a bored look on his face, pulled out his phone and punched a few buttons.

After a moment he grumbled something to Otto in German and Otto rolled his eyes. "Ja, I know there's no reception, Simon! Just play a game or something, will you? I'm busy."

With a grunt of frustration, Simon turned his back to them and bent over his phone. He chuckled happily when the dancing frogs came on to the screen and he pushed a button repeatedly, laughing again when the frogs splattered one by one.

"Kids today and their inability to be bored for even a moment." Otto said conversationally to Ryan.

He studied Ryan's throat before dipping his head and plunging his fangs into the soft flesh. Ryan grunted and struggled weakly as Otto drank deeply. After a few moments, he lifted his head and stared at him.

"I'll admit, I'm still tempted to turn you – you're rather tough for a human - but I think I'll just drain you instead. Olof will be angry if he finds out I didn't keep you for the hunt. I'll drain you and hide your body, and you'll be our little secret instead. You'll see your she-wolf soon. In fact, you'll see all of your friends. My brothers are waiting for them at the gas station. They'll capture them and hunt them in the forest, one by one, just like they did with the Lycan's companions. Think how delighted they will be when they find you waiting for them on the other side. It will be a wonderful reunion. One that will – "

He suddenly jerked wildly, his hands tightening around Ryan's arms, and Ryan lifted his head wearily and watched as Otto's skin blackened. Otto stared at Ryan with wide eyes before turning his head to stare behind him.

"Hello, motherfucker." The blond man smiled cheerfully at Otto before twisting the wooden stake further into his back. "You like the feel of my wood?"

"Simon, help..." Otto whispered before he burst into ash and blood.

Ryan crumpled to the ground and Reid started to haul him to his feet.

"Another one." Ryan whispered. "Reid, another – "

He cried out and fell to the ground as Reid was torn away from him. Simon, his face red and his fangs glistening with saliva, hissed at the big blond man as he knocked the wooden stake from his hand, wrapped his hands around his throat and lifted him into the air.

"Arschloch!" He snarled.

Reid choked and gagged as he pulled his gun from the holster around his waist. Before he could raise it, Simon ripped it from his hand and tossed it to the ground.

"Fuck you!" Reid choked out before gouging the vampire's eye with his thumb.

Simon bellowed with pain but refused to let go. Instead, he squeezed harder, grinning with satisfaction when Reid's face began to turn purple. He shook Reid happily and brought him closer to his large body.

"You're dead, human." His accent was thick and harsh and he grinned again. "I will enjoy this."

His fangs grew and he moved his hands to Reid's shoulders and bent his head toward his neck. Before he could sink his fangs in to the throbbing vein, Ryan latched on to his back like a monkey. Simon grunted in surprise as Ryan hooked one arm around his meaty throat and held tightly as his other hand wormed between Simon's body and Reid's.

"Won't miss this time, asshole." He wheezed.

There was pressure against his chest and Simon looked down to see the muzzle of the gun directly over his heart.

"Scheisse." He spoke with resigned defeat as Ryan pulled the trigger.

The blast knocked the vampire backwards and Reid landed on the ground with a hard thud. Wheezing and coughing, he staggered to his knees and crawled forward as Simon, his entire body lit up with blue fire, exploded. Ryan was lying on the ground covered in ash and blood, and Reid made a low moan when he saw the hole in his chest. The bullet had travelled through the vampire and into Ryan, and blood and blue light was pouring from the gaping wound in his chest. Reid gathered the young man into his arms and touched his shoulder lightly.

"Ryan?" He rasped. "Can you hear me?"

"Reid?" Ryan's eyelids fluttered open.

"Yeah, it's me, buddy. You're going to be okay."

Ryan's laugh turned into a cough and blood spurted from his mouth. "Got the fucker, yeah?"

"You did."

"Asshole. Killed Constance. The others are in danger."

"I know, I heard. Just stay still, Ryan." He wiped the ash from his face as Ryan stared up at him.

"I'll see Constance soon."

"Yeah, you will." Reid said softly.

"Good. I'm tired and I miss her." Ryan whispered.

He closed his eyes and Reid watched helplessly as his breathing slowed to a stop. He was about to lower his body to the ground when Ryan jerked in his arms and his eyes flew open. He took a gasping breath as he stared over Reid's shoulder and smiled happily.

"Hello, baby." He whispered.

He raised his hand and Reid, goosebumps popping up all over his body, twisted his head to look behind him. He half expected to see Constance standing behind him but there was nothing but the darkness.

He turned back as Ryan's hand dropped to the pavement with a heavy thud and the life faded from his eyes. Reid eased him to the ground and closed his eyelids.

He took a deep breath, it burned like fire in his throat, before bending and heaving Ryan over his shoulder. He placed the young man's body in the van and covered it with a blanket. He picked up his gun and Ryan's, tucking Ryan's into the back of his belt, and snagged the wooden stake from the ditch before jogging toward the gas station. He was too late to warn Chen and the others, they would have been captured by the leeches by now, but he might be able to save them.

And Selena. His mind whispered. *Selena might still be alive too.*

He picked up the pace as a small flicker of hope went through him.

Chapter 22

Chen opened the door of the gas station. The lights buzzed quietly as he stepped into the store and checked his cell phone. There was still no signal and he glanced at the others.

"Anything?"

They checked their phones and shook their heads no. As Chen started toward the counter, Mallorie wandered to the back and Paul followed her. A man, wearing jeans and a plaid shirt, stood silently behind the counter.

"Good evening." Chen said politely.

The man nodded as Chen glanced behind him. There was a second man, dressed similarly in jeans and a striped t-shirt, filling the cooler with bottles of soda and Chen nodded to him before turning back to the man behind the counter. He wore a nametag with "Billy" written across it and he studied Chen carefully. An odd shiver went down Chen's back and he had to stop himself from reaching for the sword hidden beneath his long jacket.

"I'm wondering if I can borrow your phone." He asked. "We've had some car trouble."

"The phone is for paying customers only." The man had a thick, German accent and Chen glanced again at the man in the aisle before smiling.

"I would, of course, purchase something." He placed a candy bar on the counter in front of him. "May I use your phone?"

The man shrugged and handed the cordless phone to Chen without speaking before folding his arms across his chest and leaning against the counter.

Chen held the phone to his ear before placing it back on the counter. "It doesn't seem to be working."

The man's gaze traveled over Chen's missing hand. "Service goes in and out."

"Do you have a cell phone that works?"

"Nein."

"Our little town is a long way from Germany." Chen suddenly said.

The man shrugged. "Perhaps."

Chen stared at the man. He returned his stare and Chen cursed loudly and took a step back when something dark and cold flickered in the man's eyes.

He pulled his sword free as Mallorie screamed a warning.

"Paul! Look out!"

There was a loud crash and gunfire behind him but Chen didn't turn. The man behind the counter had leaped over it and was stalking toward him, his fangs protruding from between his lips and his nails lengthening into sharp talons.

"Do you believe you can defeat me with only one hand?" The vampire hissed at him.

Adrenaline singing in his veins, Chen took another step back. He bumped into the end rack. It was piled high with cans of beans and they crashed downward, rolling crazily across the floor. The vampire in front of him kicked away a can with an impatient hiss before stalking closer.

"Lower your sword and I will not harm you." He held his hands up in a pacifying manner. "You have my word."

There was a scream of pain from Mallorie and Chen's head swivelled in her direction. He had just enough time to see the second vampire sinking its fangs into Mallorie's throat before the leech in front of him picked him up and threw him over the counter. He crashed hard into the back wall, his legs knocking the long, narrow cigarette case off the wall with a loud squeal. A grunt of pain escaped him when his stump slammed against a rack of batteries, and he fell to the floor. Packages of batteries rained down around him and as the vampire leaped on to the counter, he realized his sword was gone.

The vampire landed on him with a heavy thud, knocking him flat to the floor, as he caught the gleam of his sword just inches to his right. The vampire wrapped his fingers in Chen's hair and slammed his head against the tile floor before yanking on it viciously.

"Just a little taste before we take you to the barn, ja?" He drooled happily as he opened his mouth and his fangs lengthened. He bent his head with terrifying speed and squawked loudly when he was met by cold steel.

Chen, panting harshly, twisted his sword and shoved it further into the leech's open mouth. The tip of the sword burst through the back of the vampire's skull and it gagged loudly and scrambled to move when Chen sat up. Chen pushed the vampire on to his back and pressed both knees against its sternum.

Moving quickly, he yanked the sword from the vampire's mouth and sliced it across the leech's throat. As the sharp blade cut through its flesh like warm butter, the vampire's eyes widened, his hands drummed helplessly on the floor and blood poured from his gaping mouth. Chen pushed himself back as the vampire's head and body turned to ash and leaned against the wall. His heart was pounding, his stump was throbbing and his entire body was shaking with adrenaline.

"Paul! Are you alright?"

"Dammit! Yeah, I'm alright. I just got a mouthful of this fucker's blood and ash."

Chen took a deep breath at the sound of Mallorie and Paul's voices. A broken carton of cigarettes was pressed up against his leg and he pulled a package of cigarettes out and awkwardly ripped it open with one hand. He placed a cigarette in his mouth as Mallorie's voice rose in alarm.

"Chen! Where the hell is Chen?"

"I'm here." He called. There was the sound of footsteps and then Mallorie and Paul peered over the counter. Paul was drenched in blood and ash, and there was blood trickling down from the holes in Mallorie's throat.

"Holy shit, master! Are you okay?" Paul, wincing a little, climbed over the counter and set his sword on the floor. Mallorie holstered her gun and followed him. The two of them joined Chen, squeezing onto the floor of the narrow space.

"I'm fine."

"Fuck, those leeches were strong." Paul said. "Mallorie's bullet didn't do shit, and I was left with no choice but to stab him when he was drinking from her. I thought I was going to fucking skewer her too."

He glanced at Mallorie's ripped shirt. "Sorry about that."

"You didn't even scratch me." She fist bumped him before studying the cigarette in Chen's mouth. "I didn't know you smoked, Chen."

"I don't. Figured I'd give it a try." He shrugged.

She frowned but Paul reached over Chen's head and snagged a lighter from the display on the back counter. He shook out his own cigarette and lit it before lighting Chen's. He inhaled deeply and blew out a perfect smoke ring before tossing Mallorie the cigarette package.

Chen inhaled cautiously and Paul snickered when he coughed loudly. "Finally, something I'm better than the master at."

Chen grimaced but took another cautious inhale as Mallorie sighed and shook out her own cigarette. "When in fucking Rome, I guess."

She lit her cigarette and took a puff, coughing a little as her eyes began to water. "We're all going to die of lung cancer."

"Dying of lung cancer is the least of your worries, my pretty." A deep voice spoke above their heads.

The three of them glanced upward and Paul cursed loudly as the four vampires leaned over the counter and smiled at them.

The smallest one stared at the pool of blood and ash. "Where are Marco and Felix?"

"Did you check the bathroom?" Paul asked innocently before taking another puff of his cigarette.

Mallorie laughed and Chen's mouth twitched as the vampires scowled at them.

"Come with us, if you please." The smallest one said.

"And if we don't?" Chen asked.

"Why would you not?" The vampire gave him a quizzical look. "You're dead if you do not."

Paul, smoke drifting across his face, stared at Chen. Chen shook his head slightly and Paul's hand which had been inching toward his sword, stopped.

"Well, when you put it that way." Paul replied before stubbing his cigarette out in the pool of blood and ash. "We'd be happy to accompany you. Lead the way, bloodsuckers."

* * *

"Guten Abend. My name is Olof."

The sun had just dipped below the horizon and the vampire smiled at Mannie and the others as he entered the barn. His long dark hair was tied into a neat bun at the back of his head and his bright blue eyes glowed. He was trailed by the other vampires and Mannie counted nine in total as they stood silently in the barn and stared at the prisoners.

"I see you are finally awake." He glanced at the dark-haired vampire standing behind him. "I was afraid my brother was a little too rough when he threw you into the tree."

"I have a hard head." Mannie replied.

"Indeed. Your group is rather strong and clever for humans." Olof crouched down in front of Mannie and studied him thoughtfully. "Tell me why."

Mannie shrugged. "Maybe the humans are just weak in Germany."

Olof laughed. "I think not. In fact, we have discovered that this country is ripe for the taking. Both the humans and the vampires are pathetic, snivelling creatures."

He glanced briefly at Judd before turning back to Mannie. "When we left Germany, I told my brothers I would find us a new home. One where the women were beautiful," he smiled at Selena and Stephanie, "and the blood flowed like wine. After many months of searching, we have finally found it. I had no idea what riches there were across the ocean. Now that I have discovered it, we will take what we want. It is our birthright, after all."

"Bullshit!" Tyrone burst out. "You assholes aren't any better than the asshole leeches we already have. We kick their asses and we'll kick yours."

A fleeting look of annoyance crossed Olof's face. "The young are so rude now. Do you not agree, my friend?"

"I am not your friend." Mannie said softly.

Olof shrugged. "Fair enough."

"Where are our friends?" Mannie asked.

Olof smiled. "I'm afraid your friends are dead. My brothers and I hunted them last evening. I'll confess, it was the best hunt we've had in a while. The young ones were rather cunning and fought bitterly to the very end. So many of the humans we hunt give up too easily. It takes the fun out of it. Isn't that right, Lars?"

"Ja, Olof." The vampire answered immediately.

"You still haven't told me why your group was in the woods attacking the vampires." Olof said to Mannie.

"We didn't attack them. We were just having a bush party. They attacked us and we defended ourselves."

"Indeed. And doing a rather remarkable job at it." Olof snapped his fingers and one of the vampires, he had short red hair and his face was covered in freckles, crossed to a stall. He opened it and Mannie stared silently at the contents. The stall was filled with purses and backpacks, jackets, shoes, and a few articles of clothing. Suitcases were stacked neatly to one side and in front of it all were their weapons.

"Wooden stakes, guns with bullets filled with ultraviolet light, and," he paused again and perused Alex's face carefully, "an actual sword."

There was silence and Olof sighed softly. "Odd items to bring to a bush party."

"Are they?" Mannie asked. "We don't think so."

Anger flickered across Olof's face and he reached out lightning quick and slapped Mannie hard across the face. "Listen to me, you ignorant little worm, I have killed more humans over my lifetime than I can remember. I will not hesitate to kill you and your friends if you do not tell me what I want to know. Do you understand?"

Mannie shrugged and Olof snarled at him and grabbed him by the hair. He yanked his head forward and pointed toward the stall. "Do you see all of that? We have been here but a few short months and that stall is nearly filled with the belongings of the people we have killed. Your belongings will join them shortly. Do not doubt that.

Refusing to tell me what I want to know will not lengthen your lifespan."

"Go ahead and do it then, you blood-sucking scumbag." Mannie spat in his face. "You keep talking about killing me so just do it already. I haven't got all fucking night!"

Olof's face reddened with rage and he shoved Mannie back before standing and picking up Alex's sword from the stall. He held it lightly, studying it in the dim light before walking toward Stephanie.

"I will cut pieces of flesh from this pretty little girl until she's screaming and begging for mercy. I will not stop until you tell me what I want to know."

He held the sword against Stephanie's leg and smiled at Mannie. "I know you're hiding something. This brown beauty has been bitten before as has that one." He pointed at Luther. "My brothers and I can smell it on them so we know you are not unfamiliar with our kind. Tell me what I want to know."

He pressed the tip of his sword into Stephanie's leg and the young woman groaned hoarsely when blood bloomed through her jeans.

"Don't you tell him a fucking thing, Mannie!" She suddenly snapped defiantly.

"That's my girl." Tyrone said approvingly. Lars slapped him across the head and Tyrone grunted with pain as Olof shook his head.

"Ahh, the bravery of youth. You're a stupid girl. Brave but stupid." He raised the sword and held it over Stephanie's ankle. "This might hurt, my sweet."

"Wait!" Mannie shouted as Olof brought the sword down in a whistling arc. He stopped it just above Stephanie's ankle and smiled at Mannie.

"Ja?"

"We hunt vampires, okay? We hunt them and kill them."

"Remarkable." Olof grinned at the other vampires. "How many hunters do you have?"

"Just what you see." Mannie said bitterly. "A few of us were bitten and we decided to do something about it."

"Where did you learn the technology for the bullets?" The redheaded vampire suddenly asked.

"Good question, Klaus." Olof said approvingly. "Well?" He stared expectantly at Mannie.

"Those two are fucking geniuses." Mannie nodded to the twins and Olof rolled his eyes.

"I find that hard to believe."

"Why? Because we're black? Fuck you, you racist motherfucker." Luther said with disgust.

Olof ignored him as he stroked Stephanie's leg with the sword. "Where do you find the money for your hunting trips?"

"What's it to you?" Luther asked. "You broke or something?"

"Answer the question." Olof said sharply.

"We got a silent partner. She's a millionaire and she was more than happy to share the wealth after you assholes turned her parents and they tried to suck her dry." Tyrone replied.

"Interesting." Olof replied.

He dropped the sword in the stall and stared silently at the other leeches. "We will not hunt all of them tonight. We were too greedy last night and hunted too many at once."

There was some low grumbling and Olof held up his hand. "Brothers, you will do as I say."

The other vampires nodded immediately and Mannie watched in stunned silence when a few of them gave short bows to the vampire leader.

"Tonight, Andreas and Gunther hunt. Choose, brothers." Olof gestured to the prisoners and the two vampires walked back and forth in front of them for a few minutes.

Gunther pointed to Stephanie and she stared defiantly at him for a moment before bowing her head. Mannie could see tears dripping down her face and he spoke quickly.

"She's weak. Hunt me, instead."

Gunther shook his head. "Ich mag wie sie aussieht."

"Ja, you never enjoy working for your meals." The one named Klaus spoke in broken and halting English and Gunther glared at him as the other vampires laughed loudly.

"Sei still, Klaus!" Gunther snarled.

"Enough!" Olof said when Klaus snarled back. "Andreas make your choice."

"The brown woman is mine." Klaus said quickly when Andreas paused in front of Selena.

Andreas laughed and moved on before stopping in front of Tyrone.

"This one." Andreas said and Luther gave his twin a sick look of fear.

"It'll be fine, Luther." Tyrone said quietly. "I'll kick his ass."

"Excellent." Olof clapped his hands together. "Send the girl out first."

Lars sliced through the ropes around Stephanie's wrists with his fingernails and hauled the girl to her feet. He dragged her to the end of the barn and pushed open the small door. Ahead of them was the forest and Lars petted Stephanie's hair gently.

"You have a half hour before Gunther comes looking for you. Head into the forest, my pet." He said. "Or toward the road, it matters not. Very few cars travel this way and your hope of finding help before Gunther finds you is slim."

He smiled at her again. "Might I suggest that you do stick to the woods? More places to hide, right? Perhaps you will get lucky and find a warm, safe hiding spot until the sun rises."

Stephanie swallowed thickly and stared at the others.

"It'll be okay, honey." Selena said softly. "You can do this."

Stephanie nodded and glanced over at Tyrone when he called her name.

"I'll find you and we'll kill them together, alright?"

"Alright." She said softly. She slipped out the door and into the trees. Lars closed the door and headed toward Tyrone.

"Wait a few minutes, Lars." Olof said. "No doubt they will search each other out but let's not make it too easy for them."

Lars nodded as Olof suddenly frowned. "Where are Otto and Simon?"

"They headed into town. The human has our money for the last batch of cars."

"And Marco and Felix?"

"The store." Lars replied.

"Ja, I know. Why are they not back? I told them to close early tonight. Go and fetch them." Olof said impatiently.

Four of the vampires left the barn and the others waited patiently until Olof nodded to Lars. Lars cut through the ropes and lifted Tyrone to his feet.

Tyrone smiled faintly at Luther. "I'll be back to save your ass, dickhead."

Luther, his mouth trembling, nodded. "Be careful, numbnuts."

"Fuck careful." Tyrone replied and followed Lars to the door. Without looking at his brother or the others, he left the barn and disappeared into the forest.

Olof smiled at Mannie and the others. "Shall we make a wager on how quickly Gunther and Andreas kill the young ones?"

Chapter 23

Flanked by the vampires, Chen, Mallorie and Paul entered the decrepit old barn. Mallorie inhaled sharply when she saw Mannie and the others sitting on the floor but shut her mouth with a snap when Chen stepped discreetly on her foot. A large and powerful-looking vampire, his hair pulled into a neat bun, approached them.

"What's this? More?"

"Ja." One of the vampires grunted.

"How interesting. Lars, three more guests have arrived." The vampire smiled at Chen.

"My name is Olof. What happened to your hand?"

Chen didn't reply and the vampire leaned closer. "Come now, don't be shy."

One of the vampires still flanking them, muttered something in German before handing over their swords, Mallorie's gun and four wooden stakes."

Olof, a mild look of surprise on his face, turned to the one named Lars. "More swords. And they killed Marco and Felix — two of my best. Where do these humans come from?"

When Lars only shrugged, Olof sighed. "Tie them up with the others."

Andreas, his face a mask of excitement, approached Olof. "Olof?"

"Ja." Olof waved his hand impatiently. "Go, enjoy your hunt."

With a hiss of excitement, Andreas and Gunther ran out of the barn.

As the vampires did as he asked, Olof squatted in front of Mannie. "You lied to me. You said these were the only people in your little vampire slaying group and yet, here are three more."

"I've never seen those assholes in my life." Mannie replied.

Olof snarled and raked his nails across Mannie's face. Blood welled up and flowed down his cheeks, soaking into his t-shirt as Mannie grunted with pain.

"Do you honestly expect me to believe that these humans with their swords and their bullets filled with sunlight are not a part of your group?" Olof sneered. "I am not the fool you believe me to be, human. Now, how many more are out there? Tell me before I lose my patience completely and tear off your head."

Mannie shrugged. "I can't remember."

Snarling, Olof grabbed Mannie around the throat. Before he could rip his head off, Chen spoke loudly.

"There are only two more of us. We broke down not far from the gas station when we were looking for our friends. They're waiting for us at the van."

Olof, his eyes glowing, stared at Chen for a few moments before releasing Mannie. Mannie coughed and gagged, gasping in air through his throbbing throat as Olof stood and approached Chen.

"If you're lying to me, I'll take your other hand."

"I'm not lying." Chen said calmly.

Lars spoke quietly in German and Olof shook his head. "Not yet. Their friends will not be expecting them back yet. We will finish the hunt of the young ones, and then you and Horst can retrieve their friends and bring them to the barn."

Klaus cleared his throat loudly and Olof stared expectantly at him. "What is it, Klaus?"

"There are more, Olof. We can hunt more, ja?" He said in broken English. "The brown one, perhaps?"

Olof rolled his eyes. "You are too impatient, Klaus. Would you rather not wait until tomorrow night?"

Klaus shook his head and spoke in rapid German, glancing anxiously at Selena.

"He is right, brother." Lars said to Olof. The longer we wait, the more weak the humans grow. Let him have his fun with her tonight when she is still strong."

"Fine." Olof replied. "Release her into the woods. Give her a twenty minute start."

"No!" Mannie shouted. "I'll go! She's weak! Send me out instead."

They ignored him and Lars sliced through Selena's bonds before lifting her to her feet and herding her toward the door. Klaus slapped her on the ass as saliva dripped from his fangs and down his chin.

Selena, her face pale and her small body trembling, refused to look at him. She smiled briefly at the others, her eyes traveling over each of them as she stood just outside the doorway, before Lars shoved her harshly in the back. She staggered forward, nearly falling before regaining her balance, and flipped the vampire the bird. She jogged into the forest and the darkness swallowed her.

* * *

Reid, his large body hidden behind the oak tree, watched as the leeches marched Chen and the others into the barn. He slammed his fist against the tree, wincing when it sent a throb of pain across his freshly-healed break, and cursed under his breath. If he had just been five minutes earlier, he could have warned them. Now he was on his fucking own with at least four vampires, probably more, guarding his friends.

"Think, you asshole." He muttered to himself. He turned and scanned the forest behind him. Hannah and Will were still tracking the twins' scents and he had a pretty good idea that it would lead them here. If the twins were still alive he was nearly certain that they were in that barn.

The back door of the barn flew open and two vampires, dressed in dark suits and red ties, ran out. He shrank back behind the tree as, hissing loudly, the leeches bounded into the forest.

"Shit." He muttered again. It had been too dark for him to tell if they had been two of the leeches that had captured Chen and the others. They all looked alike in their dark suits. It didn't matter, he decided. He couldn't sit here with his thumb up his ass any longer. He needed to make a plan and -

His breath caught in his throat when the back door of the barn opened again and Selena appeared in the doorway. His heart stopped and then started up again in a fierce banging rhythm that stole his breath. Relief flooded through him in a giant wave that made his knees weak. She was alive.

He scowled angrily when the vampire shoved her in the back. She stumbled and nearly fell and he bit back his harsh bark of laughter when she turned and flipped her middle finger at the leech. She disappeared into the forest and he waited, every nerve screaming at him to go after her, until the vampire closed the door of the barn.

He took off in the direction that Selena had ran, his heart thudding, and a huge grin on his face. He darted around a tree and hissed her name, squinting in the darkness as he ran. Where the hell was she?

* * *

"Will? Wait."

"For what?" He gave her an impatient look as he jogged through the trees. "There's no time to fuck around, Hannah."

"I know." She took his arm and pulled him to a stop. "Are you alright?"

"Am I alright?" He scowled at her. "Am I alright? Well, let's see –my pack has been kidnapped and may or may not be dead. Either way, I'm deliberately leading my mate into danger when every part of me is screaming to protect her. There's a bunch of – of super vampires roaming around who are strong enough to kill a Lycan and – "

His voice broke and he turned away from her, staring into the trees as she wrapped her arms around his waist and hugged him tightly. "I'm sorry for your loss."

"I've known her since I was a child." He said hoarsely. "She joined the program because of me and I'm the reason she's dead."

"That isn't true." She said firmly. "Constance was an adult and she made her choice. You're not responsible for her death, honey. Don't go down that path."

He was silent and she inhaled deeply. They had been running steadily for nearly half an hour. The twins' scents were growing stronger, Tyrone's in particular, and she was starting to smell Selena's as well.

"We're getting closer." She said.

He nodded. "We need to keep moving."

"I know." She rested her forehead in the middle of his broad back. "I love you, Will."

"I love you too." He turned and kissed her firmly on the mouth before squeezing her hand. "Be careful with these leeches, alright? Use your swords to fight. You're doing well with the Lycan changes but your swords are still your most powerful weapons."

"I will. We should – "

A scream shattered the quiet night air and Hannah froze before pulling her swords free. Will was already starting to shift and as his clothes tore from his body, he growled, "Stay in your human form."

She nodded as he shifted fully and bounded ahead of her. She ran quickly but she was no match for his wolf and after only a minute or so he had disappeared into the darkness. She found her mate's scent easily and increased her pace but staggered to a stop when another stronger scent drifted to her on the wind.

"Tyrone?" She whispered. His scent was now impossible to ignore and, abandoning her chase after Will, she turned and followed it.

* * *

Stephanie winced as the root dug into her ass, and shifted into a more comfortable position. She clutched the broken branch a little closer to her chest before resting her forehead on her knees. She was ridiculously afraid and she was almost positive the leech would smell her fear.

She clawed up a handful of dirt and smeared it across her face, upper chest and arms. They were already black with dirt but she rubbed more in anyway. She had ran for nearly twenty minutes, until she had a stitch in her side, and then looked for a hiding place.

Hiding was her only chance. She went through the training, she was stronger and faster, but without weapons she didn't have a chance against these vampires. If she wanted to see the sun again, she had to hide.

She had stumbled on to the hollow tree by chance and immediately squirmed inside, ignoring the uneasy voice in her head that questioned what else might be lurking inside of it. It had turned out to be the skeleton of what she thought might be a squirrel and a disgusting amount of animal droppings.

Which you're currently rubbing into your face, her inner voice moaned. *You're going to catch all sorts of diseases, Steph!*

Fuck that. She'd rather have a hundred diseases than be the leech's meal. Besides, if she did make it out of this fucking mess, the first thing she'd do was bathe in a tub of disinfectant. Hell, she'd –

A branch cracked and her breath caught in her throat. She shrank backward, trying to keep away from the soft moonlight shining just outside the tree, and listened carefully. It was hard to hear over the rapid pounding of

her heart, and she tried to will it to slow down as she bit
her bottom lip and cocked her head.

There was the soft rustling of leaves but nothing else and
her body relaxed a fraction. Just an animal scuttling in
the dark, she was almost certain. The leech hadn't –

A hand, pale with nails that were long and sharp, reached
in and slid around her wrist. The leech yanked her out
through the narrow opening. She grunted in pain when
her head connected with a solid thump against the tree,
and screamed in breathless terror when the vampire
threw her to the ground. He straddled her and she stared
fearfully at him as he grinned.

"Hello, kleines mädchen. Trying to hide, were you? You
needn't have bothered. I can smell your fear." Andreas
said happily. "The others were harder to hunt. They
banded together and tried to make simple weapons. It
was fun to kill them one by one. It is a shame you make
this so easy for me."

His fangs lengthened and he opened his mouth wide as he
slowly and teasingly bent his head toward her.

Stephanie screamed shrilly, the sound echoing through
the forest, and stabbed Andreas in the cheek with the
broken branch she still held in her hand. Andreas
bellowed in surprise and pain and jerked away from her.
She scrambled to her feet, a moan of dismay slipping out
when she realized the leech was already on his feet and
reaching for the branch. He pulled it free of his flesh with
a wet, sucking sound, and she gagged when putrid

smelling blood poured from the wound and coated his lower jaw and throat.

"Not bad for a little girl." He gargled through the blood as he tossed the stick to the ground. Already the wound was starting to heal over and as he grinned at her, blood coating his lips and fangs, she turned and fled.

Don't look back. Don't look back. She chanted repeatedly to herself even as she heard the vampire chuckle softly behind her. The leech would catch her, he was incredibly fast and strong, but she refused to give in. She refused to –

There was a harsh growling in front of her and her eyes widened as the giant gray wolf appeared in the darkness. He was running straight toward her and, as he crouched and began to leap, she instinctively dropped to her knees and flung her body backward. She slid across the ground, wincing when her shirt rucked up around her shoulders and the bare flesh of her back was scraped by pine needles and stones. She stared upward in numb wonder at the thick gray fur on the wolf's belly as he sailed over her and hit the vampire with a harsh thud.

She slid to a stop and flipped to her belly, breathing harshly and staring wide-eyed at the wolf and the leech fighting before her. Despite his surprise at the sudden appearance of the Lycan, Andreas had recovered quickly and Stephanie struggled to her feet as he jabbed his long nails into the Lycan's side. The wolf howled in pain as Andreas threw his other hand over his throat to protect it from the Lycan's snapping jaws.

She searched frantically for a weapon as the Lycan fought to keep the struggling, hissing Andreas pinned to the ground. She pried a rock out of the ground and ran toward them just as the Lycan made a snarl of frustration and rage and bit the leech's fingers off. The vampire screamed as blood jetted out from the stumps and the Lycan snarled again before latching on to Andrea's exposed neck. He bit through the flesh with a loud crunch and Andreas' cries weakened as the wolf burrowed deeper into his pale skin.

With a final growl, the Lycan tore Andreas' head from his body as Stephanie staggered backward, tripped over her own feet, and fell to the ground with a harsh thud. She dropped the rock as the vampire burst into ash and the Lycan turned to face her. His face was dripping in blood and a shiver of fear went down her back as the wolf crept closer. His eyes glowed softly and he growled deep in his throat before suddenly shifting.

Will, blood dripping down his side from the five small wounds just below his ribcage, wiped the blood off his face and knelt in front of the dirty, violently-shaking woman. "Stephanie? Are you alright?"

"Yes, sir." She whispered.

"Where are the others? Are they alive?"

She nodded and swallowed thickly. "Some of us. They're keeping us in a barn, sir. They – they're hunting us. These vampires are – they're different."

"I know." Will said grimly. "Can you walk?"

She nodded and he helped her to her feet as she gave him a startled look. "Tyrone is out here too! We have to find him! There's another vampire hunting him. Please, Will – I mean, sir – we have to find him!"

Will turned his back to her and inhaled deeply. "We go this way. I'm going to shift and you're going to ride on my back. Do you understand?"

"I – I don't think – I mean, are you sure?"

"Yes!" He snapped impatiently. "Quickly, Stephanie!"

He shifted and lay down on the ground, barking softly at her. With a nervous look at him, Stephanie climbed gingerly on to his back, gasping in alarm and clinging tightly to his fur when he leaped to his feet and ran swiftly through the forest.

* * *

Tyrone paused and held his breath. He listened intently and then forced himself to keep moving when the faint sound didn't repeat itself. He needed to find Stephanie, the two of them had a better chance together than alone, but he had been walking for nearly twenty minutes and there was no sign of her. Of course, it was so fucking dark he could have stumbled past her and not even known it. Fuck, he needed to –

A shrill scream sent goosebumps shuddering across his flesh and, muttering a quiet curse, he turned and ran in the direction of the scream. He was certain that had been Stephanie, who else could it be, and he vaulted over a fallen log and landed neatly on this feet before continuing on.

As he dodged around a thick tree, a shadow flickered and there was a brief flash of red before he ran full speed into the leech's outstretched arm. He bounced off of it, pain radiating through his chest, and landed on his back in the dirt. He rubbed his chest as Gunther laughed delightedly and straightened his tie.

"Guten Abend, dark one. It's a lovely night for a walk, isn't it?"

Tyrone climbed to his feet and gave the large vampire an impudent look. "Took you long enough to find me, dickface."

The smile dropped from Gunther's face. "What did you just call me?"

"Dick. Face." Tyrone enunciated slowly. "You don't look that bright so I'll explain. It means your face looks like a dick."

Gunther hissed and Tyrone gave a strangled grunt of surprise when the leech's hand shot out and closed around his neck. He squeezed viciously and lifted the teenager into the air.

"Do not treat me like a fool." He snapped before tossing Tyrone like a rag doll.

Tyrone slammed face-first into a tree and tumbled to the ground. His head was ringing and blood was trickling from a cut on his lip but he staggered upright and grinned at Gunther. "What? Don't like hearing the truth, you fucking mosquito?"

Gunther snarled and shot toward Tyrone. He lifted the teen again by the throat and bared his fangs at him. "I will tear your throat out."

Tyrone, his eyes bulging, pulled at the leech's cold hand. Gunther set him on his feet and relaxed his grip. Tyrone pulled in a ragged, coughing breath, before eyeing the vampire.

"You're nothing but a Dracula wannabe. Your bloodsucking friends back at the barn think you're a dickface. Hell, your mama thinks you're a dickface. She told me that right before she wrapped her lips around *my* dick and – "

Gunther screamed with rage and backhanded Tyrone across the face. He flew backwards over the fallen log and disappeared. Gunther, breathing heavily, straightened his tie again and strode toward the log before leaping easily over it.

"I am going to kill you slowly. You will beg me for mercy before I am – "

He paused and stared blankly at the empty ground.

"Was ist das?" He muttered softly. "Do you think hiding will save your life, dummer junge? I can smell you."

He inhaled deeply and his steps faltered. "Eine andere Wölfin?"

There was a flicker of movement to his left and he whirled, his eyes widening in surprise at the dark-haired woman standing before him.

"Hello, asshole." She said softly. She was holding two swords and the boy was standing behind her with a look of triumph on his face.

"Oh, dickface - you're in for a world of hurt now." He said gleefully.

Gunther curled his upper lip at him and took a step back when the woman growled deep in her chest and bared sharp fangs at him. Her eyes were glowing a soft jade and he could see her sharp nails curled around the handle of her swords.

"You think I am afraid of you?" He asked. "I have killed many Lycans. Bigger and stronger ones than you."

The woman grinned at him, a cold and feral smile that sent a trickle of fear down his back. She took a deep breath and her smile widened. "You are afraid of me, leech. I can smell it."

She raised her swords and nodded to him. "Begin."

Fear was rushing through him now, strong and unpleasant and utterly foreign to him. There was something about the Lycan, something about the way she held her swords and stared so fearlessly at him, that sent shivers running down his spine. He knew with absolute clarity that she would slice him apart. For the first time in centuries, Gunther turned to flee from his enemy.

A gray wolf stood behind him. He stared wide-eyed at one of the biggest Lycans he'd ever seen as the wolf snapped its teeth and lowered its head before stalking toward him on stiff legs.

"Wait." Gunther held his hands out. "Wait, I can be of assistance to you. I can – "

His back arched as the cold steel slid into his flesh. He stared numbly at the dirty, dark-haired girl standing next to the Lycan before the she-wolf wound her hand in his short hair and yanked his head back.

"You're so weak." She whispered into his ear as her blade pierced his heart.

Hannah pulled her sword free as the vampire turned to ash. She turned and tugged Tyrone into her embrace.

"Are you okay, honey?"

"Yeah. I had it all under control." Tyrone's voice was muffled against her throat as he hugged her fiercely.

"Really? Were you planning on insulting him to death, Tyrone?" Hannah said dryly.

Tyrone laughed shakily and winced when she touched the cut on his lip. "Where's your brother?"

"At the barn. They're hunting us."

There was a soft pop as Will shifted and Tyrone nodded to him. "Hey, wolf boy. I'd hug you but you're naked and I don't want you to get the wrong idea."

"Shut up, kid." Will said affectionately as Stephanie pushed past him and threw her arms around Tyrone.

"Tyrone!"

Tyrone hugged her back before wrinkling his nose. "Fuck, Steph. You fucking reek. What the hell, girl? Were you bathing in shit?"

"I was trying to hide my scent!" She glared at him and smacked him hard on the back.

He flinched. "Careful, girl, I just got my ass kicked, remember?"

"Yeah, I remember." Her face softened and she hugged him again as Hannah gave them an impatient look.

"C'mon, you two. We need to get to that barn. Stay quiet and keep your eyes open."

Will shifted to his wolf form and Hannah caressed his large head briefly. Stephanie took Tyrone's hand and he squeezed it reassuringly as they followed Will and Hannah toward the others.

Chapter 24

Klaus sat in the tree and watched as the woman with the mass of curly dark hair walked quietly past him. He grinned when she bent and picked up a fallen branch. She tested its weight in her hand, and studied the end of it before holding it tightly and moving forward.

There was a faint scream and the woman froze like a frightened deer. It was almost impossible to tell what section of the forest the scream had come from, and Klaus shifted slightly and smiled again. At least one of his brothers had been successful in his hunt. These humans might be more skilled than others they had taken but in the end, they were still only humans. They would fight and claw for their lives but his kind would win. They always won.

The woman was almost out of his sight and he suddenly scowled. His brother had found his prey and drank his fill but if he stumbled on to Klaus' prey, he would not hesitate to take her blood as well. They had lived and hunted together for centuries but there were no rules when it came to their prey. First come, first serve, was their motto.

He leaped silently to the ground and ran. He passed by the woman in a blur of speed, the wind from his passing kicked up her hair, and she whirled around to look behind her as he concealed himself behind a tree. She studied the darkness for a moment before turning back around.

"I know you're out there, leech." She spoke loudly and, he realized with a grudging respect, without fear and he stepped out from behind the tree and into the moonlight.

"Guten Abend, lovely one."

Selena took a deep breath. Oddly enough she wasn't afraid. She was going to die tonight at the hands of the vampire standing before her but, for the first time since she joined the recruit program and began to hunt, she felt no fear. There was only one thought beating in her head like an insistent drum.

You should have told Reid you loved him.

Yeah, she should have. She did love him, had been in love with him for the last month, and she should have just told him the truth and damn the consequences. He would have run screaming but at least she wouldn't be feeling such regret now.

"I am eager to taste you. Your blood calls to me so strongly." Klaus said softly. "Do not be afraid of death, my pet. You will live on through me for all of eternity."

She closed her eyes and pictured Reid's face in her mind as she waited for the leech to stop his yapping and attack her. She wished she could see Reid one last time, hear his deep voice and feel the touch of his warm hands.

"Hello, sweetheart."

A smile crossed her face. She could almost hear his voice beside her.

"Who's your new friend?"

Her eyes flew open and she stared in silent shock at the man standing next to her.

"Reid?" She whispered.

"Miss me, sweetheart?" He grinned at her.

"What – how?" She felt extraordinarily stupid as she stared at him. He was covered in ash and blood, fresh bruises were rising on his throat, and he looked like he'd been through hell and back but he had a gun in one hand and a wooden stake in the other.

He glanced briefly at Klaus, looking him up and down with barely-hidden disdain. "You should know that I'm in one fuck of a bad mood, fanger."

The vampire stared at him in numb silence. He seemed to have been completely disarmed by the sudden appearance of the large blond man and his eyes drifted to the gun in Reid's hand as he turned back to Selena.

"I didn't think it was fair that you got to have all the fun." His voice was hoarse and raspy and he patted the gun in his waistband. "I brought you a gun."

"Who are you? Where did you – "

Klaus stuttered to a stop as Reid waved his gun at him.

"Just give me a fucking minute, okay? It's been a long fucking day, two of your motherfucking friends have already tried to kill me, and I have something important to say to the woman standing beside me. So, just shut your fucking mouth."

He turned back to Selena, ignoring the vampire completely, as Klaus' mouth dropped open.

"Selena, I love you. I know this was just supposed to be two adults having a good time and nothing more but I fucking love you, alright?"

"Reid, I – "

"Enough!" Klaus shouted. He raced toward the humans with deadly speed. There was sudden pain in his chest and he stumbled to a stop as a curious feeling of warmth pulsed through his body.

He stared at the two humans in front of him. They were both holding guns, the barrels smoking, and they lowered them as he stared down at his chest. The warmth was increasing, becoming an excruciating, fiery burn, and he clawed open his suit jacket and dress shirt. Blood and bright blue light poured steadily from the two holes in his chest and he touched them gently before collapsing to his knees.

The humans were speaking, their voices seeming to come from a great distance, and he strained to hear.

"Nice shot, sweetheart. I think mine was the money shot though."

"Bullshit, Reid. We both hit him in the heart."

The blond man laughed as the edges of Klaus' vision began to darken. He tried to speak, tried to scream his pain, but liquid fire was pulsing through his veins and he could only make a soft, gasping moan before the fire consumed him completely.

Reid stared at the pile of ash and blood before snorting derisively. "Wanker."

"Wanker?" Selena arched her eyebrow at him and he shrugged.

"I'm trying out some new insults. There's only so many ways you can call someone an asshole."

Her laughter had an edge of hysteria, and he reached out and pulled her into his embrace. He kissed her lightly on the mouth and rested his forehead against hers. "I love you, sweetheart."

"I love you too." She whispered.

"You're not just saying that because you're grateful I saved your life, are you?" He grinned at her and then yelped when she knocked him to the ground and threw herself on top of him.

"No, I love you, you jackass. And I would have been just fine. I had that vampire right where I wanted him." She said tartly.

"Yeah, that stick you were carrying looked pretty damn dangerous." He replied.

She pressed her mouth down on his, kissing him with an almost frantic, desperate need. He opened his mouth and she slid her tongue in, stroking his with firm strokes as he reached down and squeezed her small ass.

"You sure know how to thank a guy for saving your life." He murmured against her mouth.

"Shut up, Reid." She whispered before kissing him back.

He dropped his gun and squeezed her ass with both hands, pushing her against him as they kissed deeply.

"Jesus, get a fucking room, you two."

They broke apart, staring up in surprise at the Lycan and the humans standing above them.

"Vampires everywhere and you're sucking tongues in the middle of the forest." Tyrone rolled his eyes as Selena jumped to her feet and threw herself at Hannah.

The two women hugged tightly as Reid stood and clapped Tyrone on the back before nodding at the wolf. "Hey, furball."

Will growled at him, baring his teeth. Reid grinned and gave Stephanie a quick hug.

"Are you alright, honey?" Hannah scanned Selena up and down anxiously.

Selena nodded. "I'm fine. Very glad to see you guys."

Hannah hugged her again as Will barked softly.

"I know." Hannah replied. She studied the others solemnly. "It's going to take all of us to save our friends. Are you ready?"

They nodded and she gave them a confident smile. "Good. Listen closely, here's what we're going to do."

* * *

"It is taking them longer than usual." Lars remarked quietly.

Olof nodded. "Ja."

"Perhaps we should send a few more."

"There is no need. Our brothers are skilled hunters, Lars. The humans are no match for them and you know that."

When Lars didn't reply, Olof turned and studied him carefully. "What is it?"

"I have a bad feeling."

Olof laughed. "A bad feeling? We are immortals, Lars. There is no other creature, human or otherwise, stronger than us. What could you possibly have a bad feeling about?"

Lars shrugged. "I don't know. I just think these humans are – "

His voice was drowned out by the loud howl of a Lycan. The vampires stiffened and the other four joined Lars and Olof in the middle of the barn.

"Olof?" A short, gray-haired vampire spoke quietly. "Did you hear that?"

"Of course I did, Horst!" Olof snapped. "It is right outside our door."

"What do we do?"

"What do you mean?" Olof replied impatiently. "We destroy the Lycan, whoever it is."

Without waiting for the others, he swept toward the back door of the barn. He threw it open and marched into the night. The others gave each other uneasy looks before following him.

Olof stared at the three humans and the Lycan standing at the edge of the woods. He studied the swords in Hannah's hands and gave Lars a look of disbelief.

"More humans with swords. Who are these people?"

"She is no human, Olof." Lars replied.

Olof inhaled deeply. "You are right, brother."

He took a step toward the woman, ignoring the large Lycan's growl. "What need does a Lycan have for swords?"

"We're here for our friends. Give them to us unharmed, and we'll let you live." The woman replied.

Olof cocked his head at her. "Is that true?"

The woman hesitated, a brief smile flickering across her face, before shaking her head. "No. We're going to slice off your heads and watch you burn."

Olof laughed cheerfully. "How fascinating you are with your swords and your pathetic threats. I was going to kill you but I've changed my mind. I think I'll keep you as my pet dog."

The Lycan standing next to her howled loudly and the woman rested one sword against her leg before placing her hand on his broad back. Olof rolled his eyes. "Obviously I can't keep both you and your mate as pets but his fur will make a warm pelt for my bed. What are your names?"

When they didn't reply he smiled warmly at them. "Come now. I would know the names of those who would take my head."

The woman shrugged. "I'm Hannah and this is Will."

The large blond man in the group stepped forward and bowed. "I'm Reid. Nice to meet you, asshole. Has anyone ever told you that you look ridiculous in those suits?"

"Charming." Olof said dryly. "You'll be the first to die."

"What?" Reid said innocently. He stepped back next to Selena and put his arm around her slender waist. "Why am I always the guy these bloodsucking wankers threaten to kill first, sweetheart?"

"Maybe because you insult their fashion choices." Selena suggested.

"You'd think they'd *want* to know when they look ridiculous." Reid shrugged.

Olof gave him a dismissive look and turned his gaze to Hannah. "My name is Olof and these are my brothers, Lars, Horst, Gregor - "

"We don't care." Hannah interrupted. "Release our friends – now."

Olof sighed and crossed his arms over his chest. "I see you have rescued your brown-skinned friend from Klaus but where are your young ones?"

A look of pain flashed across Hannah's face.

Olof grinned happily. "Tell me, she-wolf. Don't be shy."

"They're dead." She suddenly snapped.

"How sad, but not surprising. Andreas and Gunther are excellent hunters."

"Were."

"I'm sorry?" Olof arched his eyebrow at her.

"I said they *were* excellent hunters. They're dead. We killed them and it was surprisingly easy."

Reid held up his hand. "Speaking of dead - you aren't missing a couple other friends, are you? They were about this tall, spoke German, wore suits like yours."

Gregor squeezed Olof's arm. "Otto? Simon?"

Olof shook him off as Reid nodded. "Pretty sure I heard one of them ask for Simon when I put that stake through his heart."

"Otto ünd Simon konnen nicht tot sein." Gregor whispered.

Reid nodded again. "Oh they certainly can be dead, my pale-faced friend. If you'd like, we can go for a little stroll and I'll show you the pile of ash."

Selena stared up at him. "You speak German?"

"I do." Reid grinned.

"When did you learn German?"

"College maybe? I don't really remember. Meth's a hell of a drug, Selena." Reid said cheerfully.

"You smoked meth!" Selena nearly shouted.

"No, I'm just kidding. But I did smoke pot. A lot of pot. Seriously. I'm not saying I grew some plants in the closet of my dorm but I'm not saying I didn't either." Reid wiggled his eyebrows at her.

"Enough!" Olof hissed. He turned to his brothers. "I will take the she-wolf, and Lars will take her mate. The four of you capture the humans. I want them alive."

He bared his fangs at Hannah as the other vampires rushed forward.

Chapter 25

"Do you think that was Will?" Paul asked Chen.

The Asian man nodded. "It sounded like him."

"We need to help him." Alex yanked at the ropes.

Paul scowled. "We need something to cut them. Something to – "

The front doors of the barn eased open and Luther made a harsh barking sob when Tyrone and Stephanie slipped inside.

"God, Luther. Keep it together, ya fuckin' baby." Tyrone rolled his eyes as he opened the door of the stall and grabbed Chen's sword. Stephanie picked up Paul's sword and knelt beside him as Tyrone crouched next to Luther.

"Lean forward, Luther." Tyrone pushed on Luther's back and slid the sword behind him. He sliced through the rope connecting him to the metal hoop in the wall before carefully cutting the rope around Luther's wrists.

Luther groaned with relief and rubbed at his wrists for a moment before suddenly grabbing Tyrone and hugging him tightly.

Tyrone hugged him back, clearing his throat roughly, before pushing away. "God, you're such a pansy, Luther."

"Fuck you, Tyrone."

"There was another loud howl from outside as Luther stood and limped to the stall. He grabbed Alex's sword and went to work freeing Chen as Tyrone freed Mannie.

"Hannah and Will are out there?" Mannie asked.

"Yep. So are Reid and Selena." Tyrone confirmed. They're going to kick some leech ass.

Mannie staggered to his feet. "We need to get out there and help them. These vampires are fucking strong and – "

He weaved unsteadily and Mallorie, rubbing her wrists gingerly, steadied him around the waist. "You need to sit down, Mannie." She touched the lump on the top of his head. "You've got a concussion for sure."

"I'm fine!" He insisted vehemently.

"You're not fine." Mallorie replied. "You go out there, you're just going to get yourself killed."

"I won't, I – "

"She's right." Chen interrupted. Alex and Paul had gathered around him and he stared unblinkingly at them. "Remember your training. Alex, do not let your anger cloud your judgment. Paul, keep your sword down."

"Yes, master." They replied in unison.

Chen turned to the twins and Stephanie. "The three of you will stay in here with Mannie until we are finished. Do not – "

"No fucking way!" Luther snapped. "Those fuckheads killed Constance. I'm not staying in here, Chen. You can't make me."

He stomped to the stall and picked up two wooden stakes. "I'm going out there."

"If Luther's going, I'm going." Tyrone grabbed his own stakes as Mallorie gathered the remaining guns. She stuck one in the waistband of her pants, handed the other to Stephanie and gripped the final one tightly.

She squeezed Stephanie's shoulder. "Keep Mannie safe, Steph, alright? If any vampires come through that door, make sure your shot is to the heart."

"Alright." Stephanie stood in front of Mannie. "Don't worry, Mannie. I'll keep you safe."

"Thanks." Mannie grunted before sinking to the ground and leaning against the wall. He stared at the others. "Be careful out there."

Chen nodded and the others followed him out of the barn.

Mannie struggled to his feet and held his hand out. "Get me a stake, Steph."

"You're not going out there! You can't and I won't let you!"

"I'm not." Mannie eyed Judd who was hanging limply with his head down and his eyes closed.

Stephanie handed Mannie the stake. He stood in front of the vampire and Stephanie watched nervously as he touched the leech's shoulder.

"Judd?"

There was no reply and Mannie spoke louder. "Judd, look at me."

Judd sighed and opened his eyes. "I'm thinkin'. I can't remember that fella's name. I don't know why. He was the last drink I ever had and I can't remember. Was it Terry?"

"It's over, Judd." Mannie said.

"Is it? You gonna let me go?" Judd said hopefully.

"I'm going to set you free." Mannie replied. "Are you ready?"

Judd nodded before staring over Mannie's shoulder. "It wasn't Terry. Something with a G maybe."

Mannie plunged the wooden stake into Judd's chest. The vampire's back arched and his eyes widened.

"Gary. His name was Gary." He whispered.

Mannie wrenched the stake free and stepped back. He staggered on his feet and Stephanie hurried over and led him away as Judd, a smile on his face, disintegrated into ash.

* * *

Hannah, adrenaline singing in her veins and the pure, unfiltered joy of hunting lighting up every nerve, raised her swords as the vampires advanced. Beside her, the short-haired vampire appeared in a flash and slammed into Will. Her mate gave a short howl of pain as he was driven deep in to the forest, the vampire clinging tightly to him.

Before she could turn and go after them, Olof was standing in front of her. He smoothed his hair back, a few strands had loosened from the bun, and smiled at her. "I find you interesting, my dear. Very interesting."

Vaguely she was aware of Selena and Reid being surrounded by the four remaining vampires and she prayed that Tyrone and Stephanie would free the others in time to help them. As Olof took a step closer, she tightened her grip on her swords and grinned fiercely at him.

"I don't find you interesting at all. You're just like every other leech I've met − boring, and too stupid to know they're about to die."

Anger flashed across his face. "You do not want to call me that again, Lycan bitch."

"What?" She taunted. "Boring? Stupid?"

With a snarl he dove at her. He was quick, quicker than even Samuel, and three months ago she wouldn't have stood a chance. He would have gutted her and feasted on her blood before she could have even reacted.

But she was different now. Her wolf, ruled by a simple, animalistic need for survival, surged within her and she whipped to the right with ease. The leech's hands gripped air which only seconds prior had been her smooth throat, and he blinked in surprise as he stumbled over his own feet and fell.

She laughed loudly, a sound that was half-howl, and her eyes glowed as Olof leaped to his feet and hissed angrily.

"Too slow!" She crowed at him.

She had never felt so alive or more powerful in her life. Every muscle in her body was vibrating with power, and her Lycan senses had kicked in with a rush that left her breathless with excitement. She could hear the mosquito's buzzing, the leaves on the trees trembling in the wind, and the rustling of the small creatures hiding in the forest. She inhaled deeply. Her mate's scent filled her lungs, blotting out the other smells, and she smiled happily as her fangs popped out.

She would kill this troublesome little worm and then she would find her mate. She would take him deep into the forest and they would hunt and mate until the sun began to rise over the horizon. They would –

Olof, his body a blur, reached for her and she snapped her teeth and sliced him across the stomach with the sword in her right hand. He screamed and scurried backward, clapping one hand over the gaping wound in his flesh as she howled again.

"You make this too easy, leech." She snarled.

The pain on Olof's face was replaced with amusement. A small trickle of fear slid down Hannah's spine when he moved his hand and she realized the wound had already healed. Olof straightened his torn suit jacket and tightened his tie.

"Perhaps I should start making an effort then, she-wolf." He said.

"Perhaps you should." Her voice was deepening and hair was sprouting on her cheeks as her wolf tried to take control. She fought against the shift, knowing she needed her swords, and Olof cocked his head at her.

"Why do you fight against the turning? Is it not better to let it free? What use are silly human weapons when you have a beast inside of you?"

She didn't reply and, moving more quickly than she could ever have imagined, the leech snatched her around the waist, lifted her into the air and threw her into the forest. She crashed into a tree, her head slamming against the bark hard enough to make her see stars and she yelped in pain when two of her ribs broke with a harsh snap. She dropped to the ground, panting loudly and her wolf howling for its freedom, and searched frantically for her dropped swords.

"Looking for these?" Olof appeared in front of her. He held her swords in his hands and he lifted them to the faint light of the half-moon, studying them carefully as they gleamed dully. "I'll ask you again, what need does a Lycan have for swords?"

"Fuck you." Hannah growled as she climbed to her feet. Behind her, hidden by the thick trees, she could hear her mate and the leech fighting viciously and she took a small step backward.

Olof laughed. "I'm really not that interested in you, my dear. You're pleasant looking enough but the smell of your wolf is enough to turn any man away. Now, stop moving away and pay attention. You will answer my question or I'll use your own swords to slice you apart."

He giggled like a small boy and studied the swords again. "Oh, this is going to be fun."

* * *

"Selena?"

"Yeah?"

"I was thinking when we're done here, we should go for tacos."

"Are you kidding me?"

"What? I'm starving. Don't you like tacos? I'd be willing to go for Thai food. You like Thai food?"

"Now is not the time, Reid."

"Fine, but when we're driving aimlessly around town later tonight trying to decide what to have for dinner, you're going to wish we had made the decision now."

"Reid – "

"I'm not trying to sway you or anything but you might want to consider the tacos. They've got a higher caloric value and you're going to need your energy for what I'm going to do to you later."

"Oh really?"

He grinned at the hint of curiosity in her voice. "Really, really. We're talking shenanigans, sweetheart. Lots and lots of sexual shenanigans. Until you can't stand and I have to carry you around the – "

"Halt die Klappe, Dummkopf!"

"What did he just say?" Selena asked.

They were surrounded by the four vampires and she gripped Reid's hand tightly as she raised her gun.

"He's asking me to go for drinks with him later." Reid said cheerfully.

The vampire gaped at him. "Habe ich nicht!"

"Of course you did." Reid replied. "Listen, I'm flattered - maybe even a little curious - but you see this lady beside me? She's the jealous type. And I know she's small but believe me – you do *not* want to piss her off."

The vampire made a snarl of rage and lunged at Reid. Reid pushed Selena back and fired. The leech dodged the bullet and landed on him with a heavy thud, knocking him to the ground. His gun fell from his hand and he twisted for it as the vampire pounced on him.

"Reid!"

He could hear Selena screaming and her gun firing. The vampire on top of him winced when a bullet grazed his neck, drawing a spurt of blood that spilled down his shirt, but didn't release his grip around Reid's neck.

"I am not allowed to kill you," he hissed, "but ripping your foolish tongue from your mouth will not wound you mortally."

Reid clamped his mouth shut as he reached blindly for his gun. The tips of his fingers brushed against the hot barrel and, ignoring the sizzling pain, he wrapped his fingers around it and dragged it closer.

The vampire squeezed his throat and traced his mouth with one cold finger. "Open up, Dummkopf. I will make it quick. It might not even – "

A look of fear blanketed his face, as he stared down at the gun jammed against his chest.

"Good bye, fuckface." Reid said and pulled the trigger.

The sound of the dry click made his face drop as the vampire laughed and knocked the empty gun out of his hand.

There was a soft, whistling rush of air and the vampire blinked in mild surprise. A thin line of blood appeared on his throat, and the vampire's head slid from his body and landed in a soft thump on the ground next to Reid.

Blood poured out of the vampire's headless neck and Reid groaned and shoved the body off of him. "Gross, dude."

He wiped the blood from his face and stared up at the Asian man holding the bloody sword. "Thanks, Chen."

Chen bowed slightly as Reid's eyes suddenly widened. "Selena!"

He jumped to his feet, looking around frantically, and sighed with relief when he saw her standing with Mallorie. The two women, along with Paul, Alex, and the twins, had surrounded the three remaining vampires.

As the vampires hissed in fear, Paul glanced at Chen.

"Master?"

"Begin." Chen said softly.

Chapter 26

Hannah took another step back and Olof's face wrinkled in anger. "I said not to move, Lycan bitch. Pay attention to me."

Will howled and Hannah turned toward the sound of pain and anger, her heart pumping with a sudden rush of adrenaline. Her mate needed her. He needed her and –

There was a rush of burning pain as Olof's cold hand wrapped around her throat. She looked down to see her sword embedded in her stomach and she gasped harshly as he yanked it free.

"I told you to pay attention to me." The leech said softly. He glanced at the wound in Hannah's stomach. "Do not worry, she-wolf. Your Lycan abilities will heal you and you can adapt to life as my pet."

She stared wide-eyed at him as he pushed her back against the tree and tightened his grip around her throat. "You must forget about your mate. As we speak, Lars is ripping him apart. But do not worry – I will give you his pelt as a gift to remember him."

He laughed as the skin on her face began to ripple and change. "Now you shift. It's about time. What kind of Lycan are you, anyway? I've never met one who was so reluctant to shift. In fact, I – "

He jerked and made a soft strangled noise of surprise as Hannah's jaw cracked and twisted into a long snout and dark, coarse hair covered her flesh. His hand dropped from around her neck and she growled hungrily as he stared down at his chest.

Her hand had punched through his chest and he watched as her wrist twisted and she pulled sharply. She grinned as his heart, black and bloody, emerged from the dripping hole in his chest. She squeezed it tightly, blood dripping over her fur-covered hands and her nails digging into the rotting flesh.

He stared mutely at her as she made a soft-pitched yip of excitement and tore his heart in half before shoving him to the forest floor. He collapsed on his back, his skin beginning to smoke and blacken, and stared up at the woman standing before him. Her body rippling and her clothes tearing at the seams, she lifted her head to the sky and howled triumphantly.

* * *

The Lycan, his gray fur matted with blood and his back leg held up, limped to the woman. She was staring transfixed at the glimpses of moon she could see between the leafy trees, and he nudged her hip. He whined softly when he saw the wound in her stomach and nudged her again.

She turned her gaze to him, her jade eyes glowing with a wild, fierce light, and shook her head. "It is nothing, my love."

He chuffed lightly and she blinked and shuddered all over before taking a deep breath. She seemed to really see him for the first time and, with a soft cry of distress, she knelt beside him and touched his bloody fur.

"Will! Are you alright?"

He shifted and sat on the ground, holding his leg out awkwardly in front of him. "My leg is broken."

"Oh honey." She crouched next to him, her clothes were torn and he could see glimpses of her smooth flesh between the ragged strips, and hugged him tightly before kissing him on the mouth.

"I'll be fine." He smiled at her. "How's your stomach?"

She shrugged. "Already starting to heal, I think. A couple of my ribs are broken as well."

He frowned and she shrugged again. "I'll live. You killed the leech?"

He nodded and studied the pile of ash on the ground. "I heard you howling. Did you have to shift?"

She shook her head. "No, not really. I kind of half-shifted after the asshole leech took my swords and stabbed me in the stomach."

"You let him take your swords?" He arched his eyebrow at her and she growled softly before sitting next to him.

"You'd better not let Chen know that." He grinned at her as they leaned against a tree and he put his arm around her. "He'll have you back in sword training 101. Lesson one – don't give your sword to the leeches."

She laughed, wincing when it sent sharp pain shooting across her ribs, and kissed his bare chest. "I love you, Will."

"I love you too, Hannah." He kissed her forehead. "The others are coming."

"I know. I can smell them."

There was a rustling in the trees ahead of them and Chen and the twins appeared in the dark. Paul, Alex, and Reid and Selena were behind them, and the group stared solemnly at the two Lycans before Reid cleared his throat.

"We're going for tacos. You in?"

* * *

Three weeks later

"Tyrone? Be a dear and bring out the potato salad from the kitchen, would you?"

"Sure, mom." Tyrone brushed a kiss across Natalie's cheek.

He flipped the bird at his brother when Luther snorted "pussy" under his breath.

"Language, dearest." Natalie said disapprovingly.

"Sorry, mom."

"That's alright. Why don't you go help your brother?"

Luther stood and ambled after his twin as Natalie smiled at Will. "They're such sweet boys, don't you think?"

"Uh, sure." Will laughed. "When did they start calling you mom?"

"Right after you rescued them from those dreadful vampires. We were so happy they were alive, I must have ugly-cried for fifteen minutes straight, and I insisted they refer to Jim and I as mom and dad after that. They agreed right away."

She patted Will's arm fondly. "How's your leg, dear?"

"Fine. It was completely healed within a day or so."

"That's so cool." Natalie replied. "And very handy when one is injured."

He laughed and she looped her arm around his and stared at the people laughing and talking in the large living room. "It was lovely of Heather to let us celebrate at her house, wasn't it? People needed this."

"Yes." He studied the small nose stud in Natalie's left nostril. "Was she the one who convinced you to get the nose piercing?"

"Do you like it?" Natalie touched it delicately. "Heather went with me and held my hand. It didn't hurt nearly as bad as I feared it would. I thought Jim would have a coronary when he saw it but he was remarkably blasé about it. I worried that I would look like an old woman trying too hard but now that I have it, I'm rather smitten with it."

Will grinned. "I think it looks wonderful."

"Thank you, dear boy. You know, I think she's trying to convince Douglas to get his nose pierced as well."

Will stared at the old Lycan. He was staring at Heather's nose piercing and she spoke enthusiastically before lifting her shirt and showing him her belly button piercing.

"Maybe he'll get his belly button pierced." Will grinned at Natalie and snickered before squeezing his arm.

"How cute are Chen and Andrew?"

"Very cute." Will said solemnly.

Natalie laughed and studied the sword master. Andrew, his arm around Chen's waist, leaned in and whispered something in Chen's ear. Chen nodded and Andrew kissed him lightly on the mouth as Mannie approached them. He spoke animatedly, his arms waving and his entire body swaying, as Andrew laughed and even Chen grinned at something he said.

"Chen's much happier now. In fact, everyone seems happier." She gazed around the room at the people talking and helping themselves to the food piled high on the long table set up against the wall. "It's been such a terrible few months for them, it's nice to see them happy and relaxed."

Will nodded as a loud burst of laughter came from their left. Reid, surrounded by a group of the babies as well as Alex, Paul and Mallorie, raised his eyebrows in mock innocence.

"Hand to God, that leech was hitting on me. I'm like a sex on a stick to fangers."

Will rolled his eyes as Natalie waved at Jim who, holding a plate of food, crossed the room toward them. "We're worried about her, Will."

"I know, Nat. I am too."

"She was fine when you first got back but she's grown distant with us the last few days." Natalie said sadly. "Even now, she's off by herself."

"I'll talk to her." Will promised. "I'll help her understand that she needs her human side as well."

"Thank you, dearest." She reached up and kissed his cheek as Jim stopped in front of them.

"Any word from the Board, Will?"

Will nodded. "Yes. I've been cleared. Jordan told me yesterday that they were dropping their investigation."

He hesitated. "Surprisingly, Jordan said some good things to them and made it clear he was on our side. He told the Board that he had no worries about Hannah controlling the shift, or that I had turned her for ulterior motives."

"I imagine they finally understand just how valuable you and Hannah are to the organization." Natalie said.

"Where are the boys, Nat?" Jim asked as he popped a piece of bread into his mouth.

"I sent them to the kitchen for more potato salad. They've been gone way too long."

Jim snickered. "They're probably trying to figure out how to turn the kitchen knives into some kind of replacement hand for Chen."

"Oh dear. You're most likely right." Natalie gave Will a nervous look. "Last week they created this odd knife/hook combination thing and we had to take Luther in for seventeen stitches after Tyrone accidentally stabbed him in the leg."

Jim rolled his eyes. "I'm not so sure it was an accident, Nat."

Nat tapped him lightly on the chest. "Oh hush now. Come on, we'd better go see what they're up to."

They headed toward the kitchen as Will inhaled deeply. He found Hannah's scent easily and ducked out of the living room, heading up the large winding staircase and down the hallway. A door opened and Selena slipped into the hall.

She stopped in front of him and gave him a pinched look of worry. "Hello, Will."

"Hey, Selena."

She glanced behind her at the closed door. "I'm worried about her."

"I know. It'll be alright."

"Promise?" She asked softly.

"I do."

She hesitated and then gave him an impulsive hug. He hugged her back and she kissed his cheek. "You're a good guy, Will."

"You're pretty great yourself, Selena."

"I know." She said simply and he snorted soft laughter.

"You're hanging around with Reid too much."

"Hey! Paws off my lady, furball."

Will rolled his eyes and released Selena, stepping back as she grinned at him and move toward Reid who was climbing the stairs behind them.

"Hello, sweetheart."

"Hey, handsome. What are you doing?"

"Looking for you. The food's getting cold and I'm starving."

"Alright. Let's eat."

Reid nodded to Will and took Selena's hand. He led her down the stairs as Will slipped into the room. It was the master bedroom and he walked quickly past the bed to the French doors. He stepped out on to the balcony and slipped his arms around Hannah's waist.

"Hello, Hannah."

"Hi, honey." She leaned against him and continued to stare up at the clear, night sky. It was three days until the full moon and he stared at it for a moment, feeling the powerful yearning to shift and run and hunt."

"It's so beautiful, isn't it?" She said softly.

"Yes." Will agreed. "But it's not the only thing that matters, Hannah."

"I know."

"Your mom is worried about you."

"She doesn't need to be." Hannah sighed. "I'm fine."

He buried his face in her throat and inhaled deeply. There was something off about her scent, something foreign but oddly exciting, and he inhaled again as she shifted against him.

"Are you happy, Will? Happy with this life?"

"I'm happy with you." He replied. "I know that our life together isn't perfect. I know that fighting the leeches is tiring and painful and I understand your desire for a normal life, but running from the people who love you and living in the woods as a Lycan isn't the answer. You have to hold on to your human side as well."

"I know that now." She frowned up at him. "I knew that the moment the twins and Selena were taken."

He brushed her hair back and kissed her forehead. "Then what's wrong? You've been distant and quiet for the last few days."

She stared up at him and he was surprised to see the glint of tears in her eyes before she looked away.

"I'm pregnant." She whispered.

He stiffened against her, his hands tightening around her waist, as she made a soft, anxious whine.

"You're what?"

"I'm pregnant, Will. That's why I've been acting so weird the past few days. When we were in the woods and I was spending most of my time in my Lycan form, I wasn't very good about taking the pill. At least, I don't think I was. I can't really remember."

He stared at her as she glanced up at him. "I'm sorry. I didn't do this on purpose. I wasn't myself and I just – I wasn't thinking. I swear."

She licked her lips nervously. "Say something, Will."

"You're pregnant." He whispered.

"Yes. I mean, I think I am. I was supposed to get my period this week and I didn't, and so I bought one of those early detection pregnancy tests and it came back positive. But sometimes those tests are wrong, right?"

"You're having a baby." He said stupidly. "You're having my baby."

She arched her eyebrows at him. "Yes. Who else's baby would I be having?"

He opened his mouth and she gave him an encouraging look. After a moment of silence, she sighed. "Are you angry with me, Will?"

He shook himself all over and surprised her by twisting her around and dropping to his knees. He lifted her shirt and kissed her belly repeatedly.

"Of course I'm not!" He nearly shouted. "Why would you think that?"

"I don't know, we've never really talked about kids and – "

He snorted loudly and rubbed her stomach with his warm hands.

"Hello, baby." He whispered.

She stroked her fingers through his thick hair as he kissed her flat belly again and stared up at her. "You're going to be a mom."

"You're going to be a dad." She answered solemnly.

A small, pleased smile crossed his face and he stood and hugged her tightly. She buried her face in his neck and kissed his warm flesh.

"I love you, Will."

"I love you, Hannah."

END

Please enjoy a sample chapter of Elizabeth Kelly's latest novel:

**WILLOW AND THE WOLF
(SHIFTER SERIES BOOK ONE)**

By Elizabeth Kelly

* * * *

Copyright 2015 Elizabeth Kelly

Chapter 1

"So, uh, Ms. Tanner – you've worked for Harvey Snow for the last two years, is that right?" Bishop tugged anxiously at his tie as he scanned the paper in front of him.

Mal sighed. Bishop was sweating through his suit jacket and he looked distinctly uncomfortable. Calling Bishop the strong, silent type was the understatement of the century. Grizzly shifters were known for their fierceness and their strength – not their interviewing abilities. Bishop was the muscle of their small security company and rarely spoke to their clients. He wasn't afraid of getting his hands dirty and while Mal trusted him with his life, he didn't trust that Bishop would get through the interview without passing out or throwing up.

He wished for the hundredth time that Kat was here to spearhead the interview. She was a jaguar shifter and while not that talkative herself, she at least had the ability to ask questions without looking like she was going to faint. She had led the other three interviews but a client emergency had forced her out of the office.

He forced himself to concentrate on the slender brunette sitting in front of them. She was a tiny little thing. He doubted she was taller than 5'4" and if she weighed a hundred pounds he would be surprised. Her dark hair was pulled into a bun high on her head and her light blue eyes sparkled with intelligence and humour. He wondered idly what she would look like with that dark hair drifting down her back and frowned to himself. The woman was not his type. One - she was human and two – as a wolf shifter, he preferred to take bigger, stronger women to his bed. This one looked like a strong wind would blow her down.

"That's right." She smiled at Bishop. "Harvey is a great boss."

Bishop pulled at his tie again and cleared his throat. "So, uh, why are you leaving?"

"Just looking for something different." She said cheerfully. "I suspect that working for your security firm would be more exciting and challenging than working for Harvey."

"Uh, right." Bishop gave him a frantic look and shuffled the papers in front of him as he searched for something else to say.

"Ms. Tanner?" Mal figured it was time to rescue Bishop.

She turned toward him and gave him a dazzling smile. "Call me Willow."

"I'm going to be brutally honest. We've never hired a human to work for us before."

"So why are you interviewing me?" She asked curiously.

"Harvey highly recommended you and frankly, we're a bit desperate. Our last receptionist had to leave rather abruptly and we've been scrambling to find her replacement. Our clients are mostly paranormal and you're going to see a great deal of oddity if you work for us."

"I don't mind." She said immediately. "I enjoy odd things. It makes the world more interesting, don't you think?"

"Uh, yes. I guess." He cleared his throat.

"Harvey has paranormal clients, Mr. Burke. I've dealt with shifters and the fae, even a vampire."

He smiled thinly at her. "Harvey's clients are a bit more refined than ours."

She laughed, a soft and low vibration that made his wolf sit up and take notice. "I imagine they are. Harvey is a rather high-profile lawyer. His fees alone generally bring in a higher class of people and paranormals."

"Right." He took the papers from Bishop's sweaty hand, smoothing out the wrinkles as he scanned her resume.

"So, why don't you tell us what you know about our firm?"

She sat up straighter and smiled again at Bishop. The bear shifter blushed and stared at the floor as she cleared her throat.

"You and Mr. King started the firm seven years ago. Three years ago, Ms. Frost became a partner in the firm. You provide personal security for a large portion of the paranormals in our city. Which, considering how small our city is, there are quite a few paranormals living here. Wouldn't you agree Mr. Burke?"

He shrugged. "I never really thought about it."

"I have. It's very strange the amount of paranormals that have gravitated to our city. I think it's because of the fault line."

"Excuse me?" Mal frowned at her.

"The paranormal fault line. It lies directly across our city. Haven't you heard of the fault line?" She asked.

He shook his head. "The fault line is a myth, Ms. Tanner."

"Maybe, maybe not." She said cheerfully. "I can assure you, Mr. Burke, that I am excellent at my job. I'm organized, great with clients, and I type over a hundred words a minute. I understand that your firm will require working strange hours from time to time and I have no problem with that."

"Even if it means working in the middle of the night to accommodate a vampire or coming in at dawn for the fae?"

"Yes." She said pertly. "I don't need much sleep."

"You must have an understanding husband."

He could have punched himself. Why the hell had he said that? His wolf panted happily as Bishop gave him a disbelieving look.

"I'm not married." She raised her hand and wiggled her bare ring finger at him. "I can do what I want, when I want, with whoever I want."

An image of her in his bed, naked and on her hands and knees with his hand wrapped in that long dark hair, flashed through his head and he cleared his throat roughly. "Okay, well, thank you for coming in Ms. Tanner. We'll get back to you in the next couple of days."

She blinked in surprise at his abruptness before standing and smoothing her skirt. He eyed her slender legs before his gaze drifted to her small, perky breasts in her silk blouse. Beside him, Bishop stood and extended his massive hand.

"Nice to meet you, Ms. Tanner." He gave her a nervous smile and she shook his hand firmly before extending her hand to Mal.

He stood and shook her hand, ignoring the little shiver that went down his back at the touch of her soft hand, and nodded to her.

"Nice to meet you both. I look forward to hearing back from you." She chirped.

She left the room and Bishop punched him in the arm when Mal stared at her tight ass.

"Stop it." He hissed at Mal.

Mal growled lightly at him as the door shut and sank back into his chair. "We're not hiring her."

Bishop rolled his eyes. "The way you were eyeing her, she'll never agree to work for us anyway. Jesus, Mal, I thought you were going to try and mate her right in front of me."

"I don't know what the hell you're talking about." Mal grunted.

"Whatever, man." Bishop took her resume and scanned it. "She's actually the best candidate."

"She's human, Bishop. We were only interviewing her as a favour to Harvey, remember?"

"Yeah, I remember. I don't know what the big deal is about hiring a human, anyway."

"Because humans and paranormals don't mix." Mal grunted.

"Racist bastard." Bishop snorted.

"I am not!" Mal protested. "I'm trying to protect the humans. A human always gets hurt when they start messing around with paranormals. You know that. It's why that asshole senator tried to pass that law forbidding us to have anything to do with humans."

"Don't tell me you supported that?" Bishop glared at him.

"Of course I didn't. It was a ridiculous law created by an actual goddamn racist. But you have to admit he has a point. Plenty of humans have been hurt or killed when dealing with paranormals and some of them are out for our blood."

"You think I don't know that? Protecting our kind against humans is 85% of our business, Mal." Bishop replied. "It doesn't mean all humans are against us."

"I'm not saying that." Mal answered patiently. "I'm just saying that hiring this human female is a bad idea."

"Is it a bad idea because she's human or a bad idea because you want to mate with her?" Bishop raised his eyebrows at him.

"I don't want to mate with her!" Mal snapped.

"Sure you don't." Bishop pulled his tie off and gathered the resumes together. "I'm telling Kat we should hire her."

"The Gorgon! What about the Gorgon? She was great." Mal said a bit desperately.

"Are you kidding? She has the voice of a lumberjack and she wants ten dollars more an hour than we're offering. And what happens the first time it's the Gorgon mating period? Do you really want to find yourself pinned against your desk while she tears your clothes off and has her way with you?"

Mal paled. "We'll just give her some time off during the mating period."

Bishop snorted and headed toward his office. "I'm recommending the human, Mal, and you know Kat will agree with me. She didn't like any of the other candidates. Just keep your paws to yourself, alright?"

"Thank you so much, Mr. King! You won't regret hiring me, I promise." Willow hung up the phone and grinned delightedly at her best friend.

"I got the job, Ava!"

"Congratulations!" Ava hugged her tightly. "I knew you'd get it. When do you start?"

"Next Monday. Oh Ava, I'm so happy! It's finally my chance to work with actual paranormals. Mama would be so pleased for me."

"She would be." Ava agreed. "Now, tell me about your new job."

"It's just a reception position, I could probably do it in my sleep, but once I show them what I can do, I'm hoping they'll move me further up in the company." Willow replied.

"I'm sure they will. How big is the office?" Ava poured herself more tea and followed Willow into the small and cluttered living room. She moved a pile of laundry from the armchair and curled her curvy body into the seat.

Willow flopped down on the sofa, resting her feet on a pile of papers on the coffee table, and took a sip of tea. "There are three partners, Bishop King, Katelyn Frost, and Malcolm Burke. They have a dozen employees that are in and out of the office, according to Mr. King."

She pulled absentmindedly on her lower lip. "I didn't actually meet Ms. Frost, just Mr. King and Mr. Burke."

"What were they like?"

"Well, Mr. King is a bear shifter and he was massive. He's the biggest man I've ever met in my life, Ava! I wouldn't be surprised if he was over seven feet tall. He seemed really nervous. I don't think he's very comfortable around women."

"What about the other one?"

"Mr. Burke? He's a wolf shifter and he seemed - I don't know - grumpy. I'm pretty sure he didn't like me." She laughed.

"He doesn't even know you." Ava said indignantly.

"I know but you know how some paranormals are. They don't like humans. He made sure to point out that they had never hired a human before. It's why I was so surprised that – "

She stopped as her breath plumed out in front of her like smoke. Ava shivered and leaned back in the chair as Willow turned and stared behind her.

"I can't help you if you don't tell me what's wrong." She said softly.

The room was growing steadily colder and Ava looked around anxiously. "Willow? Who is it?"

Willow shrugged. "I don't know. He won't talk to me."

Ava clutched her tea mug and stared at the corner that Willow was looking into. "That's weird."

"Yep, it is." Willow said cheerfully. She stood and approached the corner, holding her hands out in a friendly manner. "Will you at least tell me your name? Don't be shy."

Ava watched as Willow inched closer. "I want to help you. Let me – no! Don't go!"

She sighed discouragingly and turned around. "He's gone."

The room was warming up again and Ava shivered before curling deeper into the chair. "God, I hate it when that happens."

Willow grinned. "I love it."

"I know you do. You're a weirdo."

"Oh c'mon, Ava. It's not a bad thing. Think of how many spirits I've helped cross to the other side. They're hurting and I can help them. How is that bad?"

"It's not bad. It's just creepy." Ava replied firmly. "And what happens when you run into a not-so-nice spirit?"

"I've been seeing the dead for twenty-four years and not once have they ever been malicious or evil." Willow laughed.

Ava shook her head. "What about that girl two years ago? She didn't seem so nice."

"Courtney? She was perfectly nice!"

"She broke every dish in your house, Willow!"

"She was just misunderstood, that's all. She was angry and upset and she didn't know how to express it."

"So she expressed it by shattering all of your dishes?"

"Hey, you'd be angry too if your boyfriend cheated on you with your mother."

Ava rolled her eyes. "I'd need to have a boyfriend for that to be a possibility and with a body like this, we both know that's not going to happen."

"Oh hush, Ava. I hate it when you talk badly about yourself." Willow frowned at her. "Besides, it has nothing to do with your body and everything to do with your self-confidence. You're gorgeous and sweet, and you just need to get over this ridiculous idea that all men want a skinny stick in the sack."

"Says the girl who wears a size two." Ava muttered.

Willow snorted. "I'd gladly take your curves." She grabbed her small breasts and gave them a shake. "You think these little molehills are grabbing any man's attention? I'd kill to have your mountains."

Ava blushed and crossed her arms over her chest. "Yeah, and my carrot coloured hair and pale, freckle-covered skin."

Willow laughed. "I only wish I could pull off red hair. Now, let's go shopping. I need a couple new outfits for my new job."

"Willow and the Wolf" will be available at Amazon in June of 2015.

If you would like more information about Elizabeth Kelly, please visit her website:

http://www.elizabethkelly.ca

Stalk her:

https://www.facebook.com/elizabethkellybooks
or
https://twitter.com/ElizabethKBooks

Write to her:
mailto:elizabethkellybooks@gmail.com

CPSIA information can be obtained at www.ICGtesting.com
Printed in the USA
LVOW04s1456100915

453651LV00008B/149/P

9 781926 483344